ıvıa

Rising

Published by On the Wing Press

'Mapton Rising' copyright © 2016.
Sam Maxfield

Cover illustration © Sandra Lamb

To Joss Edge, for constant encouragement

Stella Struggling

Stella was trying to deter her two-year-old daughter, Gerta, from stuffing a grape up her nose when the doorbell rang.

'Mine,' Gerta wailed, snatching at the grape.

'Grapes are for eating,' Stella explained wearily. 'Not for pushing up your nose, Gerta. Remember last week when Dr Graves had to use tweezers to get that bead out of your ear. You didn't like that, did you?'

'Mine!' Gerta repeated, face contorting into a pre-tantrum grimace.

Stella braced herself but the tantrum never came as Gerta spotted Gina. Her expression changed to delight.

'Gwamma,' she cooed, holding out her chubby arms.

'Come to Grandma, duckie,' Gina said sweeping her up. 'Oh, you're getting too heavy for an old lady like me.'

Stella thought that Gina looked remarkably fit, certainly in comparison to how she'd looked four years ago when Stella had been yanked out of her London life to come look after her.

'You'll never guess what I've heard,' Gina said breathlessly.

Stella eyed her warily. She looked feverish with potential gossip.

'What?'

'You know how The Paradise has been struggling.' Stella nodded. The Paradise Holiday Park was an eyesore, even by Mapton standards.

'Well, I heard Dennis Payton's gonna make it an 'adult park',' Gina said. 'For dirty boggers. Can you believe it?'

Stella's tired mind could hardly grasp it.

'What do you mean? 'Adult park', she asked.

'A sex park,' Gina mouthed, before bending her head so Gerta could run her fingers through her hair. Gina's bright red hair fascinated Gerta. 'For perverts 'n' the like. He's applying for a licence to turn the entertainment centre into a swingers' club.'

'Oh Gina,' Stella groaned. 'Who told you this?'

'Pirate Tom,' Gina said. 'He sits on the council, don't he? So he knows.'

'Rumours, then,' Stella said. 'I can't believe you're giving credence to anything Tom Turner says. You're usually at each other's throats.'

Gina grunted. 'Don't matter who says it. It matters if it's true. It needs stopping.'

'By you?' Stella asked.

'Of course,' Gina said, as though Stella had just taken leave of her senses. 'We don't want that sort in Mapton.'

Stella opened her mouth to tell Gina she was talking rubbish when Gerta piped up. 'Me!' she shouted. 'Me, Gina. Me mummy.'

Gina laughed. 'Cheeky little bogger. Not getting enough attention? How'd you like to spend today with Grandma Gina, so Mummy can get some stuff done?'

'Yeth,' Gerta agreed. 'Go beach with Gina 'n' George.'

'That's right. We can pick up some shells.'

'And Daddy?'

'We'll have some lunch at Daddy's shan't we?'

'Yeth,' Gerta nodded emphatically.

Stella fetched Gerta's coat and shoes, as well as the large bag of nappies, food, wipes, and all the other paraphernalia that went with trucking around a toddler. She hung the bag on Gerta's pushchair.

'Me do it,' Gerta said, pushing her left foot into her right shoe. Gina kneeled down, groaning, and swapped the shoes over.

It took a few minutes to get Gerta ready and strapped into her pushchair.

Stella gave Gina a rueful look. 'Brace yourself,' she said.

Gina grinned. 'Off we go, Gerta-girl,' she said.

'Mummy come?' It was always the same question.

'No, Mummy paints on Tuesdays,' Gina said. 'Say goodbye.'

Stella leaned down to plant a kiss on her daughter.

'Mummy come!' Gerta shouted. It was the cue for her Tuesday tantrum, which, Gina assured Stella, only ever lasted to the post box round the corner when Mummy was promptly forgotten.

Cheerfully, Gina wheeled Gerta out as the tot began to a bawl for Stella. 'Mummmy!'

Each time it broke Stella's heart to let Gerta go in such seeming distress but once the wails had faded along the street and the house descended into blissful silence, she breathed out a guilty sigh of relief.

Was it normal to feel so relieved at getting rid of your child for the day?

Stella made herself a coffee and carried it up to her studio in the north turret. Henry was already there, curled up on his cushion in a corner. He

3

opened one eye, and satisfied it wasn't the noisy, tail-pulling demon that had ruined his quiet home-life, resumed napping.

Stella studied her easel critically. She just couldn't get this painting right, no matter how she tried, and yet she couldn't leave it alone either.

Since her move to Mapton, Stella's style had changed, becoming bolder, looser, and more dramatic. Before Gerta had been born she'd begun to develop this new style, experiencing a creative surge fuelled by the high of new love, and the emotional energy she'd gained by resolving old hurts with Gina.

It was hard to believe four years had flown by so quickly. The old Stella wouldn't have imagined the sort of life she had now. When Gina's accident had brought her unwillingly to the peculiar little seaside town, she'd initially hated it. Hated Gina too. But then she'd met Rick, the unexpected American running a diner on the Lincolnshire seafront, and fell in love. Soon she'd found herself racing a mobility scooter with the local scooter gang, the Mapton Marauders, against Pirate Tom's Siltby Wanderers, and singing karaoke in the local pubs. And she and Gina had faced their painful past. But it hadn't been until she returned to her life in London that she'd realised that Mapton – and the people in it – had got under her skin, and she couldn't live without them. That was when her painting style underwent a radical change, as though Stella had shed her old skin.

At first, Susan Cadman, her agent was nonplussed by the change in direction, and then alarmed as Stella began to turn down commissions to concentrate on her personal work.

Mapton began to creep into the paintings. Stella had Mapton Marauders captain, Sue Mulligan, sit for her on her mobility scooter, her toothless Yorkshire terrier, Scampi peeping out of her basket. She captured Gina, hair blazing, head tipped back in a raucous laugh. She could be seen snapping photos all over Mapton; the laundrette sign: 'Kleen & Gone'; Pam Stimpson's famous baby doll pyjamas floating on the line; George's regimentally planted petunias. People noticed and they gossiped. Stella was an outsider – what right had she to come in and stick her nose into all of Mapton's business. But they were curious about her too, and, as more than one Maptonite noted, she was an arty type, and they were known for being eccentric.

Proclivity, the London gallery she sold most of her non-commissioned work through wasn't too keen on her new style either. But it took a couple out of loyalty. They didn't sell – a first for a Stella Distry - and Proclivity were about to send them back, when Martin Salvino, hip art critic and trend-setter, sauntered into the gallery and snapped up the painting of Sue and Scampi, following up with a review of it in his weekly Evening Standard column.

Stella Distry used to leave me a bit cold. Her precise, perfect renditions of beauty are hardly the cutting edge of art. Like a female Jack Vetrianno, her work is posed, lifeless and oh, so popular. So imagine my surprise when I wandered into a certain gallery this week, fully expecting to be engulfed with the ennui of middle-brow art, when

a painting socked me in the eyes with such bold, ugly, ironic gorgeousness, I bought it on the spot.

'Sue & Scampi' takes a middle-aged woman on a gaudily festooned mobility scooter and her tongue-dripping Yorkshire terrier. Starkly placed against the grey concrete of a seaside promenade, Distry (for she is the artist!) captures the terrifying despair of the British underclass, depicted in the woman's empty grin and the dog's toothless maw. One can almost taste the delicious hint of irony, as though Distry is playing a joke on the viewer and one might find it hidden somewhere in the signature meticulousness of her details. Off to the side an ice cream wrapper blows along the ground, seemingly signifying the transience of cheap pleasures and the sadness of a fading resort.

According to the gallery, this is no one-off, but a new direction for Stella Distry. Could it be that Distry is re-inventing herself to be a late developing 'enfant-terrible' of the art world? I really do hope so.

Stella had been very glad that Sue hadn't read the piece. She could just imagine her reaction to being called part of the 'underclass'. Rick and Stella had laughed themselves silly over it after Susan had very excitedly emailed her the piece. They'd read it in bed. 'Wow,' Rick said. 'I never knew you were so deep.'

Stella had mixed feelings. She'd read enough art-criticism in her time to know how ridiculous it could be, but it disturbed her; had she meant to be ironic? Was she secretly mocking her friends in Mapton?

She didn't tell Gina about the review.

6

The result, though, was a renewed interest in her work, and requests for more paintings and limited edition prints of her recent work. Finally, Susan suggested it was time to she did a major exhibition, her first in years, and it was this that she was working towards now.

Or at least trying to.

The truth was she felt exhausted. Not just today, but all the time. Swept by a wave of hopelessness, Stella sank onto the small sofa she'd crammed into the room, pulled the yellow throw over herself, and curled up.

Henry, spotting the opportunity for extra warmth, joined her, purring.

Tuesdays were taking on a worrying pattern, Stella knew, but unable to stop herself she sank into a restless sleep.

She woke an hour later, bleary eyed and unrefreshed. Henry had drooled on her tee shirt but as Gerta had already smeared her with mashed banana earlier it hardly mattered. Stella could dimly remember when things like that had mattered; when deciding what to wear could be a pleasure and seemed important.

The exhibition was less than four months away, and this was going to be her major piece – a montage of Mapton's fair made up of ten large canvases. She'd done seven of them but was stuck on the current canvas.

She squinted at the painting. It was a fairground scene – Mapton's tatty little funfair caught at the magical hour when dusk stripped away the paltry reality and the rides transformed into illuminated enchantments. Centre stage was the ghost train which locals called the Sin Ride, due to its owner's penchant for dressing as a hooded monk and asking each rider: 'Do you dare face your sins in the dark?'

Stella wanted to capture the jittery laughter on the customer faces as they emerged from the ride to the final shock of Brother Frank leaping out at them, roaring.

Instead what she kept painting on the faces was sheer terror.

On the wall behind her easel, blown-up large, was the photograph she'd taken to work from. It was actually a composite of different shots of the fair. The photos captured the lure of neon lights and electric bulbs, the blur of the waltzer, the woo-woo scream of the ghost train. You could almost smell the tang of fried onions and hotdogs.

Gritting her teeth, Stella reached for her paints and once again began painting out the screaming faces of the ghost train riders. She was going to recapture their laughter if it was the last thing she did.

Mapton on Alert

George Wentworth was waiting for Gina and Gerta at a table outside Rick's diner. Gina's dog, Ginger Rogers, waddled out to meet them, tail wagging. A tubby corgi, she was the most placid dog Gina had ever owned, far different than her previous dog, Bing Crosby, the Jack Russell with criminal tendencies who'd long since gone on the run.

'Come here, darling.' George opened his arms to Gerta. 'Come to Granddad.'

'Don't call yourself that,' Gina snapped. 'You're not her granddad.'

George ignored her, scooping Gerta into a hug. 'What you been doing?' he asked the tot.

Gerta was about to tell him when she spotted Rick emerge from the diner. 'Daddy!' she squealed, wriggling out of George's arms and running for her father.

'Gerta gherkin,' Rick laughed, swinging her up. 'Hey baby. You had a nice morning with Gina?'

'Yes,' Gerta nodded, proceeding to burble out a tale involving crabs, ice cream, and other incomprehensible things.

Rick raised an eyebrow at Gina. 'Ice cream before lunch?' he said.

Gina pulled a face. 'She wanted it. It's natural. Kids need sugar.'

'They don't need sugar, Gina, they want it. You know we don't let Gerta eat junk on a weekday.'

Gina snorted. 'Oh, gerroff your high horse, Rick. You run a diner for God's sake. What about all them cakes you sell? Anyway, I'm her grandma. It's my job to spoil her.'

'You're Stella's grandma,' Rick needled her back. 'Technically you're Gerta's great grandmother.'

Gina had never let Stella call her Gran, or Grandma or Nana. Suddenly all that had changed when Gerta came along. Gina was ready for grandparent status but in denial about the age implications of great-grandparenting.

'Gi'over, Rick,' Gina said. 'Stop being such a mardy-arse. You're worse than Stella.'

'Gwamma said bad word,' Gerta observed.

'Well, that's your Grandma Gina for you,' Rick said. 'Bad to the bone. C'mon, let's get you something proper for lunch.' He carried Gerta into the diner.

Gina took a seat next to George. 'Bit of ice cream never did no one no harm,' she grumped.

George raised his hand to someone behind her. Gina turned to see Sue Mulligan approaching on her mobility scooter, her motley crew of scooter-riding pensioners – the Mapton Marauders – straggling behind her like ducklings.

Sue honked her horn. She was a little breathless as she drew up on her Rascal Vision. The scooter had once belonged to Gina, but she had sold it to Sue six months ago. After the fall that had brought Stella to Mapton, Gina claimed her legs had gone 'off', but once Gerta came along, and Gina wanted to take her out in her pushchair, she had miraculously regained the full use of both legs.

Still, she couldn't help eyeing her former chariot proprietorially as Sue glided to a stop by their table. She didn't approve of Sue's embellishments.

'Have you heard the news?' Sue asked.

'About The Paradise?' Gina nodded.

Sue looked a little crestfallen. 'Terrible ain't it?'

George shook his head. 'Horrible. Mapton's a family resort.'

'Tom Turner says it's coming over from the continent. Apparently they been doing this sort of thing in Holland for years.'

'Disgusting,' Gina shook her head. 'I'm sick of the EU forcing their rules on us. Like trying to make our bananas straight. Now they want us to accept their sleazy ways.'

'House prices will fall,' George said gloomily.

'We should do something about it,' Gina said. 'Protest or something. The council shouldn't allow this to happen.'

Sue nodded. 'We could start a petition. No one's asked us what we want. We could make some flyers to let people know what's going on. We can't let sex-fiends take over Mapton. This is our town.'

'We'll form a committee,' Gina declared, as though forming committees and 'joining in' was something she did every day. She was fired up.

'We'll call ourselves Mapton Knights,' George said. 'Like the Knight Templars in the crusades.' George was a bit of a history buff.

'Yes!' Sue said. 'Mapton Knights, like in Merlin.'

George didn't correct her. Sue was gazing at him with admiration, something Gina rarely did, if ever.

Rick returned with Gerta, bringing a booster seat with him. Gina looked after Gerta while he wrote down the Marauders' orders and disappeared back inside. Half an hour later he brought out sandwiches for himself, Gina and George. It was April, a fine day, but not as busy as the holiday season would get, so he had time for a quick lunch-break while his employees ran the diner. Ange, the diner's co-owner, didn't work Tuesdays.

'So whaddya talking about?' Rick asked.

'We're gonna form a committee,' Sue said. 'To stop them opening a sex club at The Paradise.'

'Aw, that ain't gonna happen,' Rick laughed. 'That's just Pirate Tom stirring you up.'

Gina shook her head. 'Dennis Payton's got an application to the council,' she said. 'It's like when they threatened to open up that asylum centre near here. We stopped them didn't we? Mapton didn't need a load of illegal immigrants.'

'I wish we had taken them. Asylum seekers aren't illegal immigrants, Gina,' Rick said. 'They're people seeking refuge from terrible conditions.'

'Well they should seek 'em somewhere else,' Gina replied. 'This country's overrun with immigrants.'

'You do realise I'm an immigrant?' Rick said.

Everyone looked taken aback.

'You're an American,' Sue pointed out. 'You talk English.'

'And I'm white,' Rick pointed out. 'Does that make it better too?'

Gina flared. 'Don't you be making out we're bigots, Rick. It's not just the coloureds; I don't like them Eastern Europeans neither. Except Grazja, she's all right.'

'Or gypsies,' Sue put in.

'Wow,' Rick said. That's quite a list.'

George said. 'I prefer live and let live, but we haven't got the resources to pay for all these people,

12

Rick. I don't think it's fair. This country's going to the dogs, what with all these immigrants on benefits, people having sex changes on the NHS and now this. A holiday park for perverts. I don't know what Britain's coming to.'

Rick sighed. 'Well, I don't think it's gonna happen in Mapton anyway. I think someone's pulling your leg. Oh, hey there, Scampi.' This last was in response to a small furry head that popped up out of the basket attached to Sue's scooter. 'It's not like you to miss food.'

Sue lifted the Yorkshire terrier gently out of the basket. 'She's getting old,' she said sadly. 'She sleeps most of the day now.'

'Scampi!' Gerta crowed. She clambered off her chair and waddled towards the dog. Ginger Rogers ambled over too, wagging her stub of a tail.

'Be gentle, Gerta,' Rick warned, although Scampi was incapable of biting, having no teeth whatsoever. 'Play nice.'

'Good doggy,' Gerta said, patting Scampi with exaggerated gentleness.

The adults watched them indulgently, and for now all talk of a sex camp was forgotten.

#

The issue was very much up for discussion at the Siltby and Mapton Town Council office. Martha Seaton, mayor and chair of the council was fuming. Her deputy, Tom Turner, had gone too far this time, undermining her authority by spreading rumours about The Paradise Holiday Park. She'd been fielding calls all morning from residents and business owners chittering on about some supposed 'sex camp'.

13

It was the most ridiculous thing she'd heard but people were taking it seriously.

Martha strode into Tom's office without even knocking. She knew he was in; she'd seen his Drive Royale scooter parked outside. If she caught him doing something unsavoury, like picking his nose or playing pocket-pool, so much the better.

Tom looked startled as she burst in but he was perfectly respectable, a mug of coffee in one hand, an official-looking document on his desk and a jumbo sausage roll for his working lunch.

'Bloody hell, Martha,' Tom said. 'Don't you knock? I almost spilt my coffee on this budget report.'

'What this nonsense I've been hearing about a sex camp at The Paradise?' Martha demanded.

'Eh?'

'Don't play innocent with me, Tom Turner. I've been getting calls all morning. At least three of them said they'd heard it from you.'

'Oh,' Tom waved her away. 'You know how people get things mixed up.'

'What did you say to get them mixed up?'

'Nothing, nothing,' Tom protested. 'Only…'

Martha gritted her teeth. 'Only what?'

'Only I had a tip-off on Monday from a friend of mine on the district council. Said there was an application in from a Mapton caravan site to licence a swingers club. I was in the cob shop when I took the call. Someone must've overheard me.'

Martha closed her eyes. 'Who's your friend in district?'

'I can't say,' Tom said. 'I promised I wouldn't.'

Martha stared at him in disbelief.

Tom smiled smugly. 'Sorry. Anyway I was going to raise the issue at the next meeting.'

'Have you asked Dennis Payton if it's true?'

Tom shook his head. 'Not yet. But you know what he's like. I wouldn't put it past him. He's been looking for ways to make a cheap buck for years, and The Paradise has always had a dodgy reputation with those Swedish type chalets.'

'Well, it's all pie in the sky at the moment,' Martha said. 'We need to ascertain the truth and cut off the rumours before they get out of control. I'll write a letter to the district council requesting information and make some informal calls.'

'Good,' Tom agreed. 'I'll have a quiet word with Dennis Payton. Put our minds at rest.'

'Right,' Martha said, heading for the door. She turned back. 'And in the meantime, Tom, keep your mouth shut.

She didn't see the two-fingered flip-off Tom aimed at her back as she left, but she felt it. It gave her a warm glow inside.

Doctor's Orders

Stella woke with a banging headache. The alarm read six-forty-five. Groaning she pulled a pillow over her head to fend off the painful sunlight filtering through the curtains. This exhibition was weighing on her. She hardly had time to paint looking after Gerta and this large house; even with Rick and Gina's help it was Stella who carried most of the workload. That hadn't been something she'd envisioned in the early days of their romance.

She'd been awful to Rick last night. Snapping at every little thing he said, taking any comment as a criticism. She hated herself even while she was doing it. It was as though the old Stella was locked inside her, helplessly watching the harpy she'd become. Today she would do better. Today would be different. When Rick came home later she'd make them dinner. They could play with Gerta, and then after she'd gone to bed, they'd watch something funny. It would be good to laugh together. Maybe she'd feel like sex. It was hard to remember how that felt.

And she'd stop eating so much chocolate and junk. She wouldn't feed it to Gerta so why did she give it to herself? All she had to do was try harder and take better care of herself.

Easy.

Forcing herself out of bed she stumbled to the shower and let the hot water do its good work.

Gerta was eating strawberries when Stella entered the kitchen, and Rick was leaning against the island drinking a mug of coffee.

'Mummy!'

'Good morning, sunshine,' Stella said, dropping a kiss on Gerta's head. Her daughter smelled deliciously of baby shampoo and her own sweet smell.

'Coffee?' Rick asked, his smile warm but a bit frayed.

'Please.'

'Me coffee,' Gerta demanded. She held out her sippy cup. Rick took it and filled it with milk.

Gerta took a gulp and let out a sigh that perfectly mimicked Rick's reaction to his first sip in the mornings. 'Coffee good,' she announced.

Rick and Stella laughed.

'We're going to raise a caffeine addict,' Rick said.

Stella accepted the mug he offered her and repeated Gerta's reaction.

'Sorry I was so grumpy last night,' she mumbled.

Rick shrugged. 'It's okay. I get it. You're worried about the exhibition.'

'I'm going to make it up to you tonight,' she said. 'I'll make dinner and then we can watch something funny and then...' she cocked an eyebrow suggestively. 'Who knows.'

Rick frowned. 'It's Wednesday,' he said quietly. 'Pop-up night in Lawton.'

Rick ran a pop-up haute cuisine kitchen at his friend Jill's deli on Wednesday and Friday evenings.

It was first come first served and people began queuing an hour before the restaurant opened.

Stella felt stupid and peevishly annoyed. Originally, the pop-up had only been on Friday evenings but Rick and Jill added Wednesdays due to demand, and because they were having so much fun doing it.

'Fine,' she snapped. 'Of course. I forgot. Stupid me.'

'Stupid Mummy!' Gerta crowed, delighted.

'Not stupid,' Rick said. 'It's a great idea. We'll do it tomorrow.' He reached for her but Stella shrugged away.

'Maybe,' she said. 'Whatever.'

'Whatever'? How old was she? Twelve? What was wrong with her? Today had hardly begun and already her good intentions had disintegrated.

'You should get over to Lawton then,' she said flatly.

'I don't need to go till mid-morning,' Rick replied. 'I was going to take Gerta to the park. Do you want to come?'

Stella shook her head. 'If you've got Gerta for a couple of hours I should work.'

Rick moved closer. 'Hey,' he said, touching her cheek. 'You can take the morning off. It'd do you good.'

'Why don't you take tonight off?' Stella said.

Rick stepped back. 'I can't do that. It's booked. It's my job.'

'Painting is my job,' Stella said. 'But you think that's different.'

Rick turned away. 'C'mon Gerta,' he called over-brightly. 'Let's give your mummy her space.'

Stella felt doubly guilty after they'd left as she spent an hour simply staring at her painting while a load of washing ran. Giving up, she picked up a trail of Gerta's abandoned toys before she impulsively rang her friend, Sarah Graves, who was also her doctor. Sarah didn't work Wednesdays, so Stella hoped she'd be there. She was, and, even better, suggested they meet for a coffee in Siltby.

After some initial small talk, Sarah said. 'So come on then, what's up?'

Stella didn't know where to begin. To her horror tears welled up.

Sarah rummaged in her bag for tissues, handed her one, and waited patiently.

Finally Stella said, 'I think I might be a bit depressed.'

Sarah smiled sympathetically. 'I've thought so for a while. Or probably more exhausted.'

'Really?' Stella felt shocked. Had it been that obvious? 'Why didn't you say something?'

Sarah shrugged. 'I thought you'd talk when you were ready. Is it the exhibition?'

Stella sighed, wiping her eyes. 'Yes, in a way. I've got painter's block. I can't get past this one painting and the exhibition's coming up fast.' She stirred her coffee. 'I've done exhibitions before, so I don't know why this is freaking me out. But I don't seem to have enough time to paint since Gerta came along – of course, I shouldn't, what's the point of having children if you don't change your life for them, it's just – well, I'm not sure Rick has changed his life much.' She immediately felt guilty for saying so. 'He has, that's unfair. He's taken Gerta out now –

I should be home painting - but then he's off to Lawton for his pop-up kitchen, which used to be once a week but now it's twice.'

Sarah said: 'We're planning to queue tonight.' She looked so sheepish that Stella smiled.

'I hope you get in,' she said. 'It's a pity I can't put a good word in with the chef but he's very strict about the first come, first serve rule.'

'Oh, I wasn't suggesting…' Sarah began.

Stella laughed and patted her hand. 'I know,' she said. She sat back to take a sip of coffee. She sighed. 'Sorry to be such a moaner. I know what a great life I've got.. It just feels like too much sometimes. I can't believe I used to have the time and energy to paint and draw every day. It sounds funny to other people but being creative takes a lot of energy and concentration. It's not simply the time I spend in the studio, it's finding the inspiration, letting ideas have time to brew quietly.'

'Not something you can do with a two-year-old,' Sarah nodded. 'I know about that.' Sarah had two boys, ten and eight. But you know you make it harder on yourself. I can't believe you don't even have a cleaner for that big house. I couldn't make do without Mrs Wooton, and my house doesn't have four turrets and look like a small castle.'

Stella sighed. 'Rick did, before I moved in. But I didn't like the idea of someone I didn't know poking around the house. It feels like having a servant.'

'You didn't mind Grazja living in as a carer for Gina,' Sarah pointed out.

It had been Sarah who'd arranged for a live-in carer to look after Gina when Stella had first come to Mapton following Gina's accident. Stella would have looked after her grandmother herself (although grudgingly) if Gina's dog, Bing Crosby, hadn't sunk his teeth into her ankle hard enough to disable her too.

Grazja Bobienski had been a godsend.

'That was different,' Stella said. 'Gina couldn't do anything for herself and I was off my ankle. We needed her. Besides, it was Grazja.'

'Well,' Sarah said slowly. 'Grazja rang me last night. Her job in Edinburgh ended. Her old lady died last month'

'Oh, that's awful,' Stella said. 'Grazja really liked her. Is she all right? Why didn't she tell us? Gina hasn't mentioned it.'

'She's down,' Sarah said. 'She could do with a change of scene. Sea air and a live-in position with light cleaning duties and childcare might do her the world of good. You know she can't cope with nothing to do.'

Sarah's tone struck Stella as a little rehearsed. 'You want me to employ Grazja as a housekeeper stroke nanny?'

'I think you should consider it.'

'Why?' Stella shook her curls, bewildered.

'Because,' Sarah said patiently. 'I think you're suffering from exhaustion and mild depression and I'm concerned that if you don't get support soon it will become serious depression.'

'Are you telling me this as my doctor?'

'As your doctor and your friend,' Sarah said. 'You haven't seemed quite yourself for a while. Look, Stella, most women, even if they only go back to work part-time, have a work place that is *not* their house. They get away from it all. The cleaning and

21

the child-care, etcetera, etcetera are there when they get back but they have a break from it. A mental break. You're not having that.'

'I love being with Gerta,' she said. 'I like watching her grow. There are loads of stay-at-home mums.'

'Yes, and they rarely have careers as super-successful artists, or if they do you can bet they use their earnings to pay for extra help,' Sarah said. 'Think about it; having Grazja around will lessen the burden for a while. She can run your household while you recharge your creative energy. And you'd be doing her a favour. Maybe only till after your exhibition?'

Stella considered it. 'I'd have to talk to Rick. And Gerta.'

Sarah nodded. 'Good,' she said. 'I think it will help both of you.'

#

On her way home, Stella popped into the new Boots that had recently opened. A Boots in Mapton had caused a stir – brand chains were a rarity around here, not because Mapton was trying for an independent business ethos, but because most chains didn't consider Mapton worth bothering with, or simply didn't know of its existence at all. So a Boots was seen as a sign of Mapton's upward mobility.

Stella liked their brand of cheap cleansers and moisturisers. She wasn't a fan of fancy beauty products.

As Stella browsed the shelves, she saw Gina's blazing red hair appear at the window. She'd been spotted. Grinning, Gina waved to her and pushed through the door.

'Hello, duckie,' she said. 'Where's Gerta?'

'With Rick,' Stella said. 'Just till he goes to Lawton. It's his pop-up kitchen tonight.'

Gina nodded. 'Dunno why anyone likes that posh food. Tastes like salt 'n' spit.' This was Gina's standard comment on Rick's haute cuisine, and said out of habit rather than malice.

'What yer doing here?' Gina asked. 'Not badly are yer? Or Gerta?'

'No, no,' Stella said. 'Just buying moisturiser. So, where are you off to?'

Gina puffed her chest out. 'I've just picked me 'n' George's lunch up from Dan's Cobstop. I'll take it up to the beach hut in a bit but first I'm going over to The Paradise to have it out wi' Dennis Payton.'

'Have it out with him?' Stella asked, alarmed. 'Why, what's he done?'

Gina looked outraged. 'I told yer yesterday. He's only going to make The Paradise into a sex camp.'

'Oh, yes. I remember. Rick said you were getting yourselves all worked up about it. I think it's just a daft rumour.'

'Well, that's what I'm going to find out, ain't it,' Gina said. 'And then we'll see.'

'By having it out with Dennis and riling him up,' Stella stated.

Gina drew back a bit, nettled. 'I'll be polite,' she said. 'Unless he has a go at me.'

Stella felt the familiar exhaustion settle like a fog in her brain. She should try stopping Gina – Gina and Dennis had a bad history since he'd banned her from Karaoke nights for heckling – but, honestly, Stella couldn't find the energy.

'Well,' she said. 'Good luck with that. I've got to go. Rick needs to be off soon.'

Gina followed her out of the shop. 'Bring Gerta to the beach hut after lunch,' she said. 'It's a nice day. You look like you could do wi' a bit o' sun.'

'Maybe,' Stella said, waving Gina off to her 'High Noon' with Dennis Payton.

#

Rick was back with Gerta, when Stella got home.

'Where've you been?' he asked stiffly. 'I tried ringing you.'

'Sorry,' Stella said. 'I met Sarah for coffee, and then I bumped into Gina.'

'I thought you needed to paint,' he said.

Stella suppressed an urge to snap back. 'I needed to talk,' she explained. 'I've been feeling exhausted. Sarah thinks it might be mild depression.'

Rick's expression softened and he unfolded his arms. 'I think she's right, babe,' he said, sounding relieved. 'You haven't been yourself. Is she going to put you on medication?'

'No,' Stella said. 'It's not that bad yet. Sarah said I need more support. More time and space to paint.'

Rick stepped back. After a moment he said: 'Okay. I get that. You want me to help out more, is that what you're saying?'

'No,' Stella nodded. 'Sarah suggested I hire Grazja to be a sort of nanny/housekeeper.'

'Huh?' Rick said. 'What? Like live here with us!'

Stella nodded. 'We've got room. She could have the annexe over the garage. She wouldn't even be living in the house.'

'Yeah but still… Anyway, Grazja's already got a gig she's happy with. What about her old lady in Edinburgh.'

'She died recently. Apparently Grazja's feeling a bit lost.'

'Sarah told you that? I didn't know she knew Grazja that well.'

Stella folded her arms defensively. 'It was Sarah who first recommended Grazja after Gina's accident. They stay in touch. She thinks it will help Grazja out too.'

'What do you want?' Rick asked. 'That's what matters. Do you want a housekeeper? God, it sounds weird just to say it, like we're Victorians. I mean, I know I had a cleaner – we should never have let her go, but still… and do you want someone else looking after Gerta?'

Stella hesitated. 'I didn't at first. It sounded mad, but the more I think about it… It's Grazja. She's our Mary Poppins. She's magic. Look what she did for me and Gina. It'd just be for a few weeks while I prepare for my exhibition.'

Rick nodded slowly. 'Lemme think about it,' he said. He approached cautiously to put his arms around her. She let him, pressing her nose into his familiar scent. He smelled good and she sighed.

Gina Wades In

Gina crossed the threadbare carpet of The Paradise's dimly lit club bar; at this time of day it was utilised by a few locals playing bingo. The caller stood on the small stage, flanked by silver tinsel curtains. He stopped when he saw Gina; everyone did.

Gina hadn't set foot in The Paradise for almost four years, not since Dennis had banned her from Karaoke nights. It wasn't as though she hadn't been warned enough times.

In the sudden silence, Gina threw back her shoulders and marched forward.

'Where's Dennis?' she demanded.

The bingo-caller jerked his head to the back of the room. All eyes watched Gina as she sailed past, and she heard the outbreak of excited chatter in her wake.

Dennis looked up as Gina barged into his dingy office at the back of the clubhouse. He didn't appear surprised.

'Well, well,' he said. 'Look what the cat dragged in.'

'That's not very polite, Dennis,' Gina said, looming above him.

Dennis chortled. 'That's good coming from you, Gina.' He nodded to the chair in front of his desk. 'Have a seat. To what do I owe this rare pleasure? Not begging to come back, are you?'

'You needn't worry about that, Dennis, although the way I hear it The Paradise needs the business.'

Dennis smiled sourly. 'We're doing all right,' he said. 'Now, what do you want, Gina?'

'The truth,' Gina said.

Dennis raised his eyebrows. 'About what?'

Gina caught sight of the girly calendar nailed to the wall behind his chair. She curled her orange lips. Dennis twisted to see what she was looking at and turned back, grinning, daring her to say something.

Gina forced her attention back to the matter at hand. 'The truth about this sex camp we keep hearing about,' she challenged him.

'Sex camp?' Dennis's gaze was intimate. 'That sounds fun but whatever do you mean?'

Gina blushed to her orange roots but held her ground. 'It means, Dennis, that there's a rumour going round – from a reliable source I must say – that you intend to make The Paradise into an adult-only site where swingers and sex addicts can come to make free. We know you've applied for the club license.'

Dennis leaned forward, folding his hands together. 'And that's what people are saying?'

Gina eyeballed him. 'That's right. Well, is it true? That's what we want to know.'

'Do you now?' Dennis said, tipping back in his chair. 'And what business is it of yours what I do with my park?'

Gina glared. 'It's Mapton's business,' she said. 'We got a reputation to keep up.'

Dennis laughed. 'Since when have you worried about 'reputation', Gina Pontin?'

'I don't give a hoot what people think of me,' Gina snapped. 'But I care about Mapton.'

'Very civic minded, I'm sure,' Dennis said. 'But it's none of your, or anyone else in this town's business what I do with my own property.'

'So it's true then,' Gina demanded. 'Shame on you, Dennis Payton. I know you're a snake but I didn't think even you'd stoop this low.'

Dennis shrugged. 'I don't have to admit or deny anything to you, Gina. Like I said, what I do with The Paradise is my own affair.'

'If you spruced it up a bit,' Gina said, 'you wouldn't struggle so much for nice families. It's a bloody tip, Dennis. You've really let it go. When are you gonna get that sign fixed?'

Dennis stood up. 'Best improvement I made to The Paradise was banning you. There's plenty who'd agree. Now, I got a ton of work to do, so if you clear off I'll be obliged.'

Gina rose. 'I was just offering some advice,' she said. 'No need to be so touchy. So, I'll tell the committee you're going ahead. We'll be taking action, you know.'

'What bloody committee?' Dennis said. 'You're not on the council.'

'We've formed an action group,' Gina said, raising her chin. 'Mapton Knights. That's 'knights' with a K. We're fighting to keep Mapton clean and decent from scum like you.'

'You and whose army?' Dennis laughed.

'Oh, you'll be surprised just how many people you've upset' Gina said. 'Mapton won't stand for this, Dennis. You mark my words.'

Dennis sneered. 'You tell your committee whatever you want. I ain't confirming nothing. Like I said, it ain't no-one's business what I do, 'specially yours.'

'We'll see,' Gina swelled. 'Prepare for a fight, Dennis, cos we're gonna take you down.'

'Ooh, I'm quaking,' Dennis shot back.

'You will be,' Gina said, and strode out of his office.

#

After Gina left, Dennis picked up his phone and dialled a number. When the recipient picked up he said: 'Gina Pontin's just been in. The ball's really rolling now.'

#

The first meeting of the Mapton Knights Action Committee (MKAC, pronounced emkac) took place on Thursday evening in the function room of The Diving Helmet. Dave Suggs, landlord of The Helmet, who got on unusually well with Gina, agreed they could use the room for free. Not only that, Sugsy was outraged about the possibility of a sex camp and wanted to sign up with the Knights. In addition to him, Gina and George, the rest of the group was formed from Sue's Scooter gang, The Mapton Marauders, the seven in attendance being the core of the gang, while others often only turned up for race nights.

George had brought along a small gavel which he banged on the table to bring the meeting to order.

'Ooh, George 'as got his knocker out,' Sue crowed.

'Put it away, George,' Andy Timmis called. 'You'll frighten the ladies.'

There was cackling. George blushed but kept his gavel out. 'Let's start the meeting,' he said. 'First

29

things first. We need to appoint a chair, a secretary to take notes, and a treasurer.'

'A treasurer?' Gina looked at him like he was mad. 'We won't be making money.'

'Ahem, yes. But we'll probably need a small petty cash fund to get started,' George said. 'For leaflets and such.'

'Sounds like you've put some thought into this,' Sue said admiringly.

'Well, yes,' George said, shuffling a sheaf of papers in his hands. 'I've taken the liberty of putting together a rough agenda, just to get us started.' He passed them out.

'That's what I like,' Sugsy said. 'Someone with a bit of initiative. Well done, mate.'

George blushed again.

'Oh, he was up all night doing these,' Gina said to cover the fact she hadn't a clue he'd planned an agenda.

'Right,' George said. 'First thing we need to do is appoint a chairperson to run the meetings. Now, as the idea to form this group was Gina's, I nominate her.'

Gina beamed at him. Another surprise but a welcome one.

The rest of the group was silent. Finally Sue said: 'But the idea for the name was yours, George, and you've produced a whole agenda. I nominate you.'

This produced rumbles of agreement.

'Oh,' George said, looking embarrassed. 'I really didn't mean…'

'No, George. It should be you. Remember how well you used to run those slide-show talks at the library?'

'That was twenty years ago,' George protested weakly.

'They were great,' Alf said. 'My favourite was 'Mapton's Monkey Witch Trial'. How did you get slides from the sixteenth century?'

'Er, the pictures were drawings out of books,' George explained, 'put on to slides.'

'Yeah but how did they do that?'

George looked baffled. 'They didn't,' he said. 'I did.'

'Amazing,' nodded Alf. 'Yeah, you should definitely be chair. I second Sue's nomination.'

'Let's vote on it,' cried Sue. 'George for chair.'

All hands shot up except for Gina's. She glared belligerently around. 'This committee was my idea.'

George leaned towards her. Apologetically, he said: 'All it means is that I run the meetings. Boring stuff. You'll be campaign leader.'

Gina considered. 'All right,' she said, raising her hand. 'George is chair. I nominate myself for campaign leader.'

'I don't think you can nominate yourself,' Sue said.

'I nominate her,' George quickly intervened.

'I second it,' Sugsy said.

A moment's ominous silence followed while the group processed the idea of Gina as leader.

Next to Gina, George stared at them beseechingly. It was the look of a man who wanted an easier life.

'I vote yes,' Sue said, raising her hand. 'As long as I can be the PR person.'

'What's that?' Mildred asked.

'Public relations,' Sue said.

'Sue is popular,' Alf pointed out. 'She knows lots of people. And she's a celebrity.'

Sue had become a minor celebrity when Channel Five made a pilot programme called Britain's Maddest Seaside Town.

'That's true,' agreed Andy. 'And I'll be treasurer.'

Babble broke out around the table. George banged his gavel. 'Order,' he cut through the noise. 'I bring this meeting to order.'

When he had their full attention he continued. 'Let's put it to motion then. Gina for campaign leader, Sue for PR, Andy for treasurer. All say aye?'

'Aye.' It was unanimous.

'Finally we need a secretary to minute the meetings and contact members.'

Mildred tentatively raised her hand. 'I was a secretary for years, George. I can take the minutes in shorthand and then type them up.' Her blue hair quivered.

'Excellent,' George said. 'Do you have a computer, Mildred?'

Mildred looked worried. She glanced at husband Alf. 'No, but I still have my old typewriter.'

'Don't believe in computers,' Alf said. 'They're rubbish.'

'Oh, dear,' George said. 'I'm afraid they're vital in this day and age. You'll need to email and word-process, Mildred. You can't be secretary without them.'

Mildred's face crumpled. Her friend, Carole, raised her hand. 'I've got a computer and I'm a whizz on the email, George. Mildred and I can do it together. She can take shorthand during the meetings and I'll help her with the computer stuff.'

'Fantastic, Carole,' George said. 'Team-work; that's what we like to see. You can be joint secretary. All say aye?'

All did. Mildred beamed at Carole. 'Pass me some paper and a pen, George. I'll start right now.'

'Ahem, number two on the agenda,' began George.

'What was number one?' Alf asked.

'What we just did,' George replied. 'Decide on the committee roles.'

'Alf,' hissed Mildred, elbowing him.

Alf batted her away.

'So, number two on the agenda,' George continued. 'What are we 'for'?'

'Stopping the sex camp,' Gina said.

They all nodded.

'Keeping Mapton as it is,' Andy ventured. 'A good, clean old-fashioned family town.'

'Ah,' said George, pointing his gavel at Andy. 'That's good. We're preserving Mapton. We're traditionalists.'

'We don't want no perverts," Sue said. 'It'll be paedos next.'

'And them dog-walkers,' Alf piped up. 'Them who like to watch.' Mildred shushed him.

'Well, there's enough of that around here as it is,' Sugsy said.

Everyone looked at him.

'That's what I've heard,' he protested.

'I believe the term is 'dogging," George said. 'I saw a documentary on it. Sickening. Let's be sure not to get that phrase mixed up with dog walking. After all most people in Mapton do walk their dogs and we don't want to offend decent folk by misapplying that term.'

Alf reddened.

'As PR person I should put together a mission statement,' Sue announced.

'A what?'

'A mission statement,' Sue repeated. 'It's what companies do. They have a mission statement to let people know what they're about – what they stand for 'n' all.'

'Sue watches all those programmes on business,' Mildred confided to the group. 'Like Hotel Inspector, The Apprentice, Bling my Business. She knows it all.' She looked proudly at Sue.

Sue swelled. 'It's amazing what you can learn from the TV,' she said. 'And of course I was on TV, so I know how the media works.'

Gina rolled her eyes. 'That should be my job,' she said. 'I'm campaign leader.'

'But I'm PR,' Sue pointed out. 'Public relations. It's my job to write stuff for publicity.'

George quickly jumped in. 'You should do it together. Gina had a great idea to leaflet Mapton residents about the camp. We can add the mission statement to that. Now, Gina's already been busy and had a meeting with Dennis Payton…'

This caused a flurry of excitement.

George turned to Gina. 'Gina, can you report your findings to the committee?'

Gina puffed her chest out. 'I can, George,' she said. She stood dramatically. 'Dennis Payton ain't got a decent bone in his body.'

'So the rumour's true?' Sue asked.

'He wouldn't deny it,' Gina said. 'Practically admitted it. And he said it weren't none of our business what he does with The Paradise.'

'Course it's our bloody business,' Andy blurted. 'If you drive in to Mapton from Siltby side The Paradise is the first thing you see. How long have we been trying to get him to fix that sign? It's a mess now. How's it gonna look wi' a load of sleazy pervs hanging out?'

'Like Mapton's scraping the bottom of the barrel, that's how it'll look,' Alf said.

'Like a slum,' Sugsy agreed.

'What else did he say, Gina?' Mildred asked.

'Called us a load of interfering busy-bodies. Said we were snobs and thought we were better than everyone else.'

'Cheeky bogger!' Sue said. 'I been going to The Paradise for Sunday lunch for years. Never again. He's lost my custom.'

'And mine,' Andy declared. 'All the Marauders should boycott him.'

Alf looked a little aggrieved. 'It's such good value though. Two courses for £4.95.'

'Yes, but the quality's slid a bit,' Mildred said. 'Last week I couldn't tell whether I was eating pork, beef, or lamb.'

'It's horsemeat,' Gina informed her. 'That's what Rick thinks. Dennis gets his meat wholesale from somewhere but it's not local. Rick says you can't sell a beef dinner for less than two pounds fifty and make a profit without summat dodgy going on.'

Mildred looked a little green. It clashed with her blue rinse.

'The French eat horsemeat all the time,' Carole said.

'Exactly,' Sugsy said. 'It's foreign. Shows Dennis Payton for what he is.'

'What's that?' asked George.

'An unpatriotic opportunist,' Sugsy replied.

Everyone looked impressed.

'Well said, Sugsy,' Gina said. 'He's insulting Mapton if he thinks he's going to get away wi' it.'

Grazja's Return

Stella had finally managed to get Gerta settled for the night when the doorbell rang.

'Oh, for God's sake,' Stella grumbled glancing at the clock. It was half past eight. She really wanted to put her feet up with a glass of wine.

She opened the door cautiously, keeping it on the chain.

'I not salesperson or mass murderer,' the woman on the doorstep said.

Stella shrieked and slipped the chain off, throwing the door wide. 'Grazja. How'd you get here so quickly? We haven't even decided yet.'

'Decided what?' Grazja asked, after Stella had hugged her.

'Whether you should be our housekeeper,' Stella said.

Grazja looked bemused. 'I don't know nothing about this,' she said. 'I just come because I want to. My old lady die.'

'I know,' Stella said. 'I'm so sorry. Come in, come in.'

'How'd you know?' Grazja asked.

'Sarah told me.'

'Oh, Sarah,' Grazja nodded. 'Yes. She worry about me, silly woman.'

'I know how fond you were of Mrs Alexander. You must be feeling awful. How did she die?'

'In her sleep,' Grazja said. 'It was good death. Peaceful. She was very ill and very old, so not a

37

surprise but still…' she sighed. 'She was hard one to crack. Even harder than Gina.'

'You could find the soft centre in a stone,' Stella said, leading Grazja into the kitchen. 'Are your bags in the car?'

'I left them in B&B,' Grazja explained. 'I not expect to be put up. I came on… how do you say it – a limb?'

'A whim,' Stella smiled. 'I can't believe you're here; you really are Mary Poppins.'

Grazja tilted her head quizzically. 'I not fly in with umbrella,' she said. 'But why you say that? What you mean about 'housekeeper'?'

'I'll make us some tea,' Stella said. 'Then we'll talk. Or would you like a glass of wine?' she added hopefully.

When they were settled on the sofa in the garden room, sipping tea, and dunking biscuits, Stella explained why she'd thought Grazja had arrived so swiftly.

Grazja smiled. 'It's good idea, me your housekeeper for a while. I like it. Give me time to think what to do next.

'I want it too," Stella sighed. Now that Grazja was here she really wanted her to stay. 'But Rick's not sure.'

'I don't have to live-in,' Grazja said.

'Well you could,' Stella said. 'We've got the annexe over the garage. We had it built for Rick's mum when she comes over. It has a little kitchenette, as well as a shower and toilet.'

'Oh yes,' Grazja nodded. 'I remember.'

'Of course, Gina will be jealous; you usually stay at hers.'

Grazja rolled her eyes. 'I only stay a couple of nights then. This is different.'

'Actually,' Stella realised, 'Gina will probably be *very* jealous. She'll see it as an insult that I haven't asked her for help, and now I'm stealing her best friend.'

'Ha!' Grazja laughed. 'So Gina. No, we tell her that you are doing this to help me out. We say I need the job.'

'Do you?' Stella asked.

Grazja shrugged. 'I like to be busy. I like to look after people. So yes, I suppose so. You don't have to pay me much though. I have money.'

'I'll pay you the going rate,' Stella assured her.

Grazja shrugged. 'We talk business tomorrow. So, Gina not know you been struggling?'

Stella shook her head. 'I've been good at hiding it. Only Sarah and Rick really noticed.'

'Sarah a doctor, trained to notice. Rick live with you,' Grazja said. 'Harder to hide.'

'That and he's more perceptive than Gina.'

Grazja grinned. 'A rock more perceptive than Gina. Oh, I miss her.'

'Why didn't you go see her first?' Stella asked.

'She not in,' Grazja said. 'Not answering her phone either. George out too.'

'Oh, that's right. I forgot,' Stella tapped her head. 'They've gone to a meeting. They've formed a committee. There're rumours of some sort of dodgy 'adult only' stuff going to be introduced at The Paradise. Gina's got herself all worked up about it.'

Grazja raised her eyebrow. 'You mean sexy stuff?'

'Supposedly. A camp for swingers. It's just a rumour,' Stella laughed. 'It'll give Gina something to be outraged about for two minutes and then everyone will forget about it. Nothing will come of it.'

Grazja's grin widened. 'I come back at right time,' she clapped gleefully. 'This I must see. Gina enraged by prospect of rampant intercourse.'

This set Stella laughing. Soon they were in tears. 'Intercourse' had once been Gina's catchphrase, although prudishly rather than pruriently. All of Mapton laughed about it.

'She doesn't use the word so often since she's been having it regularly with George.'

'Shame,' Grazja said, wiping away tears. 'Let's hope she bring it back. Now what else has been going on in Mapton?'

'Ah,' said Stella. 'Where to start…'

February had brought storms to the east coast. Violent winds drove massive waves of debris and smashed sea life onto the beach. Flooding never breached the seawall that had been built in the fifties after the devastating flood of '53, but it came close, and the beach was strewn with timbers, plastics, and the broken bodies of quite a few gulls.

The number of rescued seals treated by the Marine Life and Animal Sanctuary a mile along the coast at Golden Dunes trebled overnight until their small pools were heaving with slippery sea mammals, all in a state of distress.

'A lot of Maptonites volunteered for the clean-up,' Stella said. 'Me and Rick. Even Gina, although she got sent home for swearing at a couple of kids.'

'What were they doing?' Grazja asked.

'Just being kids.'

Grazja grinned. 'I wonder if it too late to call on Gina? Maybe she back home.'

'She might be home by now. She'll love to see you.'

#

Gina was thrilled to find Grazja on her doorstep. Already flushed with excitement after the meeting, she shrieked when she saw her friend.

'You bogger! Why didn't you tell me you were coming?'

'Spontaneous decision,' Grazja replied, returning Gina's hug.

'George,' Gina bellowed. 'George.'

Grazja winced. 'My eardrums burst.'

'Oh, go on wi' yer,' Gina laughed. 'Geooorge!'

Grazja expected George to emerge out of Gina's lounge but he came rushing out of his own bungalow across the street.

'What?' he shouted. 'What's wrong?'

'Nothing's wrong yer great idiot,' Gina beamed. 'Grazja's here.'

George, looking close to a heart attack, took in Grazja and promptly remembered his gentlemanly manners.

'Grazja,' he panted, taking her hand. 'How lovely to see you.'

'You too, George,' Grazja said, accepting his peck on the cheek.

'I'll ring Stella,' Gina said.

'No need. I see her already. I come here first but you not in. Stella say you at some meeting.'

'Oh aye, we were,' Gina said. 'Come in. We'll tell you all about it.' Her eyes shone. 'You'll never believe it.'

She told her tale to an enraptured Grazja.

'So,' she finished, 'we've called ourselves the Mapton Knights, like the knights of the round table fighting for good.'

'No, we're named after the Knights Templar,' George explained. 'Not King Arthur's knights.'

Gina rolled her eyes. 'It's all the same.'

George looked very much like he wanted to say it wasn't but backed down under Gina's glare.

'Anyway,' Gina said. 'It's all about fighting for old-fashioned British values, like decency. It's all being taken away by Europe and all them immigrants flooding in from bongo land and the like.'

'Not this again, Gina,' Grazja threw up her hands. It was an old conversation. 'I am immigrant. I pay my way. I not change your culture,' she said. 'You not want me in Mapton?'

Gina guffawed. 'Oh, gi' over. You sound like Rick. It's different. And you come from a Christian country. That's the trouble here. We're losing that and look what happens. Orgies and gays kissing in public.'

'And I think of you as being practically English,' George soothed.

'Until you open your mouth,' Gina added. 'Ain't nothing comes out right then.'

'Not my fault,' Grazja smiled wearily. 'Ain't got no good English-speaking friends.'

'Yer cheeky bogger,' Gina roared and set them laughing.

'Oh, Gina,' Grazja said. 'Only person as intolerant as you was my old lady, Mrs Alexander. She died, you know. A month ago.'

'Oh, duckie. I am sorry. What you're going to do? Sign back up with the agency?'

'I not know at moment.'

'Was she ill?' George asked.

'Yes. Very ill. She been ill for a long time. Not such a shock. I miss her though.'

'Course you do,' Gina said. 'Even if she were a bit of a cow.'

'She not so bad,' Grazja said. 'I had worse.' She gave Gina a rueful look. George understood but Gina missed it. She was thinking.

'I wonder if you could get some work around here,' she pondered. 'There's lots of cripples. Course, they want it on the NHS and you don't work for them.'

'I find something,' Grazja said. 'Don't worry. Maybe you think of someone who might need me.'

'Hmm,' nodded Gina. 'I'll put me thinking cap on.'

Genius Gina

Stella stared in the bathroom mirror at the rings around her eyes. God, she hadn't noticed how haggard she looked.

Yet, things were looking up. She had slept all the way through the night, as had Gerta; a rarity for them both.

And best of all, Grazja had moved in to the annexe and Gina thought it was her own idea.

Stella could hear Gerta chattering in the kitchen as Grazja made her breakfast. Through her haze, Stella felt a stab of guilt; she should be feeding Gerta. But the relief at being able to take a break, just for a couple of days at least, was tremendous.

'Mummy, Mummy,' Gerta squealed up the stairs. 'Breakfast ready. Come get.'

Stella was surprised to see a place set for her at the breakfast bar next to Gerta's high chair.

'Ohhh, you're getting big,' she said, swinging Gerta into the chair.

'Big girl,' Gerta affirmed, banging her spoon on the worktop. 'Me eat now.'

Grazja dolloped porridge into Gerta's plastic dish, added honey, plain yogurt, and blueberries, and placed it in front of Gerta, who stuck her spoon into it with a splat.

'Breakfast?' Grazja said to Stella.

Stella shook her head. 'Oh, no. Thanks, but I'm not hungry. I'll just have coffee.'

'You eat, Mummy,' Gerta commanded.

'Yes,' Grazja said. 'Mummy should eat too. You are thin, I notice, Stella. Not good to skip breakfast. I give you porridge.'

'No,' Stella protested, as Grazja filled her bowl. 'I don't think I can.'

'Try,' Grazja said firmly, placing the bowl in front of her. 'Will make you feel better.'

'Better, Mummy,' Gerta echoed. 'Like this.' She scooped up a large spoon of porridge and shoved it in her mouth. Most of it went down her chin and bib. Stella automatically reached for the kitchen roll to wipe her daughter's adorable mouth. 'You do,' Gerta insisted.

Stella couldn't help but smile at her. 'All right,' she said. 'I do.' Resignedly, she spooned the porridge and berries into her mouth. The sweetness of the honey and berries surprised her taste buds into delight. Suddenly she was starving. She began eating with relish and Gerta, observing her, attempted to match her, dropping much of it down herself.

Often, getting Gerta to eat rather than play with her food was a battle that could take forty minutes, but Gerta seemed inspired by her mother's gusto.

'Good girls,' Grazja said, taking their dishes away.

'Good girls,' Gerta agreed, beaming at Stella. Stella felt such an intense love for her daughter it almost knocked her off her stool.

'Give Mummy a hug,' she said, 'before I start work.'

Gerta gave her a sticky hug. 'No work, Mummy. We play.'

'Later, sweetie. Mummy's got lots of painting to finish. Grazja play with you till then.'

'Me paint with you.'

Stella looked at Grazja.

'Right, Miss Mucky Puppy,' Grazja said briskly, distracting Gerta as she deftly zoomed in with a wet cloth. 'Let's get you cleaned up.'

Stella made her escape, feeling guilty, yet exhilarated to have some time free. Time to paint. To be herself.

#

Gina was feeling very satisfied with herself. She considered her solution to Grazja's predicament sheer brilliance. She was surprised that neither Grazja nor Stella had thought of it themselves; they'd been suitably impressed when she suggested it to them.

Stella had spent Thursday morning moaning about how tired she felt, shuffling around like a zombie. It was enough to make Gina grit her teeth to stop her from slapping her out of it. What did Stella have to complain about?

Grazja suggested that she and Gina take Gerta for a couple of hours to let Stella have a rest. Gina, who wouldn't turn down the chance to show off her great-granddaughter in Mapton, readily agreed.

While Gerta ran around on the beach, Grazja said. 'I surprised at how thin Stella is. She has dark circles under her eyes. Have you noticed?'

Gina, who hadn't noticed at all, lied. 'Of course. But she's a mum and little ones are exhausting aren't they?'

'They are,' Grazja said, watching Gerta digging a hole like a dog. 'And she has that big house to clean. And a job.'

Gina snorted. 'What job? I don't think she's produced a painting for months.'

'That a shame,' Grazja said. 'She is an artist. Seriously, Gina, I am worried about Stella. She need some support, I think.'

A loud honk interrupted their conversation. Sue waved from her mobility scooter. 'Gina,' she called. 'I got the flyer sorted.'

'What!' Gina leapt up, starting up the steps to the sea wall. 'We're supposed to be doing that together.'

Furious, she snatched the paper out of Sue's hand.

'It ain't finished,' Sue said. 'It's just a draft. I was just on me way to see you and George. Get you to take a gander at it.'

'You shouldn't have done anything without me,' Gina snapped. 'There,' she jabbed her finger at the leaflet. 'What the bloody hell's that mean? 'Mapton Knights stand for good old British vales'?'

'Values,' Sue defended. 'It says values.'

'It don't,' Gina said. 'It says 'vales'.' She shoved the paper under Sue's nose.

Sue read it. 'It don't matter,' she said. 'It's only a draft. It'll get corrected. George will pick up stuff like that.'

'I'll pick it up,' Gina said. 'And it won't happen when I'm writing it. Come on, we'll go back to mine and work on it there.' She turned towards town.

'Aren't you forgetting something?' Sue asked, smiling smugly.

'What?'

'Only your granddaughter,' Sue nodded to the beach.

Swearing under her breath, Gina stamped back down the steps. She kept her voice low as she spoke to Grazja. 'Sue's making a bloody pig's ear out of the leaflet. I need to go supervise her; can you take care of Gerta?'

'Of course,' Grazja agreed. 'I love it. I need to be busy. I take her home. You no worry. You got things to do.'

'I have,' Gina said. 'I don't know what George was thinking letting Sue be PR.' She went over to Gerta. 'Gerta, duckie, Grandma's just going for a pee-pee. Grazja will stay with you.'

'Gramma going pee-pee?' Gerta said. 'Back soon?'

'Back soon,' Gina said.

'You should tell her truth,' Grazja reprimanded.

'She's two,' Gina dismissed her. 'She won't remember in five minutes, and she knows you. She'll be fine. I'll pop round and check on her later.'

When the leaflet was finally finished, and George was sitting in Gina's lounge carefully checking it through, Gina put her hand to her head.

'Me 'ead's pounding, George. That bloody Sue argued with everything I said. I had to rewrite most of what she'd done.'

'Um,' George murmured, frowning at the paper.

'Are you listening?' Gina demanded. 'I need a bit o' support. I got a lot on my mind.'

George looked up. He set the paper aside and gave her his full attention. 'Don't worry about Sue. You two'll rub along. I'll always back you up, you know that.'

'I should hope so,' Gina said. 'I'm the one you're having intercourse with. No, it ain't just Sue. I'm

48

worried about Grazja needing a job. And then she had the cheek to tell me Stella's too thin and looking tired like I hadn't noticed. Have you noticed, George?'

George nodded. 'I've thought she's looking a bit peaky of late. Not quite herself, but having a little one is tiring.'

'That's what I told Grazja,' Gina said. 'But she's not produced any new work, George. That's not like Stella, is it? And she'd got that exhibition coming.'

'No,' George said. 'Maybe she needs a bit of TLC. More childcare help. We can take Gerta a bit more.'

'But that's just it,' Gina cried. 'We're too busy right now. We got to stop this sex camp, George. I'm not letting Sue take over The Mapton Knights, cos she will if I take me eye off her for a second. It'll become the Sue Mulligan show, like she tried to do with that TV programme. But if Stella needs me, George... well, she's my flesh and blood.'

George patted her hand. 'You're too caring for your own good.'

Gina agreed. Then she sat upright. She grabbed George's arm. 'George, I think I'm a genius.'

'I don't doubt it,' he said.

'Grazja needs a job and Stella needs some help. It's perfect,' Gina said. 'Grazja can work for Stella. Stell, can afford it.'

'That could work,' George said. 'You are a genius.' He kissed her bottle-red head.

Later, when Gina was asleep, he would have to do some serious editing on that leaflet.

#

Stella worked throughout the morning, joined Grazja and Gerta for lunch, before heading back to her studio. Around three she heard Gerta's laborious steps up the stairs to her north turret studio, along with Grazja's encouraging murmurs.

There was a knock on the door.

'Come in,' Stella called.

The door opened and Gerta tottered in, clutching her blanket and her cuddly bunny, Boo-Boo. Boo-Boo was her companion in her cot and on any car journey. Boo-Boo meant sleep and comfort and the one time Stella had put Boo-Boo in the washing machine on a gentle cycle, Gerta had almost burst a blood vessel screaming.

Grazja followed her in. 'You want cup of tea?'

'You shouldn't be waiting on me,' Stella said. 'No Gerta,' she warned as the tot made a beeline towards the canvas and paints. 'Don't touch Mummy's painting things. You know that. Go sit on the sofa while Mummy cleans up.'

Gerta frowned but then she spotted Henry on the sofa, watching her with one eye, and headed towards him. He'd fled before she even reached him but by that time Stella had quickly wiped her hands and was on her way. She scooped her daughter up and sank into the cushions.

'Mummy's nap time,' Gerta declared. 'Bring Boo-Boo.' She shoved the bunny in Stella's face.

'For me?' Stella asked her. 'Boo-Boo for me?'

'Boo-Boo you,' Gerta affirmed. She threw her blankie over Stella, patting it down with her chubby hands. 'Mummy sleepy.'

'Thank you, sweetie,' Stella said. She knew what an honour this was: Boo-Boo and blankie.

Gerta popped her thumb in her mouth and grabbed a handful of fine hair, a sign she was the one who was tired.

'Come on,' Stella said, wriggling back against the sofa. 'Come have a nap with Mummy.'

'Boo-Boo too?' Gerta confirmed.

'Of course,' Stella said, wrapping her arm around her daughter.

Grazja smiled down at them. 'I get on with some housework,' she said. 'I be around if you need me. You have tea later.'

Gerta's breath was already slowing into the easy rhythm of slumber. How easily the innocent slept, Stella thought.

She nuzzled her nose against Gerta's silky blond curls and breathed in her sweetness. As she drifted off, she was filled with a sudden deep peace.

It was the last truly peaceful moment anyone in Mapton would know for a while.

The Leaflet

Saturday morning a leaflet landed on Mapton doormats. Emblazoned across the top was MAPTON KNIGHTS – STANDING FOR DECENT ENGLISH VALUES next to a logo of St George on his steed.

The leaflet read:

KEEP MAPTON DECENT

Fight plans to use The Paradise Holiday Park as a camp and club for SWINGERS.

- Mapton is a family holiday resort
- a sex club will promote the area for the wrong reasons
- it will damage our tourist trade
- it will attract undesirables and cause crime rates to soar
- Mapton does not have the police resources to deal with this
- the elderly will not feel safe to leave their homes
- house prices will fall
- it is immoral and unEnglish

DON'T ALLOW MAPTON TO BECOME THE NEW AMSTERDAM!

If you're interested in joining our campaign email us at Georgedragon2@gmail.com or come and sign our petition at The Last Resort Diner or at The Diving

Helmet. Someone from the Knights will be there to answer questions.

Further details of a public meeting to follow.

Mapton Knights Mission Statement:

The Mapton Knights Action Committee is a group of local residents dedicated to preserving Mapton-On-Sea. We are proud of our traditional seaside heritage, such as donkey rides, fish n chips, and beach huts. Mapton is a place where **decent** people want to holiday. Let's keep it that way.

REMEMBER, KEEP MAPTON DECENT

SAY NO TO SWINGERS!

Mapton Reacts

'I'm going to kill Gina.' Rick slapped a leaflet on the counter. 'Look at this.'

'What are you talking about?' Stella scanned the leaflet. 'Undesirables,' she giggled, shaking her head, 'crime rates will soar… oh, Gina… a petition at The Last Resort Diner. Oh, I see.'

'Yeah,' Rick said. 'She's gone too far this time. I better get down to the diner, warn Ange she's gonna be Gina'd'

'You want me to come with you?'

'Nah, stay here with Gerta.'

'Are you going to have it out with Gina?'

'Gina, George, Sue… whoever's there; why didn't they ask my permission?'

'The Marauders are your best customers,' Stella said. 'They won't be happy.'

Rick snorted. 'They shoulda thought of that before they put my diner on this leaflet without consulting me.'

Stella nodded. 'Still, try and be diplomatic,' she said. 'Anyway, we really don't want a swingers club in Mapton, do we?'

Rick raised his eyebrows. 'You don't believe any of this is real, do you? It's a rumour – a juicy one with sex in it – and everyone wants to be outraged and form a mob while most of 'em will be secretly rubbing themselves up against a chair leg with excitement.

'Ewwww. Gross,' Stella laughed. 'I wouldn't put it past Dennis Payton though. He's a bit of a sleaze.'

'Can't see him going to the trouble,' Rick said. 'Anyway, I'll go be 'diplomatic'.'

'Good luck,' Stella called after him.

When Rick reached the diner, he was staggered to find a crowd already milling. Gina and Sue were at the centre of the melee, seated at one of the diner's outside tables, chatting to Maptonites who were signing the petition.

Ange came out of the diner with a loaded tray. She delivered the drinks, smiling at Rick.

'Great business,' she said, coming over. 'Are you here to lend a hand?'

Saturday was Rick's day off. Two years ago, he'd offered Ange the chance to buy into the diner and now they were co-owners. Her son Mark, fresh out of catering college, was apprenticing in the kitchen.

'I just came over to warn you.' Rick waved his hand towards Gina's crowd. 'I had no idea it would already be this busy. I didn't give Gina or Sue permission to use the diner for their campaign. It's pissed me off.'

Ange gave him a strange look. 'Why? They didn't ask me either but I think it's a great idea. We're raking it in this morning. Mark's not had a moment to breath.'

Rick was taken aback. 'Yeah, but I don't want to make my money like this. I don't agree with the campaign.'

Ange stared at him. 'You want The Paradise to be a sex camp?'

Rick laughed. 'That's such a ridiculous phrase, Ange. What, are we a seventies Carry On film?'

'I don't see anything ridiculous about it,' Ange snapped. 'Think of the sorts it will attract, Rick.

People won't want to bring their kids to Mapton. We'll be a laughing stock.'

'For God's sake, it's just a stupid rumour, Ange. And I don't want my diner being used to organise some crackpot campaign, that's all. I'm just gonna tell them to move somewhere else.'

Ange looked furious. 'This is our diner, Rick. Half of it is mine, and I say they stay.'

But Rick turned on his heel, marching over to Gina and Sue, pushing through the folk waiting to sign.

'Ricky,' Sue beamed at him. 'You don't work Saturdays. You here to sign our petition?'

'That's a big fat no,' Rick said. 'I want to know why no one asked my permission about using the diner.'

His words caused a silence. Gina rose. 'Didn't think it'd be a problem, Rick,' she said. 'And Ange don't mind. Do yer Ange?'

Ange stood behind Rick, arms folded, mouth a thin line. 'I agree with it,' she said. 'I'm proud The Last Resort is a rallying point for the people of Mapton.'

Rick turned to glare at her. 'Well I don't agree with it, and don't want my diner mixed up with this or any other half-assed campaign.'

'It's not your diner,' Ange reiterated. 'I own half and I say Mapton's not a dumping ground for perverts. Mapton's on the up, Rick, and I don't want to see it slide back down again.'

This got a few cheers.

'She's right, Rick,' Gina said. 'Yer know it makes sense.'

'I don't think the rumour's got a grain of truth in it, Gina. You're just getting folk all stirred up for your own entertainment and assumed I'd be okay with you using my diner.'

Gina puffed out. 'Well, Ange owns half the diner like she says, and she agrees wi' it. Tell yer what, Rick, why don't we settle this rationally, like yer said.' She turned to the onlookers. 'Everyone who agrees wi' Ange and the Mapton Knights move to the right side of the diner. If yer don't agree wi' us the left. That's it; we can divide it down the middle, rational-like. Right side, decent people, left-side, pervs.'

There were laughs and rumbles of assent and then a bit of confusion because Gina and Sue had set up the petition signing on the left side of the diner if you were facing it, or the right side if you had your back to it and faced the sea. After some kerfuffle, the majority agreed to consider themselves to be on the right, facing the sea. One man remained on the left.

Sue called. 'I'm surprised at you, Peter. Dint think you were like that.'

'Not a matter of being one way or t'other,' Peter grumbled. 'I only came for me morning coffee, not a bloody political rally. Nothin' to do with me.'

'That's fair enough, Peter,' Ange said. 'Don't you worry about it.'

'I won't,' Peter said, shaking out his paper. He held it up in front of his face and that was that.

Gina looked triumphantly at Rick. 'See,' she said. 'Most of us care what happens to Mapton, even if you don't.'

'Oh, I care,' Rick retorted. 'And you just demonstrated exactly why I don't want my diner to be part of this sort of thing. You just told everyone here that if they didn't stand with you they're perverts. Bit of social bullying there, Gina. That's what I don't like about this sort of stuff.'

Gina opened her mouth to retort when a man wearing baggy shorts and a tee shirt with a crotchward pointing hand, and the legend: 'May I suggest the Sausage' emblazoned on it, stepped forward.

'You're a yank aren't yer? Yer got lower standards than us Brits,' he said. 'I ain't insulting yer, just saying if you want to do that pervy sort of stuff, yer should go home to the States.'

Rick looked him over, raising his eyebrows at Gina. 'That's nice,' he said. 'Very nice. See what you've started?'

Gina rounded on the man. 'You can't talk like that to him,' she said. 'You're not from Mapton, are you?'

The man reddened. 'I come to Mapton every year. I have a right to have a say, and besides, I was sticking up for yer, woman. What wasp's stung your arse?'

'That's my son-in-law,' Gina said, pointing at Rick. 'Right now, I agree, he's being a numpty, but he's our numpty, and if anyone can have a go at him then it's me.'

'And me,' Sue agreed, 'And Ange. Not you.'

The man's colour deepened. 'Mapton don't just belong to residents,' he growled. 'I been coming here most of me life, like a lot of holidaymakers, so I should get a say. I'm telling yer, if this place gets swamped with dirty perverts, you'll not see me nor my family again, and that goes for most of the folk who come on holiday here. Where will you be then?'

'Nice tee shirt,' Rick said. 'Real classy. I can see why you have the moral high ground.'

The man scowled and stepped forward, raising a clenched fist.

'You taking the piss?' he growled.

Rick squared up to him, adrenaline pumping. 'You work it out,' he challenged.

The man swung back for a half-hearted punch, when Gina stepped between them.

'Don't be such daft boggers,' she shouted. 'Or I'll take you both out.' She pointed to tee shirt man. 'You, have a paddle or something and cool off.'

The man postured for a moment, like a gorilla about to beat his chest then swaggered off, calling back. 'I'm tellin' everyone your café's shite.'

'It's a diner,' Rick shouted after him.

'You!' Gina poked Rick in the chest. 'Just what the bleedin' hell's wrong wi' yer?'

'C'mon, Rick,' Sue said, trundling over on her scooter. 'We're not trying to hurt anyone. We just want to keep Mapton the way it is.'

'The way we love it,' Gina added.

Rick sagged. 'I know you do,' he said facing them all. 'You see yourself as crusaders, but what I see is frightened people spreading their fear.' He shook his head sadly. 'If you want to continue what you're doing, that's your democratic right, but please, I beg of you, find another place to do it.'

He walked away, horribly aware that everyone was watching him.

#

At ten-thirty, blissfully unaware of the kerfuffle at the diner, George received a call from the Lawton Post. The journalist's name was Andrew Leith. He was twenty-three and raring for a juicy story to take him to Fleet Street. Nothing truly exciting had happened in Mapton since the hunt for the renegade dog gang had culminated in the now legendary donkey stampede and gas explosion that blew up the American diner. Andrew had been nineteen, doing Media Studies at university, dreaming of hitting the big time, when that story had briefly grabbed the public's attention. It hadn't occurred to him back then that his first job would be covering the Mapton community beat in deepest Lincolnshire. Apparently, unless you were well connected, you had to work your way up to the nationals. Andrew was determined to do it, but so far the chance had eluded him.

Until today. An anonymous contact in Mapton had emailed him a PDF snap of the leaflet. Andrew sat up as he read it, excitement building. No one in the newsroom had mentioned the possibility of a swingers club in Mapton. It would have been big news. If he got this scoop first...

He fired off an email to his contact, requesting information. Who had organised the Mapton Knights? The reply came: George Wentworth, pensioner, lives on Fisherman's Lane.

Pensioner, Andrew thought. He'll still have a number in the phone book. Mr Wentworth did, so Andrew rang him.

'George Wentworth,' a man said.

'Ah, Mr Wentworth,' Andrew began. 'I'm with the Lawton Post, Andrew Leith; I cover the Mapton beat. I saw your leaflet this morning. I'd like to do a story on it. Would you give me an interview, Mr Wentworth?'

'Well, erm, yes.' The man sounded pleased. 'We would like to publicise our concerns.'

'Of course,' Andrew said. 'Could you do it this morning? I can be there in half an hour.'

Mr Wentworth sounded surprised. 'Erm, I… well, I suppose so. I need to pop out for some milk if you want some tea.'

Andrew smiled. 'No, no,' he said. 'Don't bother yourself, Mr Wentworth. I don't want to put you out. Just the interview will be fine. What's your address?'

Then he rang his editor.

'This better be good,' Bob growled. 'I'm playing golf.'

Andrew told him.

'Wow,' Bob said. 'This could be big.'

'It's my story,' Andrew said.

'Of course. It's your beat. Get over there.'

True to his word, Andrew rang Mr Wentworth's bell thirty minutes later. The pensioner who came to the door was spruce, smartly dressed in slacks, shirt, and a nifty royal-blue cravat. He looked fitter than most Mapton people of any age. When he smiled his teeth were the uniform perfection of false ones.

He held out his hand. 'Mr Leith?'

Andrew returned the shake. 'Thanks for seeing me on such short notice, Mr Wentworth.' He followed him into the neat bungalow.

They seated themselves, Andrew on the sofa, and Mr Wentworth on the armchair. Andrew pulled a small digital recorder out of his pocket and laid it on the coffee table.

'Do you mind if I record this?'

'Not at all,' Mr Wentworth said.

Andrew took a notebook out of his other pocket; he'd jotted down a few questions. 'How did you first hear about the potential swingers club at The Paradise?'

'I have a good lady-friend,' Mr Wentworth began. 'Ms Gina Pontin, an active member of our community. It was she who first alerted me, but she heard it from a very reliable source, the deputy mayor of Mapton and Siltby.'

'Tom Turner?' Andrew asked. 'He told her officially?'

'Nooo, not officially,' Mr Wentworth squirmed. 'He didn't say it to her directly but she did overhear him talking about it on his phone in the cob shop. She wasn't eavesdropping, you understand, he was speaking very loudly as he often does. Oh, you won't put that bit in will you?'

'Of course not,' Andrew said. 'Don't worry. You can speak freely but the article will be very diplomatic. I'll just stick to the facts.'

'Excellent,' Mr Wentworth looked relieved.

'So you overheard the deputy mayor talking, but what else convinced you the threat of the swingers' club was real?'

'Dennis Payton.' Mr Wentworth scowled as he said the name. 'It's him that owns The Paradise Holiday Park where he wants to have his club. Ms Pontin went to see him to ask if it was true and he refused to deny it. Well, it's exactly the sort of thing Dennis would do. He's been struggling to fill that park for years. Not surprising as it's a scruffy eyesore. If he thinks he can make some money out of this scheme he...' He stopped. 'Er, don't say I said that about him.'

Andrew smiled reassuringly.

He smiled reassuringly a lot during the interview, as Mr Wentworth blithely talked away. By the end Andrew felt there were two extremely interesting stories he could mine. One was the possibility of a sex club in Mapton, but the other was equally as rich a seam, a social study on how the community would react – was reacting – to the perceived threat.

There was something ugly brewing, Andrew thought. He could almost smell it. Just the thought made him rub his hands together in glee.

Next stop, Deputy Mayor Turner.

#

Deputy Mayor Turner, or Pirate Tom as locals called him, was working a shift in the family butcher business, as he was wont to do on a Saturday morning, although his son now ran the shop full-time. He liked to be visible in the Siltby community.

Siltby, Mapton's near neighbour, prided itself on being the ying to Mapton's yang. Separated by little more than a mile along the promenade, Siltby had the seafront but none of the garish arcades and fast food outlets of Mapton. Siltbyites, considering themselves much more refined than Maptonites, were locked in an unending battle to escape Mapton's vulgar taint.

When the leaflets hit the homes of Siltby, delivered in the night by various Mapton Marauders, it caused a small shockwave. The Paradise, situated on the outer edge of Mapton, Siltby-side, was already a blight many Siltbyites would like to see

63

annihilated. The thought of it as a site for sordid goings on was unthinkable.

The butcher shop had been besieged by folk coming in to demand the truth from their deputy mayor.

Tom recognised Andrew Leith as soon as he walked in. As a councillor he had plenty of experience with the local press. He relished a good sound bite.

'I assure you,' he raised his voice. 'As deputy mayor I simply will not let this happen. It's a disgusting idea. I will fight it tooth and nail. Believe you me, I will get to the bottom of this.'

'That might be so,' Patricia Moor said. 'But I only want a pound o' mince, love, and a bone for Bobby.'

'Morning, Andrew,' Tom said, after he'd served Patricia. 'News does travel fast.'

'I got a tip-off this morning,' Andrew said. He waved the flyer at Tom. 'I'd like to get a comment on it from you Deputy Mayor.'

Tom nodded soberly. 'Ed,' he called to his son. 'I'm going out for a bit.'

Ed, wrapping a juicy bone for Patricia's cocker spaniel, rolled his eyes but said nothing.

Tom clomped round the counter, out of the shop, and settled himself gratefully onto his Drive Royale scooter. 'Gout's playing up,' he groaned.

Andrew looked startled. 'I didn't know gout still existed. I thought only characters in Charles Dickens got it.'

Tom snorted. 'It's a type of arthritis. Nothing to do with my diet, I'll have you know.' His wife didn't agree and was always trying to push rabbit food down him, silly moo. 'Let's go to the golf clubhouse,' he said, expertly manoeuvring the mobility scooter. 'I could do with a bite.'

'You play golf?' Andrew eyed him doubtfully.

Tom looked at him sourly. 'Sometimes,' he said. 'And my wife does. We're joint members.'

They settled in the bar with club sandwiches and halves of bitter. Tom would normally have a pint or two with lunch but this was business, and he wasn't having that young upstart journalist making him out to be a drinker.

Andrew took out his recorder and set it on the table. He took out his notepad and pen. 'It's quite noisy in here,' he explained. 'I'll take notes too, just in case.'

'I'd have suggested my house but the wife's got her WI girls over,' Tom said. 'It'd be like a hen-house. And you didn't give me any notice.'

Andrew shrugged apologetically. 'Got to strike while the iron is hot. I've already interviewed George Wentworth, chairman of the Mapton Knights.'

'Really?' Tom leaned forward, interested. 'What did he have to say?'

Andrew pointedly pressed the record button on the digital recorder. 'He mentioned you as source of this rumour. Apparently you were overheard talking about the application for the licence on your phone in a public place. Can you comment on that?'

'I can't comment on other people's perceptions or what they may or may not have heard,' Tom said. 'But I can confirm that there are rumours of this club and that we at the town council are currently investigating this very seriously. I am not at liberty to say more about the source of the rumour until we have got to the bottom of it.'

'The Mapton Knights, the action group that have put out this leaflet seem certain the potential site is The Paradise Holiday Park in Mapton-On-Sea. Can you confirm this?'

'I can't confirm it,' Tom said. 'But I can tell you this…' He drew himself up. 'It would happen over my dead body. It would be a ridiculous idea.'

'Why ridiculous? The Paradise and other caravan parks stand empty for half the year,' Andrew pressed. 'Perhaps some swingers' weekends in the winter would be a great way of generating extra income and introducing new tourists to Mapton.'

'That's the nature of seaside towns,' Tom dismissed him. 'We're seasonal businesses. But Mapton and Siltby have seen a growth in winter visitors over the last few years. No respectable, normal holidaymaker will want to come and stay near a sex camp whatever the season. Adults have the right to do what they like behind the closed doors of their own homes but I've been elected to protect the interests of my constituents. Mapton and Siltby are popular residences for retirees and pensioners. They'll be afraid to go out at night if swarms of swingers land in the area.'

'So you condone this new action group, Mapton Knights?' Andrew asked.

'Well, as an elected official, I neither condone nor oppose it,' Tom smiled. 'But I am proud to see local residents coming together in community spirit to preserve our traditions. I couldn't speak for other members of the council.'

Andrew cocked his head; Tom was pleased to see him take the bait.

'Are you saying there has been disagreement among the town council about the issue?'

Tom waved his hand. 'Not disagreement, no. But everyone knows that Mayor Seaton and I often take differing views. It's part of a healthy democracy. Mayor Seaton is a very kind, good-hearted lady. She's liberal and very open minded; she sometimes considers me a bit of a fuddy duddy. I'd love to live in an ideal world where you can trust people to behave decently but unfortunately we don't.'

He took a large, satisfied bite of his club sandwich, shooting mayonnaise down his shirt.

'Oh for Christ sakes,' he said. 'This shirt was only clean on this morning.'

#

'I can't believe you didn't tell me,' Gina fumed at George. 'I was only at the diner; I would have been here like a shot.'

After a long day 'campaigning' on the seafront, Gina had come home triumphantly waving pages of signatures in George's face, only to be trumped by his visit from the Lawton Post.

'What you were doing was vital, Gina,' George was animated. 'This way we had a two pronged attack. You on the ground, winning hearts and minds, me with the media, getting our cause coverage. We couldn't have had a better start to this campaign.'

'But I woulda had plenty to say,' Gina protested. 'I'm good wi' me mouth.'

'I can vouch for that,' George twinkled at her.

Gina stared at him, then barked out a laugh. 'Oh, yer dirty bogger. Gerrof wi' yer. You'll be one of them swingers next.'

Ginger Rogers woofed, as she often did at Gina's laugh, nuzzled George's shoe, and waddled to stand by her bowl, staring plaintively at it.'

George automatically reached for the dog biscuits but Gina stopped him. 'She's had people feeding her all day. She knows a soft touch when she sees one. Got George worked out, don't you, Ginger?'

Ginger wagged her tail, looking beseechingly at George, whose hand wavered over the biscuit box.

'Oh, gi' over,' Gina said, 'Bing Crosby never begged like that. You should be ashamed of yo'self.'

Ginger gave up, went to her basket, and flopped down with a disgruntled sigh.

'How many signatures did you get?'

'Yer won't believe it,' Gina brightened. 'We got Mapton all stirred up.' She flourished the pages at him.

George leafed through, whistling. 'Looks like we've got the whole town supporting us.'

'Not the whole town,' Gina said. 'Rick made a right numpty of himself when he found out we was using the diner. Caused a right scene, shouting at us all and having a go at Ange. He almost got in a fight, can you believe it?.'

George frowned. 'But he gave us permission to use the diner didn't he? You said you'd asked him.'

Gina suddenly became fascinated by Ginger Rogers's claws. 'Look at them claws,' she said. 'They need clipping. She'll be tearing chunks out of the furniture otherwise. I'll fetch the clippers.'

She turned to leave but George said: 'Gina?'

It wasn't often George put his foot down with Gina, but she'd discovered over the years that there were times when he could be unobligingly stubborn.

She recognised the tone of his voice.

Avoiding his eyes, she said: 'I meant to but time just went, and Grazja turned up, and besides, Rick's me son-in-law. He should be willing to help us out. Look at all the babysitting we do for them.'

'Oh Gina,' George groaned. 'You let me think he'd said yes. That's why I put it in the leaflet.'

'Well, he hadn't said no,' Gina cried. 'And you'd think he'd be only too pleased to help out his family.'

'We don't want to fall out with Rick and Stella,' George said.

Gina rolled her eyes. 'We won't. Remember when I floored him wi' me crutch. He forgave me fo' that didn't he?'

'I suppose so,' George said, but he looked worried. '' You say he almost got in a fight? That's not like Rick.'

'I know,' Gina said. 'It were funny though. I can't wait to tell Stella.'

Brother Frank

Rick burned with embarrassment. Had that really been him, squaring up for a fight? Publicly. In front of his own diner.

Jesus! As Gina had said, what the hell was wrong with him?

Well, that would give Mapton something else to buzz about.

Rick hit the beach at a stride, where, once he cleared the day-trippers and dog-walkers, the beach went on for isolated miles. Walking east a mile would take him to Siltby, and he couldn't face that, so he headed west, head down against the usual Mapton wind.

He guessed that things with Stella had gotten to him more than he'd admitted. She'd been snappy lately, off sex - it had been too long – and distracted. He'd been worried she was getting depressed, that the pressure of this exhibition was too much for her. After all, he knew about pressure. When he'd been a top chef he'd cracked under it.

And now he didn't know how he felt about Grazja staying. At least she wasn't in the house but in the annexe. He liked Grazja a lot, but that didn't mean he wanted her poking around their house, telling them how to raise their child, or, God forbid, rearranging things in his kitchen. Yet, if it was good for Stella it would surely be good for him, and for Gerta too.

Certainly Stella seemed cheerier already. If he was being honest, he resented that a little. He'd been trying for months to cheer her up and then all it had taken was for Grazja to waltz in.

And he couldn't believe Ange had sided against him. Publicly too. She wouldn't own half the diner if he hadn't been kind enough to sell it to her for less than what it was worth.

Gina was a different matter. His grandmother-in-law was capable of pissing off a saint. He wasn't surprised to find her at the centre of a campaign like this. Her brand of bigotry was all-inclusive; it covered anyone who wasn't close to herself or to Stella, anyone foreign (except Grazja and himself), anyone of a different colour (except Stella's best friend Lycie and her family) and pretty much everyone else. She was an equal opportunities hater.

But it wasn't as though he would welcome some stupid swingers' club. He just didn't like prudish censure and small-minded mob mentality. People got hysterical before the facts were known.

So engrossed was he by his churning thoughts, it took him a moment to register he was being hailed. He looked up to see Frank Manning, better known in Mapton as Brother Frank, proprietor of the ghost train.

'Morning, Rick,' he greeted him. 'Looked like you were miles away.'

'Sorry,' Rick said. 'I was.'

'Anything to do with this?' Brother Frank said, pulling the Mapton Knights flyer from his pocket. It fluttered in Rick's face mockingly. 'I was at the diner first thing; people were already gathering.'

Rick grimaced. 'I'm not involved,' he growled. 'Anything but. I've just had a row about it at the diner. I didn't give my permission to use The Last Resort as a meeting point for the petition.'

'Ah,' Frank said. 'Awkward.'

'Very,' Rick agreed. 'I think I just made a bit of an ass of myself.'

'Happens to the best of us.'

Rick relaxed. 'You off to open the ghost train?'

Frank nodded. 'Need to oil the wheels on the cars before I do.'

'Want a hand?' Rick asked. He wasn't ready to go home yet.

Frank looked surprised but nodded. 'Okay. Thanks.'

They walked along the beach in companionable silence for a few minutes. Rick occasionally went out for a beer with Frank but he still knew very little about the man. Brother Frank was a mystery to most of Mapton. He appeared in response to an advert in 'World's Fair', the weekly trade paper for travelling showmen and fairground operators. The Forman family, who owned the fair complex in Mapton, among other properties, were advertising for an enterprising person to lease and run the ghost train. Normally the Formans would give it to one of their own, but to their shame, the five youngest Formans had one by one escaped Mapton for the brighter lights of the city.

Frank Manning seemed to turn up out of nowhere. He took the lease and spent his first winter lovingly restoring the ghost train to glory. Then he caused quite a stir when the new season came by donning a monk's robe and addressing every adult customer with the same question: 'Do you dare face your sins in the dark?' To the kids he said: 'You'll get quite a fright, so hold on tight.'

As the years progressed, Frank drew a following among returning holidayers, for whom a trip to Mapton wouldn't seem complete without facing their sins in the dark.

He lived alone in a flat over the 'Kleen and Gone' laundrette. A single, solitary man, working in a fairground with lots of kiddies, caused a bit of ugly gossip to swirl around Mapton at first but as the years went on and nothing remiss occurred, Mapton began to see Brother Frank as one of their own. Other rumours arose, better ones, suggesting a glamorous pre-Mapton life for Frank. Some said he'd been a stockbroker, others a bad romance had driven him here. But no one knew for sure, and Frank never offered any details. Not even to Rick, who was the closest friend he had in town.

'So,' Frank said. 'Do you think a swingers club is likely in Mapton?'

Rick shook his head. 'I don't, but folk around here seem to think it is. They're certainly getting themselves worked up about it.'

Frank laughed. 'Well, that's the nature of small towns,' he said. 'Just the hint of something salacious goes a long way and news travels quick.'

'I know,' Rick agreed. 'I grew up in a small town. If a dog so much as farted the whole town knew about it within the hour.'

Frank grinned. 'You have a charming way with words, Rick.'

'Would it be rude to ask if you signed the petition?'

Frank furrowed his brow. 'Yes, I think it would, Rick, but I don't mind telling you that I didn't.'

'That's scandalous,' Rick said. 'You being a man of the cloth.'

Frank smiled. 'Ah, but mine is a broad church and I'd gain a lot of sinners to face my ghost train.'

'True. So you really don't oppose the idea of a swingers club?' Rick was surprised.

Frank shook his head. 'I think it's all pie in the sky,' he said. 'I wouldn't be surprised if someone planted it to stir up a bit of publicity for Mapton.'

'But what if it is real?'

'Playing Devils' Advocate, Rick? Well, if it is a real possibility then I'd have to give it some thought. It wouldn't be good for the family image of Mapton, and that would be bad for my business. It's families and teens who come to the fair. On the other hand, I don't think a private club will cause Mapton to be consumed by fire and brimstone like Sodom and Gomorrah. '

Rick looked at him. 'Bible talk. It's like being back in the Midwest, but there they'd say Mapton will definitely burn if swingers come to town.'

'Ah, sounds like my childhood too,' Frank said. 'I can't say I actually think a sex club/swingers camp, whatever you'd call it, would be a good thing but it would befit Mapton's better nature to hold back on the judgemental scaremongering until the facts are known.'

Rick nodded. 'My feelings too.'

They'd reached the small fairground. Frank unlocked the side gate to let them in. Other fair workers were setting up their stalls and rides. Frank waved to them or said hello. Mike on the Hook a

Duck called. 'Heard there's a coachload of care kids coming in. Should be a good day. Ay up Rick, thinking of changing jobs?'

Rick laughed. 'Nah, I'll stick to flippin' burgers. Just giving Brother Frank a hand.'

'More money in flippin' burgers,' Mike said. His expression showed he meant it.

Brother Frank undid the padlocks and slid out the bars keeping the ghost train doors locked on both sides. He pushed through the swing door and flicked on a light.

'I prefer to oil the wheels inside,' he explained. 'Where no one will see it or slip on it if a bit drips.'

Rick followed him inside, intrigued to see the mysterious inner-workings of the ghost train. He knew it was a small ride but under the merciless glare of naked hundred-watt bulbs he couldn't quite believe just what a small space it really was. And how bare.

Brother Frank turned a sharp, crazy corner and disappeared for a moment. 'Just getting the oil,' he called, leaving Rick with the cars parked nose to nose on the track and a maniacal axe-wielding clown staring down at him.

'Hey dude,' he said nervously. 'Chill out.'

Brother Frank came back with a couple of cans of WD40. He handed one to Rick. 'Just oil the wheel on the axle,' he said, crouching to demonstrate. The wheels on the cars were tiny.

'So,' Brother Frank began, and this time it was he who sounded nervous. 'I'm sure I saw Gina's friend at the Co-op. The Polish woman. Is she visiting?'

'Grazja?' Rick said. 'Yeah, she's staying with us. You remember her?'

'Oh,' said Brother Frank. 'Yes. I recognise her. Um, is she staying long?'

Rick's interest was piqued. Brother Frank had an oddly strained tone to his voice.

'Yeah, truth to tell she's helping Stella out for a bit. Looking after Gerta until Stella's big exhibition is over.'

'When's that?'

'September.'

'All summer then!' Brother Frank sounded pleased.

'I guess,' Rick said. 'She's staying in our annexe. Not in the house which I'm kinda glad about.'

'You don't like her?' Brother Frank looked up sharply.

'Grazja? She's great. I just don't want anyone living in our house with us.'

'Doesn't her husband or partner mind her living away?'

This was so obviously a fishing question that Rick had to stop himself laughing.

'Nah, she's been free and single as long as I've known her,' he said. 'Goes where her work takes her.'

Brother Frank nodded, trying not to look too curious.

Rick smiled to himself. Brother Frank and Grazja; now that was a thought. He couldn't wait to tell Stella.

It went a long way to dissipating the unpleasant aftertaste of this morning's fight with the 'Knights' and Ange.

Dirty Business

Mayor Martha Seaton was furious. She had just read the Monday morning Lawton Post. Tom Turner had practically implied she was all for a swingers camp. He was such a sneaky, slimy snaky, he'd do anything to make life hard for her. It drove him mad that she was voted mayor every year while he always had to play second fiddle as her deputy; he was always finding petty ways to cause her trouble.

She read the lines again:

When asked if the town council was all in opposition to the sex camp the deputy mayor responded: 'Mayor Seaton is a very kind, good-hearted lady. She's liberal and very open minded but everyone knows that Mayor Seaton and I often take differing views'

Deputy Mayor Turner made his own feelings on the prospect of a sex camp in Mapton clear: 'It would happen over my dead body. It's a ridiculous idea.'

'I'm going to kill him,' Martha spat. 'I'm going to bloody kill him.'

She slammed the paper down on her desk, with the headline blaring up at her: **SEX CAMP THREATENS MAPTON'S REPUTATION.** Crossing to the window she stared out, oblivious to the view. She needed to regain her composure before she tackled Tom.

Drawing a deep breath, Martha forced herself to calm down.

Martha was trim and fit, her hair cut into an immaculate crop. She had run for the council in her early forties, after getting involved in a drive to clear the beach of litter. She was unusual for a local politician in that she hated waffle in meetings, was decisive, and driven by a genuine desire to serve the community rather than raise her social standing.

Tom Turner hated her. He saw her as a usurper; a woman who'd abandoned her hometown for over twenty years and then waltzed back in and stole his crown.

But no one in Mapton and Siltby knew the truth of her early life, and the pain her first marriage had brought her. Only her grown children and her husband, John Seaton, knew that, and not all of it. That is exactly how Martha wanted it to stay.

Martha went back to her desk, looked up a number in her diary, and punched it into her phone.

'Hello, licensing applications,' a voice answered.

'Hello, is that Gerald?'

'Speaking,' the man confirmed.

'Hello Gerald, it's Mayor Seaton again; we spoke last week about a sex establishment application for Mapton. I wondered if you've found anything out yet?'

'Ah, yes, Mayor Seaton,' Gerald sounded keen. 'I've seen the Post this morning. It sounds like things are a bit crazy in Mapton, but I've checked through all the applications and I've found no sign of one for Mapton or Siltby. Nor one in the inbox waiting to be processed. It seems to be just a rumour.'

Martha closed her eyes gratefully and mentally sighed.

'Thank you so much Gerald,' she said. 'You've been a great help.'

'I've already had that journalist call this morning,' Gerald said. 'I told him the same thing. He wasn't pleased like you are.'

'I'll bet he wasn't,' Martha chuckled. 'There's no story now. Thank you again.'

'I'll let you know if anything comes in,' Gerald said. 'Although I doubt it will.'

'I hope not,' Martha said. 'Have a lovely day, Gerald. Goodbye.'

She sighed. Oh thank God. Now she could call a meeting and declare it all nothing but a rumour and be done with it.

And she could deal with Tom Turner.

She straightened her skirt, patted her hair, and stepped across the hall to his office.

She should have known he'd be ready for her. As soon as she opened his door he was half way across the room, coming towards her, palms up, and a concerned expression. She noted the newspaper on his desk.

'Martha,' Tom said. 'We've been shafted. Have you seen the Post?'

She eyed him coolly. 'Unfortunately I have, Tom.'

'That damned journalist,' Tom shook his head despairingly. 'Took my words all out of context. He's made it sound as though we've got opposing views on this, Martha.'

'And how exactly did he do that, Tom?' Martha asked drily. 'Are you denying you spoke to him?'

Tom hung his head with chagrin so faked it made Martha grind her teeth in an effort not to clobber him.

'He turned up in the shop Saturday morning,' Tom said. 'He'd seen that daft leaflet George and Gina put together and came around sniffing for a story. I told him what I knew, and then we were just chatting off the record. I'm shocked Martha, at how he's twisted my words out of all recognition.'

'It's strange how that always seems to happen, Tom. When I'm interviewed it seems pretty straightforward. Of course, I wouldn't have given him anything until I talked to my colleagues and got all the facts straight. The facts, as they are, Tom, is that district have just confirmed that there are no applications in for a 'sex camp' or any such nonsense, so it appears it is just a silly rumour after all and we could have been saved this embarrassing sort of publicity if you'd held your tongue in the first place.'

Tom stepped back. 'Well, that's great news, Martha,' he said. 'You're right, of course; I'm always naïve when it comes to the press. I don't know when I'll learn to be less trusting. You'd think I'd know by now.'

He smiled his oily smile and Martha smiled back just as insincerely. 'You would think so,' she agreed. 'I'll write a press release to undo the damage now we know there's no truth to it.' She turned to go.

'Fantastic,' Tom said. 'This is good news. We don't need this sort of sordid problem sullying our reputation. Particularly yours.'

Martha, just reaching for the door handle, turned back. 'Why mine particularly?' she asked slowly.

Tom looked shifty.

'Oh, well, you know…' he said.

'I don't,' Martha said. 'You'd better enlighten me.'

Tom looked at her with feigned compassion. 'All right,' he said, 'I've had a few sleepless nights worrying about it. With the press attention a swingers club would bring, it wouldn't be long before they started to snoop into people's pasts, and you know, yours is…'

Martha's heart sank. 'Mine is what?' she asked tersely.

'Well,' Tom said, 'You have a bit of history with that sort of thing, don't you?' He was struggling to keep his compassionate face. It was clear he wanted to crow. 'We don't want that to get out. It'd be the end of your political career.'

Martha felt sick but she held it together. She looked at Tom coldly. 'I have no idea what you're talking about, Tom Turner,' she said, and left.

As soon as she closed the door to her office her knees started to shake and she had to sit down. Because she did know what he was talking about and she had no idea of how he'd found out.

Grazja's Secret

'I just put Gerta down for her nap,' Grazja said, as Stella came into the garden room. 'She even more demanding than Gina.'

Stella grinned to see Grazja collapsed on the sofa. She was usually on the go.

'Yes, but Gerta will grow out of it, I hope. Gina's stuck like that. Shall I make us a cuppa?'

'Please,' Grazja groaned.

Stella returned with tea and two brownies. 'I found these in the kitchen,' she said. 'The fairies must have left them.'

'I bake them last night in my little kitchen,' Grazja explained. 'I couldn't sleep.'

'No wonder you look exhausted,' Stella said anxiously. 'Is it Gerta? Are you finding her too much? Don't feel obliged to stay.'

'No, no,' Grazja smiled. 'I love it. Gerta just the challenge I need to keep my mind off things. She so sweet. And I love being back in crazy-town.'

'So what is it?' Stella asked, handing her a mug.

Grazja grimaced. 'It is embarrassing. I not talked about it to anyone.'

'You can tell me if it helps,' Stella said. 'I won't tell Gina or Rick, if you don't want me to.' She was burning with curiosity. Grazja was tight-lipped about her past, and although they knew she was a widow, she never talked about her husband or any children. Would it be something to do with that?

But what Grazja said took Stella by complete surprise.

'I am rich woman,' she announced unhappily.

'What do you mean?' Stella said. 'How?'

'My old lady,' Grazja sighed. 'Mrs Alexander. She left me money in her will.'

'But that's fantastic,' Stella cried. 'She must have really appreciated you.'

'No, it not 'fantastic'. She didn't just leave me some money, she left me *all* of her money.'

Stella digested this. 'But her family,' she said. 'You told me they couldn't wait for her to pop off so they'd inherit. She had a niece and nephew. Are you saying…?'

'Yes,' Grazja said. 'She cut them out of her will and left it all to me.'

'Wow.' Stella sat back, stunned. 'They must hate you.'

'Yes,' Grazja agreed. 'They do.'

'Did you know beforehand? Had she mentioned it?'

'Of course not,' Grazja snapped. 'I would never have let her. I would have told her solicitor she had lost her…' she made a small sphere with her thumb and index finger and gestured irritably.

'Marbles,' Stella supplied. 'Had she?'

'No', Grazja laughed bitterly. 'She knew what she was doing. She hated her family and did it to spite them. It was her last nasty joke.'

'But she made you rich,' Stella said softly. 'She must have thought a great deal of you to leave you everything.'

'She like me, but that not why she did it, Stella. You not listening. She did it to make trouble even after she was dead.'

'Don't you want it?' Stella asked. 'Can you give it back?'

'Oh,' Grazja snorted. 'She thought of that. The will stipulates that I can give nothing to the family, neither can I give it all to charity.'

'She really thought it through.'

Grazja nodded. 'She was an old spider, sitting in her web, just waiting. I thought I'd truly befriended her. Now I see I was trapped fly all along.'

'I'm so sorry,' Stella said. 'I suppose the family will contest.'

'They have already started. And they harass me. I get new phone this week so they not have my number. They send me hate texts and leave messages.'

'That's horrible,' Stella said.

'That's why Mrs Alexander hate them. They horrible just like her. It runs in that family. If she'd had children it would have been much harder to cut them out by Scottish law. You know they paid my salary?'

'The niece and nephew? But why? She had plenty of money.'

'To show what good family they are. Look, we take care of elderly aunt. It never occur she won't leave them everything and leave it to me. Mrs A has last laugh, yes?'

'A pretty cruel laugh,' Stella said. 'So, what do you do now?'

'Nothing,' Grazja sighed. 'I just wait for law to decide and not spend the money meantime.'

'Well, I'm glad you came back to us,' Stella said, hugging Grazja. 'Between Gina's campaign and Gerta's demands, it'll certainly take your mind off it.'

'Yes,' Grazja agreed. 'Now, let's eat brownies.'

Nose for a Story

Andrew Leith had been disappointed to discover no evidence of an application for a sex establishment but he wasn't going to give up on the story so easily. Something was off – his journalist's instincts told him so – and he would place a bet that Tom Turner was involved somehow. He didn't doubt that Tom was against the actuality of a sex camp in Mapton but he'd seemed suspiciously pleased about the rumour, and, certainly, if George Wentworth was to be believed, the first person to speak of an application, despite Tom's refusal to deny or confirm it.

Dennis Payton, proprietor of the Paradise, had been out of town on Saturday, but Andrew was on his way to see him. He hadn't called ahead.

The Paradise loomed, its clubhouse a flaking, dubious orange. The second 'a' of Paradise had gone years ago, and the 'e' had finally dropped off last summer, narrowly missing a holidaymaker and litigation.

Andrew grimaced at the sight; it was a seedy introduction to Mapton-on-Sea in its current state. A few caravans were occupied but the majority were empty, and although it wasn't the height of the season, most other parks were half to three quarters full by now.

A greasy smell of bacon and eggs lingered in the clubhouse as Andrew entered, mixed with the odour of years' worth of stale beer spilled on the carpet.

Andrew wrinkled his nose as he headed towards Dennis Payton's office. He paused outside the door, listening for any conversation inside - eavesdropping was second nature to him – but hearing none he knocked, hoping Dennis was in. He was gratified to hear a grunted, 'Come in,' and pushed open the door to be greeted by the sight of Dennis, feet up on desk, chewing a limp-looking bacon butty. He had brown sauce smeared on his chin.

'Who are you?'

'Andrew Leith, from the Lawton Post, Mr Payton,' Andrew said, offering his hand. 'I was wondering if you'd be willing to talk about the rumours of a planned sex establishment at your park.'

Dennis eyed Andrew's hand, and for a moment Andrew thought he would refuse to shake, but then he kicked back from the desk, rose, reached over, and grasped it.

''ave a seat,' he said, swallowing a last, large remnant of his sandwich. 'I saw your piece in the Post, Mr Leith. You seem to know more about all this than me.'

'You're saying you don't know anything about it?' Andrew asked, drawing up the proffered chair. 'That you're not planning a sex establishment?'

'You tell me,' Dennis said. 'You're the reporter. You're the one who put my name in the paper.'

'I was only reporting on what I'd been told by George Wentworth of the Mapton Knights Action Committee.'

Dennis smirked. 'Those codgers. You know his squeeze, Gina Pontin, is notorious around here. I banned her from my clubhouse years ago for anti-social behaviour.'

'Really,' Andrew leaned forward. 'What did she do?'

Dennis snorted. 'What hasn't Gina Pontin done? I banned her for heckling other singers during Karaoke. She'd had plenty of warnings. I'm surprised nobody's slapped an ASBO on her. She's had run-ins with most people in Mapton at some time or the other.'

'So you think Mrs Pontin may have started the rumours to get back at you?'

Dennis's eyes gleamed. 'I'm sure there's a bit o' that,' he agreed. 'She marched in here last week all high and mighty, like some bloody re-born Mary Whitehouse, demanding to know if the rumours were true.'

Andrew frowned. 'So she didn't start the rumours herself then,' he said. 'Not if she heard them from someone else.'

Dennis shrugged, unfazed. 'Who knows? Wouldn't put it past her to pretend she'd heard it from someone else to stir it up.'

'George Wentworth claims she overheard Deputy Mayor Tom Turner talking about an application for a sex establishment licence for the Paradise.'

Again Dennis shrugged. 'I don't know about that. Weren't there.'

'So you categorically deny the rumour? You have the opportunity here to set the record straight in the Lawton Post.' Andrew said.

Dennis cocked his head and eyed him ruefully. 'Like I said to Gina Pontin, I don't have to admit or deny nothing. What I do or don't do with my own business is my concern and no one else's.'

Brilliant, Andrew thought, fighting to keep the excitement off his face. This is just what I wanted.

'So you won't say you're not considering a sex establishment?'

'No, I won't say that,' Dennis said. 'But I won't say I am, either. Like I said, it's no one's business but mine.'

'Surely something like that would have an effect on the town?' Andrew said. 'It would affect the reputation of Mapton as a family resort.'

'I'm not willing to comment.'

They looked at each other and Andrew saw he'd reached an impasse.

'Off the record,' he said, relaxing back. 'I've been doing a bit of research into these swinger clubs. Seems like there's much more of a demand for places like that than you might think. There's a club in Sheffield, for example. People pay top dollar to go to it. And then there's a farmer in Norfolk who built a clubhouse and a caravan park on his farm for swingers and he's raking it in. Says he'd never go back to farming. Says the swinger community are much better behaved than families. They leave the caravans clean; no litter; no dog mess; no damages.'

Dennis raised an eyebrow. 'Is that so?'

Andrew nodded. 'Apparently it's a hidden and mainly untapped market. Mostly couples and

89

single women are allowed and the number of single men is strictly controlled, so you don't get fights breaking out. Oh, and they don't usually drink alcohol, so again, no puking, no fights. Most of them are professionals too – lawyers and doctors, etcetera - so they're willing to pay. Anyway,' Andrew finished, 'from what I've learned it's certainly a good earner if you don't mind running that sort of thing. And,' he laughed. 'You get to watch while you work.'

Dennis grinned lasciviously. 'Do your readers know you're a perv?'

Andrew rose to go. 'Oh, 'he said. 'That's not my scene. I'm just saying if it was then it'd be a perk of the job for sure.'

Off and On

'That was Mayor Seaton,' George said, placing the phone in its cradle. 'She says there's been no application to the council for a sex establishment licence, and she's calling an emergency meeting to 'put an end to this nonsense for once and for all'. That's what she called it – 'nonsense'.

'It ain't nonsense,' Gina huffed. 'I bet she hasn't even talked to Dennis Payton. And maybe he don't need a licence.'

'George cocked his head thoughtfully. 'Well, I suppose people can do what they like in the privacy of a caravan but I think if they want to use the clubhouse for 'adult entertainment' he does need one.'

Gina eyed him. 'You know a lot about this, George. You turning into a dirty bogger?'

George reddened. 'Of course not,' he said. 'But I've been doing some research online. You can't fight a battle, Gina, without knowing your enemy. It's recon.'

'Well, as long as that's all it is, George Wentworth,' Gina said tartly.

'Of course, of course,' George said hastily. 'But you'd be amazed, Gina, what folk get up to. There's even a UK Swingers Society on the net, making out it's all above board and respectable.'

Gina snorted. 'Respectable my arse. Just you be careful you don't get addicted to stuff online, George. It happens. You start off looking at fluffy bunnies and end up addicted to porn. You read about it all the time.'

Rick nodded to Julie Taynor, Town Clerk, and general dogsbody for the town council. 'Morning, Julie, what can I do for you?'

'Morning Rick, can't stop. Just wondered if you'd mind putting this notice up in your window? Mayor Seaton's calling an emergency town meeting to set everyone straight about that daft sex camp rumour. Thursday 7pm in the community hall.'

'Sure, leave it with me,' Rick said. 'I'll put it on the door. So, the rumour's not true then.'

Julie rolled her eyes. 'I only wish it was, Rick. Could do with spicing things up around here.' She gave a merry kick of her heels before making a swift exit.

Rick grinned at Frank, who was sipping his coffee at the counter. 'I couldn't tell if she was joking or not.'

Frank laughed. 'You never know with people.'

'So, a town meeting,' Rick said. 'You going?'

'Probably,' Frank nodded. 'I never get to go when the season's on and this'll be a juicy one. You?'

'Nah,' Rick shook his head. 'After Saturday I think I'll keep my head down or I might get lynched. Anyway, if I'm in, Stella can go to keep an eye on Gina. With me at home with Gerta she could take Grazja too. Give them both a laugh.'

He watched Frank out of the corner of his eye. Yes, he definitely perked up at the mention of Grazja.

#

The news of the meeting flew around Mapton and Siltby. By Thursday there was an atmosphere of anticipation in the air so thick the sharp sea breeze couldn't cut through it.

Martha Seaton had redirected her phone calls to go straight through to Tom. That should keep him occupied and out of her way.

She'd hardly slept for the three nights following their last conversation, wondering just how much Tom knew and how he was planning to use it. With the local elections just around the corner he was up to something. If she could at least cut this rumour off at its root and stop the parish gossips, she'd be able to concentrate on how to outmanoeuvre Tom.

Gerald had kindly rung twice since Monday to reassure her there was still no sign of any application.

Tom had been out of the office mostly, and she'd had no feedback from him on his promised talk with Dennis Payton. In fact, she'd been trying to get hold of Dennis herself, but he wasn't taking calls. When she'd paid a visit to the Paradise on Wednesday, Teddy Suspring (whom everyone called Teddy Surprising) calling Bingo to a few pensioners in the clubhouse, told her Dennis had gone to Sheffield for a couple of days to see his old mum.

Looking around the clubhouse, Martha was pleased to see no sign of any recent improvements that might suggest a new direction in business. It was as tired-looking and tatty as ever.

"Do you have any idea where the swingers' camp rumour started, Teddy?' she asked.

'First I heard about it was that leaflet,' Teddy said. 'Never heard it from Dennis, that's for sure. He's as tight-lipped as they come. Tight-fisted too.'

The more Martha thought about it the more likely it seemed that Tom had deliberately started it himself. Who better to have overhear his phone call than Gina Pontin, a woman whose outrage could echo from one end of the beach to the other. And who would be one of the first people Gina would tell but Sue Mulligan, a waggle-tongue on wheels.

Oh, Tom, she thought. I bet there was no one on the end of that phone. You started this, didn't you, and you want to be mayor. You want to get rid of me.

Her stomach lurched; perhaps this emergency meeting wasn't such a good idea. Still, it was too late now. She would handle it strongly, make it short, and shut down the rumour before Tom could get his two pennies' worth in.

Her mobile rung. It was Gerald. Answering she turned pale. 'Oh no,' she said, dropping into her chair. 'Oh, please tell me you're joking.'

\#

Stella and Grazja surveyed the mobility scooters parked outside the community hall. There were two distinct groups on either side of the door.

'The Marauders and the Wanderers are here,' Stella noted. 'Moon's full so it must be a rumble night.'

'That still going on?' Grazja laughed. 'I thought the police put a stop to it.'

'Oh, they've been turning a blind eye,' Stella said. 'I think there's been a bribe somewhere. Pirate Tom most likely. He's chummy with the chief. Bet they're Masons.'

'Secret handshakes,' Grazja said.

'Dressing up in stockings and suspenders,' Stella added. They giggled.

Inside the hall was packed. This was the most exciting thing to happen in Mapton since the Channel Five cameras left.

More scooters lined the back of the hall - the people who really couldn't walk further than a couple of steps without them - and most of the chairs were already taken.

Stella spotted Gina's red hair bobbing on the front row, sitting between George and Sue.

'I'll just pop up to say hello,' Stella told Grazja. 'See if you can find any seats.'

Grazja gazed around, looking for two empty seats but the rows were full. Then a man tentatively waving caught her eye. He sat on the back row, three along. Beckoning to Grazja he nodded at the two vacant seats to his right.

Grazja smiled, vaguely recognising him as a Maptonite she'd seen around but didn't know, and made her way over, politely squeezing past the first three people as they stood to let her pass.

'Thank you,' she said. 'I didn't think we would get a seat. My friend will be along in a minute.'

The man nodded, smiling shyly. 'You're Grazja, aren't you? Rick told me Stella and you were coming so I saved these seats. I'm Rick's friend, Frank.' He offered her his hand.

Grazja took it. The shake was a bit awkward sideways on but she smiled graciously. 'Nice to meet you, Frank. It good of you to think of us.'

'Not at all,' Frank said.

They sat in silence for a few moments, as everyone chattered around them.

'So,' Grazja said. 'This will be exciting, yes? I never been to town meeting before.'

Frank nodded. 'It'll be lively all right. Mapton folk have plenty of opinions.'

'Especially about a possible sex camp,' Grazja laughed. 'Although I heard this meeting is to stop that rumour.'

Stella arrived before Frank could reply.

'Sorry, thanks, thanks,' Stella said as she pushed through. 'Oh were they your toes, Frank? Sorry.'

When she was seated she said: 'Well done on getting these seats, Grazja. I thought we'd be standing.'

'Frank saved them for us,' Grazja said.

'Really?' Stella gave Frank a probing look. 'That was nice of you, Frank.

'Rick said you were coming,' Frank said, dropping his eyes under Stella's gaze.

'Ah,' Stella said. 'You've introduced yourselves? Frank runs the ghost train in the fair, Grazja.'

'Really?' Grazja raised her eyebrows. 'You the monk?'

'I am,' Frank admitted.

'Though not a real one,' Stella teased.

'Er, no,' Frank blushed. 'Of course not.'

'Where you get idea?' Grazja asked.

'Oh, I don't know,' Frank said. 'It just came to me.'

Grazja had just opened her mouth to say something else when Mayor Seaton rose to call a start to the meeting.

She, Tom Turner, and other council members were aligned behind a bench table on the small stage at the end of the hall. Julie Taynor, the minute-taker, sat to the left.

#

Mayor Seaton waited for the chatter to die down before speaking. She stood straight and poised before the townsfolk.

To her right she was aware of Tom Turner's smug smile

'As you know, concerns have arisen regarding the possibility of Paradise Holiday Park becoming a centre for adult entertainment and a swingers' camp. Understandably, a rumour of this nature has caused quite a stir in our community. Mr Wentworth and Ms Pontin here,' Martha said, nodding to the front row, 'have taken it upon themselves to form a group opposed to the idea. I'm sure you've all seen the leaflet they sent round on Saturday.'

There were murmurs of affirmation as well as a laugh or two.

The mayor waited for the room to settle before continuing.

'I'll be honest; I called the meeting to reassure you all that the rumour is unfounded. Certainly there had been no record of an application to the district council for an adult entertainment licence, and no confirmation from The Paradise of Dennis Payton's intention… until late this afternoon.'

The room went very still.

'At 4.45 today I received official word from the district council. Dennis Payton has put in an application for an adult entertainment licence for the Paradise Holiday Park.'

For a moment the only sound was the clatter of Derek Wilson's false teeth hitting the wooden floor. They were constantly falling out as they weren't made for him but for his late wife, whose mouth had been considerably smaller than his.

Then the hall erupted into sound.

Mayor Seaton was braced for it. She turned to look at Tom and was grimly satisfied to see his smug smile had been wiped out. He looked entirely taken by surprise, and, she noted, angry.

So, not part of your plan, she thought. Interesting.

'I knew it,' Gina Pontin stood up. 'I tode yer he were a snake.' Her voice carried over the hubbub. 'So what's the council going to do about it? The Mapton Knights are going to fight.'

Most people cheered Gina, although a few jeered.

Mayor Seaton held her hands up for quiet. When things had settled enough to begin she kept her voice low and quiet, forcing the few chatterers to shut up as others around hushed them to catch the mayor's words.

'Let me be very clear; I know I speak for all the town councillors…' she briefly turned to glare at Tom Turner, 'When I say we are all one mind in this matter. Mapton and Siltby Town Council absolutely oppose the proposal to turn The Paradise into a centre for adult entertainment, whether that means a swingers' camp or a strip club, or anything else. We are very clearly a family holiday resort and intend to remain so.'

'Yeah, but it's not up to the town council, is it?' Gina said. 'George has been looking into it and it's up to district, and look at the sort of places they let Skegness have.'

'Has George been checking out the strip-bars?' some wag shouted, causing a ripple of laughter.

'Wash yer mouth out,' Gina yelled back. 'This is serious and George is doin' something proper about it so gi' him some respect.'

A few folk clapped, and Sue called. 'You tell him Gina.'

'We should send Gina to Lawton; she'd whip 'em into submission.' Sugsy called from way back. 'That's what we need, a strong leader.'

This idea seemed to appeal to some and appal others. Again the hall erupted.

Martha took a moment to look at her fellow councillors. Except for Tom, she had called each one to apprise them of the situation before the meeting and to propose a measure she was going to raise.

They gave her the nod. Tom, catching the exchange, scowled, realising something was afoot, and that he'd been excluded.

She would pay for this, Martha knew, but right now she had to take action.

Again she waited for people to quieten down.

'It is vitally important that we work together, which is why I propose that key members of the Mapton Knights be officially co-opted as a steering group to work with the town council to oppose the plans for the Paradise,' Mayor Seaton said.

'I second the proposal,' Councillor Stan Martin called, avoiding Tom Turner's furious glare.

Mayor Seaton looked down at George and Gina. 'What do you say Mr Wentworth?'

George looked delighted but Gina grimaced. 'What does steering group mean?' she asked. 'It don't mean you can control us?'

'Of course not,' Mayor Seaton said. 'A steering group works with the council to advise them. As we'll all be working towards the same goal it makes sense to do it together. Don't you agree?'

'I do,' George said. 'Absolutely'.

'Do we get to keep the name?' Gina said. 'Mapton Knights.'

'Certainly.'

Gina looked at George uncertainly. He nodded enthusiastically.

'All right,' Gina conceded. 'We'll work with yer.'

'Let's put it to the vote then,' Mayor Seaton raised her voice. 'Council members, raise your hand if you agree with the proposal to co-opt the key members of The Mapton Knights into a steerage group for consultation with the town council.'

As she thought they would, over half the audience raised their hands too, but it was the council members she was looking at. All raised their hands except for Tom Turner.

Mayor Seaton looked at him, waiting. Thunder-faced he finally raised his finger in a yes. Voting no or abstaining right now would prove very unpopular with the mood of this audience. She had forced him into an impossible position.

Good.

'The proposal is carried,' she said, smiling. She would enjoy this brief moment of triumph.

And then...

Mapton and Siltby residents flooded out of the community hall in a state of noisy agitation. Far from the reassurance most of them had expected from the mayor, she had lobbed a stick of dynamite into their midst, or rather, to be fair to Mayor Seaton, Dennis Payton had.

And the bogger hadn't even attended the meeting to face his actions.

Many people had the idea to go up to the Paradise right now and demand to see him, but apparently he was out of town, the coward. What had Gina Pontin called him? 'A snake'. Well, most weren't normally in agreement with Gina, but she got it right there. And she was prepared to stand up and fight for Mapton. Who would have expected that?

If there were dissenters in the townsfolk they wisely kept their mouths shut. They might think that Dennis Payton had hit upon a good idea; a way of making some money for the town. Others might welcome a bit of adult entertainment – more than one man relished the possibility of a lap-dancing club – but now wasn't the time to pipe up in support. There was a slight whiff of lynch mob in the air tonight. It was a very good thing for Dennis Payton that he was out of town.

Stella and Grazja waited in the carpark for Gina, George, and Sue. Frank waited with them.

'Wow,' Stella said. 'That was some meeting. I can't believe it's true. I can't wait to tell Rick!'

Grazja laughed. 'Yes. So much excitement. I think Mapton might explode. They all disgusted but they look so happy.'

Frank smiled. 'People love a good protest, and this is a juicy cause.'

'What you mean 'juicy'? 'Grazja asked.

'Well, you know,' Frank coloured. 'About sex.'

'Ah,' Grazja nodded. 'Yes. This is very 'juicy'.'

'Gina's going to be unbearable,' Stella sighed. 'Working with the council. I hope Mayor Seaton knows what she's doing. She could be creating a monster.'

'Did you see Tom Turner's face?' Frank asked. 'Like thunder.'

'He hates being second-in-command, especially to a woman,' Stella grinned. 'But every year the council vote Martha in as mayor.'

'There's Gina,' Grazja said. 'See if she can get head through door, it's swollen so much.'

Stella laughed. 'Oh Frank, you must think we're terrible, being mean about Gina. We do love her, you know.'

Frank wisely just smiled.

Sue reached their group before Gina, whizzing up on her scooter. 'Bloody'ell,' she said. 'What d'yer think of that? Dennis Payton's got some bloody cheek, eh?' Her face shone with delight. 'He's going to regret the day he even thought about a sex camp, I'll tell yer. The Mapton Knights will put him right.'

Stella noticed her scooter basket was empty. 'Where's Scampi?' she asked. 'You never go anywhere without her?'

Sue's face fell. 'Oh, she's at home. Been off her food today, poor love. Dint want to get her cold. And she don't like noise no more.'

Stella said nothing but patted Sue's arm. Scampi was an old lady now.

Gina arrived with George. 'Did you hear me, Stella?'

'Very impressive,' Stella said.

'I tode em dint I? Can you imagine, me working with the authorities?'

'We all are,' Sue said, nettled. 'But George is the chair, so he'll be in charge, Gina, not you.'

'Yeah, but it were me that spoke up, weren't it George?' Gina retorted, eyes flashing.

'It was,' George said, squeezing her shoulders. 'You did us proud.'

Gina glowed.

'You tell Rick to stop being such a mardy-arse and sign that petition,' she said to Stella.

Stella rolled her eyes. 'I'll pass your good wishes on.'

A young man approached the group. 'Mr Wentworth,' he said to George. 'Andrew Leith; I interviewed you last weekend.'

'Of course, of course,' George said, beaming. 'Gina, this is the young reporter I told you about.'

Stella could've sworn Gina fluttered her eyelashes.

'Shoulda talked to me,' Gina said, touching her hair. 'George is too nice. I'da tode yer straight. I knew that Dennis Payton were a dirty bogger and I've been proved right.' She looked the reporter in the eye. 'And yer can quote me on that.'

'Now, Gina,' George began but Andrew interrupted him.

'Have you got a few minutes, Ms Pontin? I'd like to interview you.'

Gina puffed up like a woodpigeon. 'Go on then,' she said.

'My car's just there,' Andrew nodded to his Fiesta. 'It'll be quieter if we just sit in it for a few minutes.'

Even as he said this people were stopping, wanting to talk to Gina or George about the meeting.

'Oh, I think I should come with you,' George said, looking worried.

'Don't be daft,' Gina said. 'You're not planning on any funny business, are yer?' she asked Andrew.

Andrew looked puzzled, then, her meaning dawned. 'No! God no, I mean...'

'Well there you are then,' Gina said. 'I'll be back in a minute, George. Don't go without me.'

The group watched Gina steer Andrew towards his car.

'It's not any 'funny business' I'm worried about,' George sighed.

Stella nodded. 'It's what she'll say,' she said.

'God help us,' Grazja agreed.

'We need to run this campaign cleanly,' George said. 'I don't want Dennis Payton to sue us for slander.'

'What's that?' Sue asked.

'It's publically insulting someone falsely or maliciously, thereby damaging their reputation.'

105

'Oh,' Sue shrugged. 'Gina does that all the time.'

'But not in print,' Stella said.

'Indeed,' George sighed again. 'Not in print.'

#

Tom Turner was furious. How dare that Seaton bitch upstage him. Any quibbles he might have had about using the information he had on her were gone. She deserved to be publically shamed. He'd ensure it, but first he was going to give Dennis Payton a mouthful.

Dennis answered his mobile on the fourth ring. 'Figured I'd be hearing from you,' he said.

'Bloody right you're hearing from me,' Tom yelled. 'What the effing hell do you think you're doing? I said 'be mysterious', 'don't deny the rumours' not put in an application for a bleedin' sex licence.'

'I had a rethink,' Dennis said. 'Been doing a bit of research. Swingers' camp, adult entertainment, there's money in it. I fancy a change. Going to spruce up the Paradise and attract a new clientele.'

'Load of pervs and a load of bad publicity is what you'll attract,' Tom spluttered. 'What's got into your head, man? I think you're forgetting who runs things round here, and who's been keeping you afloat. Without my supplier you'd have never been able to sell all those Sunday roasts for nowt and still make a profit. Not to mention the favour I did you recently.'

Dennis was stonily silent for a moment. 'I appreciated the 'favour' Tom, but that don't mean you own me. You planted this idea in my head and I've decided it's a good one after all.'

'What? A good idea to taint Mapton and Siltby with sleaze? We'll lose our family holidaymakers.'

'I lost most of 'em years ago,' Dennis said. 'I can't stand all them kids running around bawling. Adult only works perfect for me.'

'You selfish bastard,' Tom growled. 'After all I've done for you.'

'You've done nowt for me that didn't benefit you 'n' all. I've made me mind up. The application is in with the district. Anyway, what does it matter? You set the rumour to stir up trouble for the mayor, and this don't change that and whatever you've got on her, I won't interfere. I have no love for Mayor Seaton.'

'But I never wanted an actual sex camp,' Tom said. 'You better pull the plug on this application, or I'll be forced to tip off the authorities about a few of your shady dealings. Don't forget I'm a Mason. I got connections.'

Again the silence. 'I don't think we need to get nasty, Tom,' Dennis said. 'You go about your business and I'll go about mine but you try to blackmail me and we'll see what the authorities think about your meat supply. Never looked too carefully at it myself, but I never ate it either. Not much convinced of its origins.'

'There's nothing wrong with the meat I supplied you,' Tom said quickly. 'It was just cheap because they were the cuts most folks don't buy, but still good all the same.'

'Won't be a problem then if I voiced my doubts to the media – maybe that young blood, Leith from the Lawton post. He seems hungry for a scandal.'

Tom felt the veins pulse in his forehead and wondered, briefly, if he was about to have the sort of aneurysm that had killed his father. He forced himself to take a deep breath.

'Fine,' he said. 'You're right. There's no need to get nasty. You'll never get that application approved by council anyway.'

'That may be,' Dennis said. 'We'll just have to wait and see.'

#

Martha dropped onto the sofa beside her husband, John. 'The shit is about to hit the fan,' she said.

It doesn't matter,' John said pulling her close. 'You'll still have me.'

Hitting the Fan

George's worry about slander or libel proved unfounded because Gina's interview wasn't even published in the Lawton Post. By Saturday a new story had broken. Instead the headline read: **EXCLUSIVE: MAPTON MAYOR'S SHOCKING SWINGER PAST**

By Andrew Leith

As an application for a swingers' camp in Mapton is confirmed, Mapton and Siltby residents reel from disclosures of Mayor Seaton's sordid past.

Cloris Spellman told the Lawton Post she had recently retired to the area, and recognised Mayor Martha Seaton on the local news.

'I couldn't believe it,' Mrs Spellman said. 'Her hair's a different colour, but it's definitely her. She was Martha Courier back then and in the early 80s she and her husband Mike held weekly swingers' parties at their house in Southend. Me and my husband used to go regularly until it all went a bit sour.'

Mrs Spellman explained she would never have said anything if she hadn't seen Mayor Seaton on BBC Look North opposing the application for a sex camp in Mapton-on-Sea.

'It seemed a bit rich,' she said, 'hearing Mayor Seaton saying they'll fight the application given her background. There were rumours back in the day that Mike and Martha were using their parties to groom young women for a prostitution ring. I stopped going after that. Swinging's about a bit of fun, nothing exploitative. It's misunderstood enough as it is. You don't need people like that involved.'

Investigation by the Lawton Post has discovered that Mike Courier was successfully prosecuted for running a prostitution ring in 1985, although Martha Courier was never charged.

This news will rock Mapton and Siltby who have a genuine trust in their mayor. Mrs Seaton has done a lot for the area over the past few years, as Deputy Mayor Tom Turner acknowledges. 'Mayor Seaton is a very popular figure. I find it very hard to believe these accusations. Local people would feel bitterly betrayed if they were true. It's unfortunate they've arisen at this difficult time. We need to be united against the sleaze threatening to engulf Mapton if this application is approved.'

It was only on Thursday that Mayor Seaton invited Mapton's anti-sex camp action group the Mapton Knights to work as steerage group with the council to oppose Dennis Payton's application to the district council for an adult entertainment licence for the Paradise Holiday Park. Campaign leader for the Mapton Knights, Gina Pontin, expressed shock when the Lawton Post alerted her of the accusations against the mayor. 'It's the first I've heard of it,' she said. 'Mayor Seaton doesn't strike me as that sort, but if it's true she'll have to go.'

So far Mayor Seaton has been unavailable for comment.

#

'It's getting ugly,' Rick said, slapping the Post down on the diner's counter.

Ange had rung him with a migraine and asked him to take the morning shift. They'd made up during the week following last weekend's tiff. It wasn't the first they'd had and neither would it be the last, but the friendship was solid.

Frank was the only customer in this morning, the weather having turned foul overnight. He sat on his usual stool at the counter and took the paper.

'Good God,' he gasped, reading the article. 'Poor Martha. This will kill her.'

'I doubt many people will react like that,' Rick said. 'She's in for a rough ride.'

'She's a good woman,' Frank defended her.

'I don't really know her,' Rick said. 'Do you think any of it's true?'

Frank hesitated. 'Everyone has a past,' he said. 'And everyone deserves a chance at redemption.'

The door opened and a gust of rainy wind accompanied Stella as she wheeled Gerta's pushchair in backwards, followed by Grazja.

They were all dressed in raincoats and wellies.

'Horrible weather,' Stella panted.

'Daddy!' Gerta called, struggling to unclip her chair strap.

'Heya, Gerta-gherkin!' Rick laughed swinging her up. 'Ooh, you're all wet. Let's get you out of that coat.'

'Nasty day, Daddy.'

'It is, honey. It really is. It's good of you to come out and see me.'

'Yeth,' Gerta agreed. 'Eat time, Daddy.'

'Want a bit of lunch? Okay, hon, let's see what we can rustle up.' He flew her over the counter and into the kitchen.

'Hi Frank,' Stella said, dropping her dripping coat on the back of a chair. 'Thought you were a diner early bird. Bit late for you today.'

'Took me a while to face the weather,' Frank smiled.

'Tell me about it!' Stella ducked under the counter. 'Be back in a min,' she said. 'Just see what Rick and Gerta are up to in the kitchen.'

This left Frank with Grazja. He smiled at her shyly.

'Hello,' Grazja said, hopping up on a barstool. 'How are you?'

'Fine, thanks.'

'Oh,' Grazja said, pulling the newspaper towards her. 'The Big News.'

'You've seen it?'

'Gina call me last night. Reporter tell her. It's not nice.'

'You mean the accusations against the mayor or what she supposedly did?'

Grazja cocked her head. 'I mean not nice to drag up past. No one is perfect. Past should stay past.'

Frank beamed at her. 'I think so too.' Then he added. 'Unless it was a crime that's been got away with.'

Grazja looked at him coolly. 'True. But Mayor Seaton not charged. Husband was, yes, but not mayor, so she not criminal otherwise they would charge her. Besides, nothing as it seems I think.'

Frank's smile couldn't get any wider.

Grazja looked unsettled. 'Why you smile like that?'

'Because it's nice to meet someone who doesn't immediately judge or jump to conclusions.'

Grazja tossed her head. 'I judge,' she said. 'But I don't like media. Not always tell the truth. They like to …' she mimicked stirring a pot.

Frank laughed. 'That they do, and most people enjoy a bit of stirring.'

Grazja shrugged. 'I do too,' she admitted. 'But not nasty. I don't like that.'

'What about your friend, Gina?' Frank asked.

Grazja grinned. 'Oh, she like to do very big stir. Gina naughty.'

'I've heard that,' Frank said. 'Rick's told me, but I don't know her very well.'

'Oh, I get her to come on your ghost train,' Grazja said. 'She can confess her sins but it might take a few rides.'

Frank laughed again. 'You should come too,' he said.

'Oh, I never confess my sins,' Grazja said. 'And I hear you are very scary. Stella found you terrifying at first.'

Frank looked a little crestfallen. 'I feel quite bad about that.'

Grazja snorted. 'Why? You should be pleased. You run ghost train, no? Your job to terrify.'

'Only for fun.'

'I don't think she permanently damaged.' Grazja teased. 'So don't worry.'

'I won't,' Frank smiled back. They held eye contact for a fraction longer. Grazja broke it.

Abruptly she leaned back and yelled. 'Any chance of getting coffee here. Service is terrible.'

Her face was flushed.

#

'Don't you even think about doing your business inside,' Gina said, eyeballing Ginger Rogers. 'I know what you're like. Flowerpots; under the bed; anywhere but go out in the rain. Not today missy.'

She opened the back door to the howling rain. Ginger looked up at in her disbelief, as though saying 'you expect me to go out in *that*' but Gina gave her a light kick up the bum. Ginger shot forward with an indignant yelp and Gina shut the door behind her.

A pitiful scraping started at the door.

'Not till you've done your business,' Gina shouted. 'Go on, I'll let you in when it's done.'

A whine. More scraping.

'The longer you do that the longer you'll be out there.'

Silence.

Gina nudged aside the gingham curtain to peer out. A pair of pleading brown eyes met hers.

'I can tell by the way you're walking you need to go,' Gina shouted. 'Stop being so soft and gerron wi' it.'

Finally Ginger forced herself into the wind and rain to her favourite shrub, disappeared behind it, trotting back a couple of minutes later.

'Good girl,' Gina said, opening the door. 'That weren't so hard were it?'

Ginger swept back in with an icy blast of rain and a disdainful look. She refused to look at Gina, taking her revenge by shaking her coat hard enough to spray Gina with droplets.

'Oh you little bogger,' Gina laughed. She grabbed the towel she kept for Ginger. 'Let's get them muddy paws wiped.'

Ginger deigned to let Gina rub her down and clean her paws. She cheered up when Gina picked up the grooming comb and led her into the lounge.

Warm again, dry and about to enjoy her favourite thing apart from eating, Ginger snuggled next to Gina on the sofa.

Gina picked up the comb and began running it through Ginger's short coat.

It was as much to sooth her own mind as it was to fuss Ginger.

She had hardly slept with excitement for the last couple of nights.

'I'm an important person, Ginger,' she said. 'I'm on the council. Well, not on it exactly but part of a steering group. Me! Gina Pontin. Can you believe it? What would them girls who used to sneer at me at school say now, eh?'

Ginger pricked her ears back to show she was listening, eyes half-closed in blissful pleasure.

'Nobody knows the long way I've come,' Gina continued. 'Not even Stella. When I was little I used to long for the pretty ribbons other girls had in their hair. Mine were rags cut out of old dresses. I only had one pair of knickers. I washed 'em out every night but they still smelled fusty because we didn't have central heating to dry them in the winter – no one did then – and I was too embarrassed to dry 'em next to the fire. If me dad had seen 'em he'd have teased me horrible. He were a nasty drunk; did you know that Ginger?'

The comb moved rhythmically as Gina talked and the rain hit the windows. Ginger huffed contentedly.

'But I raised a daughter on me own, and a granddaughter. I own me own house and now I'm helping my community.' The comb paused as Gina suddenly laughed. 'Which is funny,' she said.' Because most of the community don't like me.'

Ginger raised her head. Gina resumed the grooming and Ginger sighed.

'I just say things like they are, Ginger,' Gina defended herself. 'People take it the wrong way. But they're gonna need a gobshite like me to stand up for what's right. Can you imagine a holiday camp for swingers? They'll be making the beach nudist next thing you know and having intercourse all over it. It makes my blood boil. Right out there in front of the kiddies. Filth. George thinks so too.

'George is chairman of the Knights, Ginge, but I'm the leader. I can't help it. I'm a natural. George is the brains but he ain't got my charisma. That reporter saw that Thursday night. Made a beeline for me. If it weren't for the scandal with the mayor, my interview would have been top story. What do you think about that? I can't believe it meself. We only had a meeting with her yesterday morning, and she seemed such a respectable sort. Speaks lovely; not as posh as Stella but nice. Can't imagine her being involved in anything dirty, but then you just can't tell. George says the posher they are the more likely they are to be into kinky stuff. It don't surprise me.

'I just can't believe it about the mayor, but they say they have proof, and when I think about it, people are never what they seem. I expected the tea and biscuits she supplied for our meeting would be a cut above but I saw the packets. Lidl. Mucky foreign brands. You'd think the mayor could afford McVities. I was hoping for Foxes.'

Ginger tipped back her head to gaze adoringly at Gina.

'I know. Shocking ain't it? If the mayor goes, does that leave Tom Turner in charge? He's already got a head as big as a hippo. It don't need inflatin' anymore.

'If I was mayor, Ginger, there's all sorts I'd get done. First off, I'd kick Dennis Payton outta town. I'd make it illegal for cats to wander about in other people's gardens – that'd be one in the eye for Pam Stimson. I'd make sure English people got first pick of all the jobs. Them kids who hang out in the prom shelters after dark – they'd have to go. Men who walk about topless in summer – unless they're on the beach. I think it's disgusting. Women can't do it, so why should men? I never know where to look.'

Gina contemplated. 'I'd make George deputy mayor,' she finished. 'He could look after Siltby. I'm not bothered about them.'

#

Andrew Leith could not believe his luck. He'd been pleased about the merest hint of the sex camp story last weekend, delighted with the

117

outcome of the meeting on Thursday, chuckling after his interview with Gina Pontin, and rubbing his hands together in anticipation by the time he'd got home to write his story up.

And then he'd got the tip off. A text from a private number and a name to call with information regarding the mayor. Then after speaking to the eye-opening Cloris Spellman ('no 'h' in Cloris darling') Andrew spent the rest of the night trawling the online British Newspaper Archive until he found the article on Mike Courier's prosecution.

True, Martha Courier hadn't been charged, wasn't even mentioned other than she and Mike hosted swingers' parties in Southend. There was no evidence to indicate that she had known about Mike's prostitution ring but it seemed unlikely to Andrew that she wouldn't have known. Maybe even solicited herself.

Mayor Seaton! God, how many boring mayoral duties had he covered with Mayor Seaton fine and upright with her perfectly controlled hair and immaculate dress-sense? To think of her as a swinger made him grin. Well, well. Naughty Mayor Seaton.

Tom Turner must be made up. Of course it was him that sent the tip-off. Andrew wasn't fooled by the withheld number. Who else but Tom Turner had it in for Martha Seaton? He'd had his finger in this pie all along, though Andrew couldn't prove it.

Still, Tom clearly hadn't expected the application for the adult licence to go ahead. What was going on there and how was Tom connected to Dennis Payton?

Andrew yawned, stretching like a self-satisfied cat. The landline on his desk rang.

'Newsdesk.'

'Is this Andrew Leith?'

'Speaking.'

'Mr Leith, I'm from the Daily Mail …'

#

By midday the local BBC and ITN news vans arrived outside Mayor Seaton's house. The curtains were drawn and no one came to the door but the reporters, with their bloodhound senses, knew she was in there, and after a period of ringing the bell and shouting through the letterbox, settled in to wait or interviewed her neighbours and the growing number of Mapton people gathering on the street. Andrew Leith joined them around one, and spoke to various reporters about his breaking story.

At four PM the front door opened, and everyone scrambled forwards.

Mayor Seaton stepped out, looking tired but smartly dressed. Her husband, John, joined her. Together they stood resolutely.

Blinking at the flash bulbs, Mayor Seaton refused to speak until the volley of questions died down, and then she gave her statement.

'I have done my utmost to serve the constituents of Mapton and Siltby to the best of my abilities, and I believe, that for the most part I have achieved a great many positive things over the past decade for the area. I hope that in future these achievements will be the legacy of my time as mayor, and I shall be remembered for these, as opposed to mistakes I made when I was very young ...'

This last caused an outbreak of questions but Mayor Seaton held her hands up for quiet and refused to go on until she got it.

'I have no comments to make on the article published in the Lawton Post this morning but in the light of the current fight against the application by Mr Dennis Payton for an adult entertainment licence to turn the Paradise Holiday Park into a venue of an adult and sexual nature, I recognise that many will feel I am unsuitable to lead the fight. It is because of this, and because I have a great respect for my constituents, that I am tendering my resignation as mayor and town councillor for Mapton and Siltby, effective immediately.

'Thank you. That is all I have to say.'

Mayor Seaton turned her back on the clamour and walked into her house, John following her. The door closed quietly, but firmly, behind them.

Aftermath

The ranks of the Mapton Knights swelled significantly after the Thursday meeting. Sunday night Sugsy's function room was jammed with Maptonites and Siltbyites wanting to join the campaign. Those who couldn't fit in over-spilled into the rest of the pub. The whole place buzzed; people chattered excitedly about Mayor Seaton, Dennis Payton, the sex camp and all the rumour, speculation and gossip in between.

George had trouble controlling the meeting until Gina stood up and roared 'Shut up everyone. We got important business to sort and we can't do it with you boggers gibbering on like chimpanzees in a monkey house.'

'You can't talk to us like that, Gina Pontin,' someone yelled back. 'We're here to help.'

'You can help by keeping yer gob shut,' Gina said. 'We value all your opinions but only one at a time. Poor George can't hear himself think. Anyway, what's there to talk about? We're here to organise action. We're already agreed ain't we? Mapton don't want no sex camp. So let George tell us what he's got planned and get on and do it.'

This was greeted by an outbreak of applause.

'Thank you, Gina,' George said, when it had died away. 'This is what we would like to do...' He outlined the plan of action. This resulted in another burst of applause. The rest of the evening was spent chaotically trying to sort out the logistics of who would do what and when, but when it was finally sorted the locals had organised themselves into a serviceable protest group.

So it was that by the time Tuesday came round, word had got round town that a protest would gather outside the Paradise Holiday Park on a daily basis.

Over six hundred people gathered on the first day in the scrubby car park outside of the Paradise, wielding placards and waving banners that said things like: Families First. No Sex Camp' and 'Keep Mapton Decent', and 'Swingers are Sinners'.

Two men held a huge sign that read:
'WE DONT WANT NO PURVURTS'

George groaned when he saw it. 'It makes us look like idiots.' he sighed.

'Why?' Sue asked. 'It's true ain't it?'

'It's spelled wrong,' George explained. 'People will see it on telly and laugh at us.'

'I wouldn't worry about that,' Gina gasped, pointing towards the Paradise clubhouse. 'They're gonna be lookin' at that.'

The clubhouse was graffitied with a caveman's version of the Karma Sutra; stick people equipped with huge breasts and genitalia were drawn in various positions, going at it like rabbits.

'Dear God!' George said.

'Dirty boggers,' said Gina.

'Can you really do it like that?' Sue asked. 'I never imagined.'

There was a commotion from the crowd.

'Sue,' Alf panicked. 'Mildred's fainted.'

'I'm coming,' Sue shouted and took off on her Rascal Vision to resuscitate Mildred.

Andrew Leith arrived in his Fiesta, closely followed by BBC TV's local news van.

'Have you got the petition?' Andrew asked, as he drew close.

George held the sheaf of papers in his hand. He nodded dumbly.

Andrew caught sight of the clubhouse wall. 'Wow.'

Vanessa Baro, Look North's roving reporter, hurried up with her cameraman.

'Is Dennis Payton here?' she asked, but before George could reply she continued. 'I'll do a preliminary interview here with you before you present the petition. We'll get some footage of the protesters too. Might want to get them doing a bit more than shuffling their feet. Get them chanting or something.'

As though hearing her, a sudden ripple of chatter and movement went through the protesters, rising into an angry wave of calls.

They turned to see what had caused the commotion. Dennis Payton had emerged from out of the clubhouse and strode towards them, face livid.

'Get this,' Vanessa told her cameraman, who was already on it, lens fixed on the action.

'Your Knights do that?' Dennis demanded, pointing to the graffiti.

'What, of course not,' George burbled. 'It's …'

'It's vandalism on private property,' Dennis snarled. 'That's what it is. You lot have got a lot of nerve drawing stuff like that on my clubhouse.'

'Don't be daft yer twot,' Gina jumped in. 'Why would we be drawing filth like that? That's your sort o' thing, that is. Mapton Knights stand for decency. It's us who's trying to stop you bringing down the morals of Mapton. Wouldn't be surprised if you dint do it yerself, Dennis Payton.'

Dennis laughed sourly. 'Oh aye, I'm going to deface me own property. It's you that's daft if yer think anyone's gonna believe you're the moral voice of Mapton, Gina Pontin.

'And all of you are on private property. My property. I'll call the police if you don't clear off.'

'Come on now,' George interceded quickly. 'There's no need for this. We are here to reason with you Mr Payton. We have a petition to give you signed by over a thousand Mapton and Siltby residents opposing your plans to make the Paradise into a camp for adult activities – namely for swingers.'

He held out the petition. 'We'd very much like to give this to you in good faith, and hope you might rethink your position.'

Vanessa took this opportunity to position herself between them. She stuck her microphone in Dennis's face. 'Will you accept this petition, Mr Payton?'

Dennis peered down, as though seeing her, and the camera, for the first time. He smiled. 'Oh aye, I'll be happy to, love.' He took the papers and began to thumb through the signatures. Smirking, he said: 'There's a few names here I could tell you like a trip to Skeg's strip clubs now and then, but I'm a gentleman and won't reveal them. There's nothing wrong with a bit of discreet, tastefully done adult entertainment. I don't what the fuss's all about.'

'This is a family resort,' someone shouted.

Dennis looked at the protesters. 'How d'yer think families start?' he said. 'Wi' a bit of slap 'n' tickle o' course. And if Mapton's such a decent place why've I got vandalism on me clubhouse? Someone from Mapton or Siltby's done that. It's a damn sight kinkier than anything I'da thought up.'

Everyone seemed to contemplate the pornographic stick-art for a moment.

'We can't show that at 6.30, can we?' Vanessa said to her cameraman.

He shook his head.

'Pity.'

#

Gina came round to Stella's to watch the six-thirty local news. George had needed a lie down after a day protesting but Gina was energised.

Stella had never seen her look so alive.

She, Gina, and Grazja gathered around the TV. Gerta danced around on the carpet in her pyjamas, fed, washed and ready for bed.

Rick remained in the kitchen cooking dinner. He said he'd watch it on his iPad as he chopped.

Gina wouldn't stay for dinner. 'Me 'n' George already ate,' she said when she arrived. 'We had the Golden Oldie two for one at The Helmet. You know I can't be doin' eatin' late. I like my tea by five-thirty.'

'It's starting,' Grazja said, as the countdown music began.

Stella turned up the volume.

The newsreader: 'A very good evening to you. Thank you for joining us. Welcome to Look North. The headlines this Tuesday night: Hundreds of locals gathered outside Paradise Holiday Park in Mapton to protest a planning application to make the park into a site for swingers.'

Film of the protesters flashed onto the screen. Gina's hair stood out like a flame.

'There I am,' she screamed. 'Gerta, come here. Your grandma's on the telly.'

The image changed to Dennis Payton. 'It's a storm in a teacup,' he said. 'People are over-reacting. All this talk of a 'sex camp' is nonsense.'

'What?' Gina yelled. 'Where's me 'n' George?'

'Shush,' Stella said. 'It's only the headlines. They'll come back to you in a minute.'

'Also tonight,' the presenter said. 'Police are cracking down on mobility scooter users blocking up roads, after a pensioner delayed traffic on a major Lincolnshire road for four hours.'

'Of course I use the middle of the road,' said the pensioner. 'It's too mucky and bumpy on the verges. I've as much right as any to travel on 'em. I've paid my taxes all my life.'

Back to the presenter. 'Elsewhere, Yorkshire villagers stumped by mysterious theft of pond ornaments.'

'They've been going missing all over the village,' a woman commented.

'Where Gwamma?' Gerta shouted over the next headline.

'She'll be on next,' Stella said.

'I better blimmin' be,' Gina nettled.

The countdown music blared to a climax. The newsreader stared seriously into the camera. 'Good evening. A protest in Mapton over the application for a so called 'sex camp' got heated today. The seaside town has been embroiled in scandal recently when revelations about the mayor, Martha Seaton, rocked the community. Mayor Seaton resigned on Saturday amid allegations that she had once embraced a swingers' lifestyle, and possibly been linked to a prostitution ring.

'The revelations came about at the time that Mapton and Siltby Town Council publically confirmed their opposition to plans to make a local caravan park a holiday site specifically for swingers.

Local businessman, Dennis Payton, who owns Paradise Holiday Park, has put an application in to the district council for an adult entertainment licence.

'A resident group, calling themselves the Mapton Knights, have organised a petition and protest against Mr Payton's proposals.

'To tell you more our reporter, Vanessa Baro, is on the spot.'

The picture changed to Vanessa Baro standing outside the Paradise, with its 'a' and 'e' missing from the sign.

'This modest (some might say a little shabby) caravan park behind me was the scene of angry protests earlier today. Alleged plans by owner, Dennis Payton, to make the park into a holiday destination for couples who like to swing, have enraged many of the locals. So much so that they have organised themselves into an action group, called the Mapton Knights.'

The film cut to George, looking a bit dazed, flanked by Gina and Sue.

'Here we go,' Gina crowed.

'What do the Mapton Knights stand for?' Vanessa asked, shoving the microphone in George's face.

George had a startled, trapped-in-the-headlights look 'Well, er, let's see now... we stand for, erm, decent British values. Mapton's an old-fashioned English seaside resort, appealing to families with young children. A sex camp wouldn't be very sleazy. No, no, I mean it would be. Sleazy, that is.'

The film cut back to Vanessa. 'But 'decency' doesn't seem to describe some of the things we've seen today. Mr Payton was shocked and horrified to find his clubhouse had been daubed with pornographic graffiti – so explicit in fact that we can't show it. The police have stated that this was likely done by teenagers messing around but Mr Payton is unconvinced. He believes that the Mapton Knights did it for publicity purposes and to stir up trouble.'

The image flicked to a shot of Dennis in his office (minus his girly calendar) looking solemn.

'One of the ringleaders is Gina Pontin,' he said. 'She's after revenge because I banned her from The Paradise some years ago. She's been waiting for her chance.'

Vanessa asked.' What was she banned for?'

'Heckling the other customers on karaoke nights,' Dennis said, looking pained. 'I gave her plenty of warnings but in the end her behaviour just wasn't fair to other people and I banned her.'

'Today, Ms Pontin verbally attacked Mr Payton.'

The footage shifted to a red-faced Gina, yelling at Dennis. Her red hair whipped wildly in the wind. 'Don't be daft yer BLEEP. Why would we be drawing filth like that? That's your sort o' thing, that is. Mapton Knights stand for decency. It's us who's trying to stop you bringing down the morals of Mapton. Wouldn't be surprised if you dint do it yerself, Dennis Payton.'

Then back to Vanessa. 'As you can see, emotions are running high here in Mapton. Mr Payton claims that if his plans are approved it will improve the commerce of Mapton and won't have any impact on the family side of the resort. To quote him: 'It will be a civilised, quiet getaway for consenting adults in a private setting and won't bother anyone else. This is all a storm in a teacup and a chance for petty revenge.'

Vanessa finished. 'Whatever the outcome, it seems clear that until the district council make their decision, this 'storm in a teacup' is going to rage on a while longer.

'This is Vanessa Baro reporting for Look North, Lincolnshire.'

In the stunned silence that followed, Stella hit the off button on the TV remote and waited for the explosion.

Gina sprang out of her chair, puffing out like a threatened cat. 'That little cow,' she bellowed. 'She made it look like I was the wrong un. I'm gonna kill her, and Dennis Payton.'

Gerta burst into tears. Stella scooped her up.

'Calm down, 'she said to Gina. 'You're frightening Gerta.'

Gina ignored her. 'I've a good mind to ring the BBC,' she ranted. 'I don't pay my licence fee for that kind of crap. And beeping me out. All I said was 'twot'. That ain't even the rude version. They made it sound like I was swearing me 'ead off. Well, I'll give em something to chuffin' bleep out.'

Gerta wailed louder. Stella looked at Grazja. 'I'll take her,' she said. 'You stay with Gina.'

Grazja nodded.

Stella carried Gerta across the hall to the kitchen where she found Rick collapsed in tears. Unlike Gerta's, his were tears of mirth.

Stella shot him a disapproving look. 'You watched it, I see.'

Rick, wiping his eyes, gulped back a laugh. 'Gina looked like a mad woman.' He sobered up. 'Oh, baby,' he said to Gerta, lifting her out of Stella's arms. 'What's happened?'

'Gwwww Gwamma shout,' Gerta sobbed.

'Gina's hit critical mass,' Stella explained.

'I'm not surprised,' Rick started to laugh again. 'George came across as a doddering old fool and Gina like a banshee. Only Dennis Payton appeared reasonable.' He rocked Gerta as he spoke until her sobs sniffled away. 'Have you seen the graffiti?'

Stella shook her head.

'It's gone viral,' Rick grinned. 'People were taking about it in the diner today and getting it up on their phones.'

'What's it like?'

'Crude but instructive,' Rick said. 'Lots of 'intercourse' in different positions.'

Gerta had fallen asleep on his shoulder.

Stella pulled the iPad towards her.

'Type in 'Mapton's Karma Sutra',' Rick said.

Stella did and found a link. A photo came up.

'Wow,' she said, peering at the drawings. 'That must've taken them all night. And they must've had a ladder.'

'I know,' Rick cracked up again. 'I love this town.'

Finally Mayor

Acting mayor, Tom Turner, stared down at page four of the Daily Mail. Things weren't going as he'd imagined they would when he'd set this ball rolling.

Originally he'd thought just the whiff of the rumour would give him a cause to heroically lead – he hadn't expected the bloody Mapton Knights – gilding him in the eyes of the public. More importantly he'd chosen the swingers theme with care.

He'd met Cloris Spellman at a Meat Management awards 'do'. She was no spring chicken, but still a nicely preserved old bird and he enjoyed a bit of flirting over their Beef Wellington. Phyllis was being charmed by Graham Spellman, so it was a congenial evening of bawdy jokes, flowing wine, and a little harmless flirting.

Neither Phyllis nor he dreamed that Cloris and Graham might suggest anything more. The most Tom had hoped for was a bit of a surreptitious grope with Cloris behind the toilet block and some tongue. No harm in that. So he'd continued to top up her wine glass and work his magic.

Cloris had edged closer to him throughout each course. After coffee she snuggled right up and whispered. 'I know a secret about your friend, Mayor Seaton.'

Tom forced his eyes away from her enticing cleavage (only a little crepey) to her mouth.

'What's that?' he wheezed. Her perfume was setting his asthma on but he didn't mind.

'Moons ago we used to go to her parties. She threw them with her husband, Mike. They were *house* parties.'

Tom's booze and sex befuddled brain tried to understand her emphasis on 'house'.' And who was Mike? Martha's husband was John.

'Uh?'

Cloris walked her fingers up his thigh. 'They were private parties,' she whispered. 'For couples only. Do you know what sort of parties I mean?'

She looked directly in his eyes.

'Uh!' Tom repeated. His crotch was on fire and his head swam. Blimey! Was she suggesting…

'How dare you?' Phyllis's screech cut through his fug. The next thing he knew she'd thrown her wine over Graham Spellman and was demanding to go.

In retrospect Tom was glad Phyllis had put a stop to what might have been a costly mistake – he was in public office after all. Once he'd sobered up, Cloris's indiscretion about Martha Seaton had fully sunk in.

He'd rung up Cloris to apologise for Phyllis's behaviour, saying it had all been an unfortunate misunderstanding, and worked his way round to talking about Martha, pretending to be concerned for his colleague.

Cloris had been only too happy to talk but promised she wouldn't tell another soul for now.

Then Tom had set to work. Given what he knew about Martha – who had year after year been voted in as mayor by his council colleagues –

starting a rumour about a swingers' camp was intended to unsettle her. Once she understood Tom knew about her past, he was sure he'd be able to persuade her to quietly 'retire', not only from her mayoral role, but stand down as a candidate for councillor at the next election.

It would be in her own interests, and that of Mapton and Siltby. Then he, Tom Turner, would be the obvious choice for mayor, as was only fitting given his standing in the community, especially when people saw him emphatically defeat any plans to bring a swingers' camp to Mapton.

Only it hadn't gone like that.

His secret ally, Dennis Payton, had stabbed him in the back. He'd been so angry at Martha Seaton for undermining him at the public meeting that he'd tipped off Andrew Leith in a fit of pique. Martha had resigned, true, but in a blaze of scandal.

Now there was the matter of a vacancy on the town council with Martha gone. Legally they had to advertise it, but Tom hoped that the ten electors needed to call an election wouldn't bother and they could co-opt a member to the council – a member loyal to Tom. He would make damn sure of that. No more mistakes!

He was finally mayor. Well, acting mayor. And what he had on his hands was a bloody mess.

The local news last night was a debacle. Mapton protesters looked like a mob of yokel simpletons, led by blundering George Wentworth and rabid Gina Pontin, while Dennis came across as a beleaguered businessman.

Today it had gone national, and Mapton was the butt of the joke.

The headline in The Mail screamed out at him.

IS THIS BRITAIN'S SLEAZIEST SEASIDE TOWN?

It was time for him to take control.

Tom reached for the phone.

'Stan? Call everyone together. It's time for a crisis meeting.'

Town Council Noticeboard

NOTICE OF VACANCY IN OFFICE OF COUNCILLOR

MAPTON & SILTBY TOWN COUNCIL
MAPTON NORTH PARISH
WARD
NOTICE IS HEREBY GIVEN

that due to the resignation of Councillor Seaton, a vacancy has arisen in the Office of Councillor for the Town Council.

If by 12 November (14 days after the date of this notice) a request for an election to fill said vacancy is made in writing to the Returning Officer at the address below by TEN electors for the said Parish Ward, an election will be held to fill the said vacancy, otherwise the vacancy will be filled by co-option.

Dated 30 October
Sam Davis
Returning Officer
Town Hall
Lawton
LN11 4PQ

An Unexpected Turn Around

Gina felt it like a blow when George told her.

After last night's television, the morning's Daily Mail – which made George swear, and George never swore – it was the final straw.

She'd rung up local BBC this morning and given the girl on the phone a piece of her mind but she wasn't able to get through to Vanessa or her editor.

This latest was the hardest to swallow. After noon, Councillor Stan Martin had rung George to let him know that, under Acting Mayor Turner, the council members had voted to disassociate the council from the Mapton Knights. There would be no steerage group.

Stan had been apologetic; he said he felt terrible, truly, and that he admired what the Knights were doing but the media coverage yesterday had been an embarrassment to the town. It would be best now to call off the protests and let Mayor Turner go through the proper channels. After all, he knew everyone in the district council. Let's get this application blocked quietly and efficiently, there's a good man.

Poor George had a bit of a turn and had taken to his bed. Gina, enraged, had set off for the council office to have it out with Tom Turner. It was more than just indignation; Gina felt it as bitter rejection. For the first time in her life she'd felt respected – or near to it. Despite her mouthy bravado, inside Gina lived a girl who was always the butt of school jokes, a child who never got a gold star or a part in the nativity – not even the peripheral ones, like a sheep. The teenager who the boys saw as easy and the girls looked down on. An unmarried mother; a firebrand; a loose cannon; tough as nails; brassy; common as muck. These were all the ways people saw her.

A joke. An embarrassment.

But these past few years she'd found a place in Mapton. She'd reconnected with Stella, met George, loved little Gerta to bits.

She was still abrasive, gobby, and often offensive – still herself – yet Gina was a part of the community too. For the first time in her life.

She wasn't going to let any journalist, any TV reporter, or any acting mayor, put her back in her place. She was not going to be the butt of their jokes anymore.

So Gina did what came naturally – did what had got her into so much trouble so many times. She went on the attack.

Or at least that was how she started off, marching into town with the steam virtually whistling out of her ears.

Some in her path took one look at her face and scurried out of the way. Others called greetings, or words of support. Many Maptonites had been angered by the news report. Gina didn't hear any of them, not even the odd couple of insults thrown her way.

She was intent on confronting Tom Turner.

Yet, in the end, she didn't confront him.

Not because he wasn't there, or because she was refused entry to the building. Neither of those things brought Gina to a stop next to the town council noticeboard.

It was the seagull that shat on her face which did it.

The superstition that a bird pooping on you is lucky proved to be true for Gina.

Naturally she was furious, letting loose with a string of expletives before digging in her handbag to pull out a packet of Femfresh, her all-purpose wipes for most occasions.

Wiping savagely at her cheek she faced the noticeboard. That's when she saw it. Not once in her years in Mapton had Gina stopped to read this noticeboard, and nor would she today if the seagull hadn't let loose at the precise moment it did.

Gina's eyes focused on the cream paper behind the glass, nestling amongst the notices as though it didn't want to be seen.

NOTICE OF VACANCY IN OFFICE OF COUNCILLOR

MAPTON & SILTBY TOWN COUNCIL
MAPTON NORTH PARISH
WARD
NOTICE IS HEREBY GIVEN

She read on carefully.

Gina read it three times, took out her phone and took a photograph of it.

Slowly, as though in a daze, she walked away from the council office.

Gina had a new plan.

In the Diner

Grazja had got in the habit of taking Gerta to the diner mid-mornings.

With the October half-term finished, and November weather settling in, most of the seafront shops and cafes had closed for the season, boarded up against the bitter storms of winter.

Only The Last Resort stayed open on the seafront, being popular with locals as well as tourists.

Its warm glow was a welcome sight on dark, dreary days and a place to come and chew the fat.

The Last Resort was larger than Rick's old diner, which had blown up in the Great Donkey Stampede of four years ago. There was usually a booth or two free on off-season mornings, where Grazja and Gerta parked themselves so Gerta could draw, or play with Play-Doh, or spend an age going through the compartments of Grazja's large bag, itemising everything she found before eventually returning them and starting again. Grazja kept this bag especially for her, and carefully selected the objects in it, learning on her first day of playing the game that lipstick was a particularly bad idea with a two year old.

Grazja always packed a large piece of PVC fabric to spread on the table, and plenty of wipes.

After the usual enthusiastic greeting between Gerta and her daddy (or with her Auntie Ange on Wednesdays) today Gerta chose to make Play-Doh sea creatures, using her plastic moulds.

Brother Frank entered.

Grazja wasn't sure whether she felt pleased or irritated.

Hadn't Stella said he was an early bird? But here he was turning up mid-morning for the third day running.

Grazja wasn't stupid. She'd picked up Stella's unsubtle hints that Frank liked her.

He could like her as much as he wanted to; it wouldn't make a difference. Romantically, Grazja's heart was closed for business. She'd turned the key in that lock when her husband had died and had no intention of reversing it.

Frank seemed a nice man and she liked talking to him. His face was pleasant, although his hair was thinning and she liked a good head of hair.

Still Frank had nice eyes.

Her husband had had beautiful eyes, and beautiful hair and beautiful hands and a beautiful heart. Until disease robbed of him all these except for the goodness of his heart.

Everything else it stripped from him viciously.

Grazja shook herself. She hardly ever allowed herself to think about the past. No good would come of doing it now.

Frank smiled at her from the counter where he was talking to Rick. He waved.

Grazja smiled neutrally back.

Yes, a hint of mooniness about his smile. Oh dear, didn't she have enough to worry about with the trouble caused by Mrs Alexander's pernicious will. At least since she'd changed her phone, the texts and calls had stopped. But they would find her eventually. They were not the sort of people to let that money go, no matter how airtight the will appeared to be.

All she'd wanted since she left Poland was to work in a job where she could use her nursing skills, do someone else some good, and earn enough money to get by without being noticed.

It was enough, wasn't it?

She did *not* need a middle-aged man making calf's eyes at her.

Not even if she did feel a little bit flattered. Well, who wouldn't? It had been a very long time since any man had looked at her that way.

Her life was simple – or had been until recently – and that was the way she liked it.

'Ga Ga!' Gerta interrupted her thoughts. She couldn't say Grazia, so had settled for 'Ga Ga'. 'Watch.'

Grazja obliged, watching Gerta's pudgy little fingers patting down her purple starfish.

'That beautiful, Gerta. Can you make me fish?'

'Yeth,' Gerta said. Laboriously, gasping and omitting small grunts she used the fish cutter to produce a wobbly fish shape. 'Eat.'

Grazja picked it up and pretended to eat it. 'Yum yum, Grazja love fish.'

'Nuff,' Gerta said, grabbing the fish and squishing it into a ball.

'Hungry, honey?' Rick materialised by the booth. 'How about Daddy rustles you up some cheese and apple?'

Grazja cleaned Gerta up before Rick returned with a plate of chopped apple and cheese cubes.

'There's a coffee and muffin with your name on it, Grazja' he nodded at the counter. 'I'll take over here while it's quiet.'

Grazja looked over to see Rick had left her coffee next to Frank's seat.

'I know what you doing,' she muttered to Rick. 'I not interested.'

Rick feigned innocence. 'Not interested in a free coffee and a muffin? That's just madness, Grazja. Go on, take a break.'

Rolling her eyes at him, Grazja slid out of the booth and walked over to the counter, hoisting herself up on the stool next to Frank.

Act like Gina, she told herself. He'll lose interest then.

She peered down at his weak, milkless tea, and said. 'Look like fly piss.'

Frank blinked at her, taken aback. His mouth tugged up at the corners.

'Thank you,' he said. 'But the saying's gnat's piss.'

'Oh,' Grazja said. 'Same thing.'

'Well, I'm sure an entomologist would argue the point with you, but I think what you're really saying is that my tea looks too weak.'

'Not tea,' Grazja retorted. 'Stained hot water.'

'Maybe so,' Frank said, turning his amused brown eyes to hers. 'But it's the way I like it. Why should it bother you? I'm not asking you to drink it.'

He did have pretty eyes. She'd concede that. Suddenly she felt ashamed.

'Sorry,' she said. 'Was rude of me.'

'Don't worry. I've heard it plenty of times. I thought it was just the British obsession with tea you can stand a spoon up in. I didn't know it was an international thing.'

Grazja smiled sheepishly. 'Tea very big in Poland too.'

'How long have you lived over here?' Frank asked.

'Oh, years,' Grazja replied. 'I like it so I stay.'

'*Zguba Polski jest naszą zyskiem,*' Frank said hesitantly.

Grazja jolted. 'What?' she said, almost vehemently.

'Oh,' Frank went red. 'I thought I was saying Poland's loss is our gain. Did I say something else? My Polish is very rusty.'

'You said it very well,' Grazja recovered. 'No one English has ever spoken it to me in the UK. I surprised that all. When you learn Polish?'

'Oh, a long, long time ago,' Frank said. He looked down at his tea. 'For work. I lived in Warsaw for a while.' He stood up suddenly. 'Is that the time? I didn't realise. I have to be going...'

'But...' Grazja began, before realising she didn't have any reason to say 'but'. He was leaving and surely that was good. Perhaps her Gina approach had worked after all.

'Bye Rick,' Frank called as he all but lunged for the door.

Rick looked up bemused. 'What did you say to him?' he asked Grazja. 'That was the fastest exit I've seen since Andy Timmis heard the pickle-onion cart had overturned on the crossroads.'

'I say nothing,' Grazja said. 'One minute he talking in Polish, next minute he out the door.'

'He can speak Polish!'

'Yes. He lived in Warsaw years ago.'

'Grazja,' Rick said in wonder. 'You've learnt more about him in two minutes than I have in six years.'

Grazja squirmed under his gaze. To change the subject, she asked. 'Pickle onion cart?'

The Plan

The town council's request that the Mapton Knights cease their protest outside the Paradise was roundly ignored. In fact the numbers of protesters continued to swell over the week.

Maptonites, stung by the media locally and nationally, needed an outlet. Chanting and waving placards outside the Paradise provided it.

Stella had been down to the site with her camera and taken loads of shots. She'd also brought large thermoses of tea and coffee, as well as biscuits and paper cups, which proved very welcome.

She handed a cup to Sue.

'I can't believe the numbers,' Stella said.

'I know,' Sue agreed. 'One in the eye for Tom Turner. He told George we should stop and let the town council handle it. Stupid twot. Got yer camera I see.'

'Yeah, I thought I'd capture a bit of the action. I might get a painting out of it. Light's good today.'

Sue nodded, cradling her tea. 'Bout time we had a bit o' sunshine. Still colder than a witch's tit when you're hangin' about. This is welcome, duck. Thanks for thinkin' of us. Come from Rick's did it?'

'I asked Ange if I could fill the flasks,' Stella said. 'Rick's over in Lawton.'

'Oh, yeah, it's Wednesday,' Sue said. 'Never did sign our petition, did he?'

Stella laughed. 'He doesn't like group-think, Sue.'

Sue snorted. 'Group-think! He's a 'nana. He don't mind groups like the Marauders when we're buying his food.'

'He doesn't want to feel pressured into doing something just because everyone else is. The more you pressure him to sign that petition, the more he'll resist.' Stella explained.

'Yeah, but some folk think it's because he's one of *them*.' Sue lowered her voice. 'Talk of you and him being secret swingers, like Mayor Seaton, you know. She moved down south when she were young and looked what happened to her. You're from London and Rick's an American. It makes people suspicious, Stella. And then him refusing to sign … It's good you've come down today. Let people think Rick's sent the tea and coffee. That'll shut 'em up.'

Stella was stunned. 'Sue!'

'I'm just telling you what I've heard, duckie. I'm not saying it's true.'

'Well it's not true,' Stella hissed. 'But supposing it was. What me and Rick may or may not do is none of anyone's business. Swingers aren't criminals, Sue. What they do is legal. It's only sex between consenting adults for Godsakes.'

'Oh, I know, duckie,' Sue said. 'If I'm honest I shagged half the town in me younger days, and half the ones I shagged are here today, but it's not the same as having a *camp* fo' it on your doorstep, is it?'

'I don't want a camp for 'it' on my doorstep either,' Stella said. 'Mostly because I don't want to have to explain it to Gerta in a few years, but I don't think you should be suggesting Rick has to be seen to supporting the campaign or else it's assumed he's a swinger himself. And if he was, what then? Are people going to hound him out of town?'

'Don't be daft,' Sue said. 'Although, you heard what happened to Martha Seaton this morning, right?'

Stella felt a chill. 'No. What?'

'Someone sprayed 'whore' across her house in red.'

Stella felt sick. 'Oh no. That's awful.'

'It is awful,' Sue agreed. 'But feeling's running high.'

#

George was feeling pretty ropey but he didn't want to let Gina down so he said nothing of it and chaired the meeting of the Knights. They'd kept it to the original committee as there was an idea he and Gina (mainly Gina) wanted to 'float' with the inner-circle before unleashing it on Mapton.

His digestion had been playing up for days, as was his heartburn.

Starting the Mapton Knights had seemed such a good idea; a crusade for common decency and a positive step. He wasn't a prude, Lord knows not, although he'd prefer to make an honest woman out of Gina if only she'd consent. Yet, this hadn't stopped them having sexual relations out of wedlock. It was the twenty-first century after all! But the idea of a sex camp right here in Mapton was ludicrous and degraded.

Starting a campaign had appeared to be the most sensible course of action. Enlisting the mayor's help had been a coup, until the mayor resigned under a cloud of sleaze. The TV, the Daily Mail (he'd be cancelling his subscription), the disregard of the town council, and now the horrible vandalism on Martha Seaton's house, it was all too much. The vandalism had upset him the most. It certainly wasn't the noble action of a Templar Knight upholding honour and virtue!

Events were snowballing so fast, George felt unable to cope but he didn't want to admit it to Gina. Especially not now. She was beginning to bloom, just the way he'd always thought she would.

There was more to Gina Pontin than most people understood. George had seen it from the beginning despite her rudeness to him.

The Knights were in rambunctious mode, geed up by the swelling support of the locals. It took George three attempts with the gavel to bring them to order.

Mildred was poised to start taking the minutes.

George began. 'Thanks for attending everyone. Alf sends his apologies. His lumbago is playing up again. Make a note, Mildred, that we all send him our best wishes.'

'She can tell him herself,' Andy said. 'She's his wife.'

'Let's keep this proper,' George said. 'Right, first item on the agenda. Everyone approve last week's minutes?' Everyone did. 'Second item. Progress report on the campaign from Gina.'

'Well, no offense to Sue but PR's been crap,' Gina opened. 'We all know that, but even so we've got over six thousand signatures on the petition and more protesters every day.'

This sparked off a discussion, with Sue staging her own protest. It went on for fifteen minutes with every member chipping in, and would have gone on for longer if George hadn't used the gavel again.

Wearily he said: 'We need to decide how to take the campaign forward, especially in view of Acting Mayor Turner's decision to cut us from the steerage group.'

'Bastard,' Sugsy said to general agreement.

'It was certainly short-sighted of him,' George said. 'But Gina has some ideas we'd like you to listen to.'

Sue pursed her lips, looking as though she was about to kick off, but Gina waylaid her with an unexpected statement.

'When I said PR's been crap, I didn't mean it was Sue's fault. It were a great idea to get the news in for the handover of the petition to Dennis. That little cow from the BBC shafted us, that's all. And who could have known about Martha Seaton?'

That started them all twittering again.

George, fighting a tightness in his chest, didn't reach for the gavel. He didn't need to, as Gina shouted. 'For God's sake shurrup! I got some proposals for yer. Just listen.'

She continued. 'First up, we need to find someone proper to do PR.' Sue bristled but Gina held her up hand to forestall her. 'Not one of us knows how to really do it. We need to find someone who knows how to handle the press. Someone who knows how it all works, and can write press releases and the like. A professional.'

'How do we pay for that?' Sugsy asked.

'I dunno yet,' Gina said. 'There must be one person in Mapton and Siltby who has some proper experience and might want to help us out. Sugsy and Andy I want you two to check that out.'

'Who made you boss?' Sue demanded. 'George's chair.'

'I'm campaign leader,' Gina retorted. 'Which brings me to my second proposal.'

George, despite his chest, felt a glow of pride in her. Look at her taking charge.

'I'd like to nominate Sue to take over as campaign leader.'

'What?'

'Sue!'

'But you're campaign leader.'

Sue's expression transformed from resentment to disbelief to flattered.

'Me?'

'Yes,' Gina nodded. 'Sue may not have been much cop at PR but she's a natural at organisation and leadership. Just look at the Marauders. Who organises you? Sue does. Who's been out on the protest lines every day, rain or shine? Sue has. Who knows almost everyone in Mapton? Sue does.'

'That's true,' Mildred piped up, looking at Sue fondly. 'It's Sue who organises all our days out, the rumbles, the prizes. Everything. We Marauders wouldn't exist without her.'

Sue blushed with pleasure as a spontaneous little burst of applause broke out.'

'What do you think Sue?' Gina asked. 'Will you do it?'

'Yes.' Sue looked thrilled. 'I will.'

'Vote on it,' George rasped. 'Hands up for 'aye''

All hands went up.

'Motion carried,' George said, fighting to find his breath.

In the excitement no one noticed.

'But what will you do Gina?' Sugsy asked. 'You're our driving force.'

Even Sue nodded.

'Ah,' Gina said, puffing up. 'That's my big surprise. Since Martha Seaton resigned there's a casual vacancy on the council. I am going to run for councillor.'

This was greeted by a stunned silence.

Then George fell forward onto the table, clutching his chest.

Stolen Thunder

'How is he?' Stella said, rushing up to Gina.

She and Rick had got to Grimsby hospital as fast as they could, leaving Gerta at home under Grazja's care.

'Keep me up to date,' Grazja had insisted as they left.

Gina threw herself into Stella's arms, sobbing. 'I dunno,' she cried. 'They took him in half an hour ago and no one's told me nothing. The paramedic thought it was a heart attack but they weren't sure.'

'It'll be alright,' Stella reassured her. 'C'mon, let's sit down.'

Gina allowed herself to be guided back to a chair. Stella and Rick took the ones on either side of her. Each held her hand.

'He woke up in the ambulance,' Gina said. 'He looked so frightened, Stell.'

'George's tougher than he looks, Gina,' Stella soothed. She didn't know if that was true but Gina's white face under her blaze of hair – grey roots needed touching up Stella noted vaguely – scared her. Gina looked so vulnerable.

George had been very good for Gina. Loyal, caring, and a stabilising influence, he'd given her genuine love, no matter how hard she made it for him at times.

Stella dreaded the effect losing George might have on Gina, and guiltily recognised the selfish kernel of that was really: 'what would the effect of a destabilised Gina have on her?'

Mentally Stella slapped herself. It was George who was important here.

'People survive heart attacks all the time,' she said. 'We need to be prepared to help George with anything he needs.'

Rick agreed. 'Sure we will,' he said. 'Anything we can do.'

A doctor came through the swinging doors and approached.

'Mrs Wentworth?' he said to Gina.

'Near enough,' Gina said, standing. She wiped her face with a tissue.

'Tell it to me straight, doctor. No sodding around.'

'Er, fine,' the doctor smiled. 'The good news is it wasn't a heart attack. The bad news is that Mr Wentworth does have angina – it was a bad angina attack – so does effectively have coronary heart disease.'

'What's that mean?' Gina demanded.

'It means that his arteries have thickened and hardened so that blood can't flow properly to his heart muscles. Ultimately this can lead to a heart attack or stroke, but although we can't cure it, we can minimise the risk of those outcomes by treating the angina with medicine.'

'To stop him having a heart attack,' Gina clarified.

'To minimise the risk,' the doctor stressed. 'And at the moment we don't know whether he has stable angina, or unstable. We are going to keep him in overnight for some more tests tomorrow, and then make a further diagnosis.

However he has responded well to a dose of glyceryl trinitrate and is no longer in pain.'

'Can we see him?' Stella interjected.

'Visiting hours are over,' the doctor said. 'But I'll see what I can do.'

'I'm going to see him,' Gina said. 'I won't go home till I have.'

The doctor just gave her a bone-weary look and disappeared through the swing doors.

All the puff went out of Gina. Her knees buckled. Rick caught her and lowered her into the seat.

'It's alright, it's alright,' Stella said, putting her arms around Gina. 'He's okay. They're keeping him for tests but he's alive and kicking.'

'I'll give him a kicking,' Gina sniffled, 'frightening me like this.'

Stella smiled at Rick over Gina's head and hugged her grandmother harder.

#

Twenty minutes later, when Gina had begun to chafe, a porter wheeled George through on a trolley.

'I'm taking him to Birdseye ward,' the porter said cheerily. 'You can have a quick word now, then see him tomorrow. Give reception a ring in the morning and ask for the ward sister. She'll tell you what's happening.'

George lay wan against the pillow, but he smiled at Gina.

'Still here,' he rasped.

'Course I'm still bloody here, George Wentworth,' Gina said. 'Where else would I be.'

'I meant me,' George said.

Gina blinked back tears. George reached for her hand. She grasped it.

'I don't know,' she said, getting herself under control. 'You certainly rained on my parade.'

George's smile wobbled. 'Stole your thunder, didn't I?'

'That you did,' Gina said. 'And you can expect a right rollickin' when you're home.'

George waggled his eyebrows suggestively.

'Oh, yer dirty bogger,' Gina whispered, leaning down to kiss his forehead. 'I do love you.'

They watched the porter wheel George into the lift.

'What thunder did George steal?' Stella asked, as they turned to leave.

'Eh? Oh! I'll tell yer tomorrow, duck.'

Developments

Tom was in the golf club bar when his phone buzzed. He checked the caller. Julie, the town clerk.

'If it's bad news I don't want to know,' he greeted her.

'It's not bad news,' Julie said chirpily. 'We're going to have a by-election.'

Tom sat up. 'Tell me you're joking,' he said.

'Nope, twelve electors' letters hit the mat this morning.'

'Twelve.' Tom ground his teeth. 'Who from?'

'From residents of course,' Julie sang. 'They seemed to have come up with a standard letter between them. You'd know most of the signatories as the friendly rivals to that little motability club of yours.'

'The Marauders,' Tom growled. 'They want to play silly buggers with me, do they?'

'I wouldn't know about that,' Julie said. 'It's quite normal for local residents to take an interest in electing their representatives. I think it's good. Shows a sense of civic duty.'

Tom bit his tongue. Julie did all the town admin and he needed her on his side to run the council smoothly.

'You're quite right love,' he said. 'Losing Martha on the council was such a shake-up I was hoping for a bit of calm. Still, needs must and democracy rules, so better get on with.'

'I'll get on to the elections office right away,' Julie said.

He was sure he could detect laughter in her voice.

#

'I can't believe Gina is going ahead with this after your heart attack,' Sue said to George. They were sipping tea in George's lounge. Normally George would enjoy two or three chocolate digestives with his elevenses, but doctor's orders forbade too much fat and sugar.

Ginger Rogers snuggled against him. Gina had brought her round to give him some company while she went out on her errands.

Then Sue had arrived unexpectedly with a bunch of flowers, a crossword book, and a jigsaw puzzle of flamingos.

'There's only two pieces missing,' she said. 'It'll still keep you entertained.'

George didn't actually want to be kept entertained. He just wanted a few days of quiet.

There was no chance of that with Sue. She had a great deal to tell him.

'It wasn't a heart attack,' George explained again. 'It's angina.'

'Practically the same thing,' Sue said. 'I thought Gina would want to take the time to look after you. She's going to be terrible busy running for councillor.'

It was one of the rare days when Scampi came out with Sue. Once inseparable, Scampi normally stayed home while Sue gallivanted. Today was one of her good days and Sue thought she might enjoy a run out to see George.

Scampi, pink tongue protruding, snored gently next to Ginger Rogers. She looked as worn-out and ragged as George felt.

If only, he thought, Sue would go, he, Scampi, and Ginger, could just snooze through the rest of the morning together quite happily.

'I want Gina to run,' George said. 'She offered not to but I think it's important. Someone needs to keep Tom Turner in his place.'

'But d'yer think she can really win?' Sue looked doubtful. 'I mean I like Gina, you know I do, but she can rub people up the wrong way.'

George smiled. 'I think folk round here are ready for a change. They want someone who will tell it like it is.'

'She don't always tell it like it is,' Sue said. 'She tells it as she sees it, which ain't always the same thing.'

'She always means well,' George defended Gina.

Sue gave him an incredulous look, but conceded. 'She's been a lot better since Gerta was born. Bit softer. Still,' Sue looked sideways at him. 'If I had someone as good to me as you are to Gina, George, I'd be spending my time making sure you was well, not fixing to get myself elected.'

George coughed. He wished Sue would go away, but he was too much of a gentleman to say so.

'Erm, how is the campaign going?' he asked instead. He regretted it because it set Sue off talking for a good hour.

By the time Gina got home to find Sue still there, George felt like the shrivelled remains of a deflated balloon.

'I saw my Rascal outside,' Gina said, bustling into the lounge. 'So I knew you were here.'

'It's my Rascal,' Sue said. 'I bought it fair and square.'

'You know what I mean,' Gina said.

'I just came by to check on George,' Sue said, struggling to rise. 'The Knights are concerned about him.'

'That's nice,' said Gina. 'You liked your card, didn't you, George?'

'Lovely,' George said. The card was on the sideboard with many others. He had been touched to get them all.

'I brought him a crossword book and a puzzle to keep him occupied while he's resting up.'

'And those flowers?' Gina's mouth curled down as she nodded to the mixed bouquet.

'Something to brighten the place up,' Sue said, finally getting to her feet.

'Arthritis bad today?' Gina asked. 'Shame. You need to go home and put your own feet up. It's time for George to have his dinner and his medicine.' She looked at George. 'You look like you need a nap, duck.' She crossed over to plump up his cushions in an uncharacteristically caring manner. 'Oh, ay up, Scampi. Didn't see you there.'

Gina turned to Sue. 'Scampi's looking a bit rough, Sue. She alright?'

Sue gathered Scampi up protectively. 'She's old,' she said. 'That's all.' She shuffled to the lounge door. 'See yer George. You make sure Gina looks after yer. I'll come by again to make sure of it.'

'No need,' Gina bristled. 'I take lovely care of yer, don't I George?'

'Splendidly well,' George said forcing himself to sound cheery. 'Thanks for coming Sue.'

Gina saw Sue out.

'D'yer like them flowers?' she asked.

'Not really,' George answered wisely. 'I think they're giving me hay fever.' He produced a small sneeze.

'I'll get rid of them,' Gina said, snatching up the vase. 'I'll bring over some of my nice artificial ones.'

'What's for lunch,' George asked.

'Cornish pasties,' Gina said. 'Grazja said I shouldn't be giving you stuff like that, but I said it would do you good. They got meat, veg, potatoes, and pastry. What's wrong with that?'

'Not a thing,' George said happily.

Rick on the Rocks

For the first part of the morning Rick felt cheerful. Last night he and Stella had had sex. Yes, actual, full-blown sex, with laughter and talk after, and no feelings of guilt because he'd felt he had to persuade her to 'let him have it' as though it was a quota she must fulfil.

He had to admit that employing Grazja was working out well.

This morning Stella had been up in her studio before he left for work. He and Gerta had climbed the stairs to the north turret to find her. Stella had been taping photos on the wall, her face glowing with anticipation of the day's painting ahead.

It had been months – no a couple of years – since he'd seen that look.

Stella had her mojo back.

Rick didn't think it was just down to Grazja. Damn, the woman was good at taking care of people, but not that good. Rick knew it was the recent goings on in Mapton. He didn't like most of it. The atmosphere in town was weird with a growing edge of hysteria. Stella found it disturbing too but it also fascinated her. It was the stimulation she'd needed to get her painting again.

If Grazja had provided Stella with the time and space, Mapton was her muse.

A goddamn ugly muse, as far as Rick was concerned. His mood soured.

He'd come to Mapton to escape from drama and high emotion – his own admittedly – and he didn't want that to change.

Plus he hated mobs. There was definitely a mob mentality developing recently. He wanted nothing to do with it.

Poor Martha Seaton's name was mud, her house vandalised; not only the graffiti, but now someone had lobbed a brick through a window. Martha herself hadn't been seen in the area for a week, or her husband, John. Who was going to patch up the window, Rick wondered. The police?

He would drive by later to see for himself.

Actually, thinking about it, he decided to give Frank a call. Maybe he'd be able to check it out this morning. The fair was closed for the season.

He was saved the trouble when Frank appeared at the diner's door, holding it open for Grazja to wheel Gerta in.

'Daddy!' Gerta cried from her pushchair. 'Coffee time'.

The customers laughed, including the grey-haired couple in the window booth. They were day-trippers.

'Bit young for coffee, isn't she, Rick?' Andy Timmis called. He was sharing a table with Carole.

'It's special coffee,' Rick grinned. 'Also known as milk.'

'Hello Gerta,' Carole called. 'Come and show us your lovely coat.'

Gerta, always pleased to do a spin for anyone, waddled over to their booth for inspection. Soon she was up on the seat next to Carole burbling away.

Rick brought over a sippy cup of milk. 'Let me know when you've had enough, Carole. She can be a handful.'

'Ooh, she's a cherub,' Carole said, giving Gerta a squeeze. 'She'll be fine here for a bit, Rick.'

Andy didn't look so enthusiastic Rick noted. Gerta was cramping his style. Rick smiled; Andy fancied himself one with the ladies but the ladies generally seemed oblivious to his advances.

Rick returned behind the counter.

'The usual?' he asked Frank, perched on his stool.

'Please,' Frank said.

Grazja was staking a booth, laying her coat on the red seat, and getting various supplies out of the bag hanging on the back of the pushchair.

'So?' Rick cocked an eyebrow. 'You been taking a walk with Grazja and Gerta?' He dipped a teabag into a mug of hot water, barely let them say hello before whipping it out and adding a splash of cold. He placed the mug in front of Frank.

'What? Oh no,' Frank said. 'Just bumped into them outside the diner. Actually, I've been busy. Have you heard about the Seaton's house?'

Rick grimaced. 'Brick through the window.'

Frank nodded glumly. 'I went over there and boarded it up. Got a call from John this morning; he'd had a call from the police. They've been staying in Aberdeen with one of their kids.'

'Great minds,' Rick said. 'I was gonna call you and ask you to go out and take a look. I hope they catch the bastards doing this.'

'Probably just teens,' Frank sighed. 'Easy target.'

'The graffiti still there?'

'Yeah. I'm going back later to see what I can do about it. See if I can scrub it off or paint over it.'

'Scrub what off?' Grazja said, appearing at the counter.

Frank told her.

Grazja looked impressed so Rick added. 'He's already been out and boarded up the broken window.'

'Broken window?' Grazja asked.

So Frank told her about that too. Grazja frowned. 'Some nasty people,' she said.

She looked at him speculatively. '*Jesteś dobrym człowiekiem,*' she said.

Frank took a moment to register. He blushed, shaking his head. '*Dziękuję, ale nie jestem.*'

Rick was amused. 'Hey guys, can anyone play the alien language game or is it private?'

'Not alien, Rick,' Grazja said primly. 'Polish. I tell him he is nice person for doing what he is. He say 'not today, postman.''

'I did not!' Frank spluttered. 'Did I?'

Grazja smiled. 'No. You say 'Thank you but I'm not.' Too modest, yes Rick?'

'Sure is,' Rick agreed. 'I'd like to help out, Frank. Let me see if I can get some cover for the afternoon, and I'll join you. I feel real bad for Martha Seaton. The past has a habit of catching up and biting you on the ass when you least expect it.'

'She shouldn't have done what she did,' Andy piped up.

Rick hadn't realised he was listening.

'C'mon Andy. We don't even know her side of the story.'

'Pretending to be all holier than thou about the Paradise when really she used to be a prostitute.'

Frank stood up abruptly, face thunderous. 'Martha has never pretended to be 'holier than thou,' he said. His quiet voice hummed with barely contained anger. 'As to your last accusation, where's your proof of that?'

'It were in the papers,' Andy protested. 'We all read it.'

'It was not in the papers,' Frank said. 'All that was in the papers was gossip and speculation.'

'Her husband got sent down for running a prostitution ring.' Andy said. He'd risen from the booth. Carole and Gerta stared at him open-mouthed.

'Her *ex*-husband,' Frank pointed out. 'There were no charges brought against Martha. And Andy, you know how it is with exes. Are you responsible for Jackie's actions?'

Rick sucked in his breath. Frank was pushing it now.

Jackie, Andy's ex-wife, had paid a local farmboy to drive a tractor through the window of a rival fancy goods shop. The boy blabbed as soon as the police tracked the vehicle to him but Jackie tried to blame the idea on Andy. It didn't stick because the lad admitted that Jackie had paid him with sex, as well as a tits mug. It had happened years ago, but Andy had never married again or recovered entirely from the humiliation. He still ran the shop but refused to sell tits mugs, despite their eternal popularity with tourists.

Andy jabbed his finger in Frank's face. 'Where do you get off talking about me like that? Who knows anything about you, anyway? Sounds to me like you and Martha Seaton are as thick as thieves. You know what they used to say about you, don't yer? Working around all them kiddies.'

'Hey,' Rick jumped in. 'Cool it, Andy. You're upsetting my kid'. And indeed, Gerta began to wail, upset by the raised voices. She scrambled away from Carole and flew towards the gap under the counter so she could reach her father.

Rick scooped her up.

'See?' he glared at Andy and Frank.

Frank looked startled, then embarrassed.

Andy stepped back but thrust his head forward.

'You didn't sign our petition,' he hissed at Frank. 'And neither did you.' He jabbed at Rick. He looked at Grazja. 'And I bet you didn't either.'

'So? Rick said. 'What are you saying Andy?'

'I'm just saying we know.' Andy walked back to the booth to collect his coat. 'We know who's with the Knights and who's not.'

'And?' Rick pushed him. He kept his voice calm while he held Gerta. 'Is that some kind of threat, Andy?'

Andy swaggered to the door. 'I'm just sayin' is all. We *know*.' He glanced back at Carole. 'I'll wait outside for yer, Carole. Best we got back to the protest. Someone's got to keep Mapton decent. And English.'

He left.

Carole, ruddy-cheeked, got up, grabbing her coat and bag. She slid out of the booth.

'Sorry,' she whispered to Rick. 'I'll pay up.'

'I thought Andy was treating you?' Rick said. They'd had a large breakfast each. 'I'm not going to let you foot the bill, Carole. Have it on the house. It's the last time I'll be letting Andy set foot in this diner for a while anyway.'

'Oh Rick,' Carole breathed. 'Don't say that. He's just passionate about the cause.'

'He practically called Frank a paedophile. Carole. But it was the 'English ' that was the clincher,' Rick said.

Carole looked puzzled.

'I'm American, Grazja's Polish, and Frank's Irish, 'Rick explained. 'It was a xenophobic insult, Carole.'

Carole smiled anxiously. 'I dunno what that means, Rick. Andy just meant Mapton needs to be more English in general; he didn't mean it about anyone in here.'

Rick looked at her blankly.

'Let me pay for mine at least,' she pleaded. 'I feel awful.'

But Rick shook his head. 'It's fine, Carole. Thanks for playing with Gerta.'

He turned away.

#

Andy's version of his row in the diner became more self-righteously embroidered every time he told it.

He told it to a great many people that afternoon. It spread through the protest group like the norovirus on a cruise ship.

By the time Sue arrived it was already a strongly held belief that all Mapton Knight protesters were banned from The Last Resort.

Resentment and anger shimmered in the Autumn air.

'That's bollocks,' Sue pronounced. 'Ricky wouldn't ban us, especially The Marauders.'

'Well he did,' Andy said. 'Din't he Carole?'

Carole protested weakly. 'It was only actually you, Andy.'

'There you go, then,' Sue said. 'What did you do, Andy?'

'Nothing!' Andy said indignantly. He stomped off to a group he'd recently become matey with.

Sue watched him. 'He's got a wasp up his bum,' she said to Carole. 'I hope he don't make trouble. I never knew leadership could be so hard.'

#

The grey-haired couple came up to pay their bill not long after Andy's departure.

They looked to be late fifties, fit and tanned. Rick saw that the woman's hair was less grey, than highlighted. She had a pretty face with intelligent blue eyes. They wore matching fleeces.

'Is it always like that round here?' the man asked, as he paid.

Rick pulled his mouth down sheepishly. 'Nah. Sorry you had to see that. Things are a bit heated round here at the moment. We're not normally like that.'

Grazja had taken Gerta home, and Frank had left with them.

'We saw the protest as we drove in,' the woman said. 'We'd seen it on the news but it's got a lot bigger. People must feel very strongly.'

'Yeah,' Rick agreed. 'I guess they do. I have no problem with the protest at all but when people start graffiting hate messages and lobbing bricks then I have a problem.'

'We didn't see any of that,' the woman said. 'But then we didn't stop. We came to walk the beach.'

'It's a great beach.' Rick said. 'And a great time to come if you want it mostly to yourself, although Sundays they hold racing on it, so I wouldn't come then if you want to hike.'

'Racing?' the man said.

'Motorbikes and quads,' Rick explained. 'It's a good day out.'

'I'll remember that. Just in winter is it?'

'Yeah,' Rick said. 'Off season. You here for the day or staying?'

'Just the day,' the woman said. 'But we thought we'd check Mapton out. Think about it for the spring and summer.'

'Cool,' Rick said. 'I hope the little incident hasn't put you off.'

'Bit of local colour,' the man laughed.

'And your food was delicious,' the woman added. 'I didn't expect it to be so good.'

Rick laughed. 'We aim to please. But I can't take the credit today. My apprentice is on kitchen duty.'

'Do you think this swingers' camp is a real possibility?' the man asked.

'Personally, no. The council will kick the application out.'

'But the protesters are taking it seriously,' the woman pointed out. 'What do they call themselves – the Mapton Knights.'

'People take UFOs, yetis, and the Lochness monster seriously,' Rick said. 'That doesn't make them real.'

The couple laughed. 'Well, it was nice meeting you ... ' the man stretched out his hand.

'Rick,' Rick said, shaking. 'And you too.'

'You look familiar to me,' the woman said. 'Have we met before.'

No ma'm,' Rick said. 'Not as I can recall.'

'You must have one of those familiar faces,' she smiled.

Not too familiar, Rick hoped, as he watched them leave. Only Stella still knew he'd once been the famous Michelin-star chef, Richard Blake.

He preferred his quiet life.

The door opened and Ange came in.

'Hey,' Rick said. 'I was just about to call you. That's the second time that's happened today.'

He noted Ang's pinched expression. 'What's wrong?'

'Did you ban the protesters from the diner?' Ange demanded.

'What! No.'

'Andy Timmis is spreading it around that you banned him and the rest of us.'

'Us?' Rick raised his brows. 'You been out on the line, Ange?'

'It's my civic duty,' Ange said. 'So what did you do to Andy?'

'What did *I* do?' Rick glared at her.

She backtracked. 'Alright, what did Andy do?'

He told her about Andy and Frank. 'It was his word about keeping Mapton English that riled me. Nationalistic crap. Making out the three of us didn't belong here.'

'Oh, he probably didn't mean it like that,' Ange said. 'I don't think you should ban him for that.'

'I didn't ban him,' Rick snapped. 'I told Carole it would be a long time before he could eat here again, but I was blowing off steam.'

Ange sighed. 'Right now he's on the protest-line winding everyone up. I thought I better get here before they do.'

'They bringing their pitchforks?' Rick asked. 'Going to burn down the diner?'

'Not if I serve 'em lunch,' Ange said. 'I think I'd better take over. At the moment you seem to be rubbing people up the wrong way.'

'Thanks!'

'I don't know what's got into you.'

'Thanks again!' Rick scowled. 'Good to have your support.'

'Is Mark in the kitchen?' Ange ignored his sarcasm.

'He's on a break. He'll be back in a minute.'

'Good. You should get going before the horde arrive. I'll give Maria a call – see if she can work an extra shift.'

Rick hesitated. 'I should stay. You might need me if folk are riled up.'

'They're riled up at you, not me,' Ange said. 'I'm one of them. Don't worry, I'll set 'em straight and put Andy right too. He *will* be banned if he does something like this again.'

Rick nodded. 'Okay, thanks Ange. I was gonna ask if you could take over anyway. I'm helping Frank scrub off the graffiti on the Seaton's house.'

Ange shook her head ruefully but said nothing. Not until Rick was at the door.

'Rick,' she called. 'You really should just sign the petition.'

Rick slammed the door behind him.

Stella gets her Mojo Back

Stella stood in front of a fresh gigantic canvas, its white surface begging for colour.

She had torn down the photos of the fairground and plastered the wall of her studio with the new photographs she'd taken of the protest outside the Paradise. She wasn't intending to copy them but use them as inspiration. Her creative sap was rising and something was coming – she wasn't sure what – but when she put her brush to the canvas she knew it would come.

The feeling was exciting, a little dangerous even. It made her jittery and nervous. Energised.

Dipping her brush into an electric blue, Stella made the first stroke on the canvas.

She painted feverishly all morning, barely hearing Grazja leave with Gerta, or their earlier than usual return.

At one point she heard Rick talking to Grazja and wondered vaguely why he was home, but it barely registered, and since he didn't appear in her studio she forgot about it.

The sound of the hoover made no dent in her concentration; neither did Gerta singing as she followed Grazja around.

All Stella saw was the canvas and the images as they unfolded before her.

She became faintly aware of hunger pangs and thirst, then, just as she could ignore them no longer, she heard footsteps on the turret stairs and a knocking at the door.

'Yes?'

Grazja's voice: 'Open door for me. Hands busy.'

Stella, wiping her hands with a rag, went to let her in.

Grazja bore a welcome tray of lunch.

'How do you always know?' Stella asked, taking the tray with relish.

'What? How I always know people eat at lunchtime?'

Stella, glancing at the clock was surprised to find it was gone two.

'It's past lunchtime,' she said. 'But you knew that I was ready now, not earlier.'

'I not 'know',' Grazja said. 'I just not bothered earlier. Now I start getting worried. You no take a break yet. Like you were in Gina's caravan, remember?'

'Yes! And you took care of me then too.'

'I nosy,' Grazja dismissed her. 'I come to see what you do? Not another Gina monster I hope?'

'No,' Stella laughed. 'Although if she really does run for councillor I might do one.'

'You don't believe she will?'

'I'll believe it when I see it. Gina's always coming up with crazy ideas that she doesn't follow through.'

'She seem serious about this one,' Grazja said. 'George too.'

'George doesn't need the stress,' Stella said.

'Maybe that his plan,' Grazja sniggered. 'Gina out campaigning, George get some peace and quiet.'

'Could be,' Stella laughed. 'Poor George.'

She peered at the tray. 'That's a lot of sandwiches, Grazja. You trying to fatten me up?'

'No,' Grazja said reaching for a sideplate. 'I eat with you. Gerta napping. I got gossip from this morning.'

Stella sat down. 'Tell me,' she said eagerly.

Grazja described the scene in the diner.

'That's awful,' Stella said. 'Mind you, mentioning Jackie to Andy is waving a red rag at a bull.'

'That what Frank said,' Grazja agreed. 'He felt ashamed. But he was defending the Seatons.'

'It's horrible about their house,' Stella shook her head. 'It could be someone we know but it's more likely kids.'

Grazja nodded. 'Not many seem bothered. People not very forgiving.'

'It's nice of Frank to care,' Stella said. 'I didn't know he knew the Seatons so well.'

'He said John Seaton did some carpentry work for him.'

'Frank's telling you a lot.' Stella gave Grazja a sly nudge.

Grazja ignored her. 'I not tell you rest yet.'

'There's more?'

Grazja teased her by taking a bite of her sandwich and chewing slowly. When she'd washed it down with some coffee, she said: 'Rick come home before going to help Frank.'

'I thought I heard him,' Stella said.

'He hopping mad. Andy stir up all the sex camp protesters and tell them Rick had banned them from diner.'

'No!'

'Yes. So Ange march in and want to know why Rick ban protesters. He explain but she decide it better if she take over and Rick leaves. Then she will let the protesters in and feed them like normal. But as Rick go out door she tell him he should sign the petition.'

'That bloody petition!' Stella groaned. 'I wish I'd never signed it now. Not if it's going to be used as a Nazi 'who's one of us' list. Poor Rick. Why didn't he come up and tell me?'

'He say this is first time he seen you like 'old' Stella in too long. He not want to disturb you.' Grazja shrugged. 'Me. I wait as long as I can to come up before I explode.'

Stella laughed. 'Rick's gone to help Frank?'

'Yes. They try.'

'I wonder if the Seatons will sell the house?' Stella mused.

Grazja got up to look at the new painting. One part showed a billboard featuring an azure sky and a man and woman throwing a beach ball across yellow sand. It was fifties in style, the couple blooming with health and wreathed in smiles. They were naked. The typography of the billboard read: Come to Mapton for Sun, Sea, and Sex. It stood before the crumbling facade of The Paradise, with its missing letters and tacky tiles. Beyond that the sky was grey, the sea leaden, the beach a winter desert. This only took up a portion of the enormous canvas and lacked the fine detail that Stella would add.

'Topical,' Grazja nodded.

She wandered over to the painting of the ghost train that was part of the collage and pondered it.

'These people look terrified,' she said, bending to peer at the passengers.

Stella sighed. 'I know. They're not meant to. I've painted out the faces a hundred times and they still come out the same way. I want them to look exhilarated.'

'This is Frank's ride, yes?'

'Yeah.'

'I wonder what he think if he see this?'

'I don't know,' Stella said uncomfortably. 'He might be offended.'

Grazja 'hmmmed' 'I think if you keep painting the faces like this you see some truth.'

'I was depressed.'

'Maybe,' Grazja said. 'But your pictures tell the truth. Gina not a monster but it was the truth of how you saw her.' She examined the monk in the painting.

'Frank really look creepy like that. Can't see his kind eyes.'

'It's the way he says 'Do you dare face your sins in the dark?'' Stella conceded. 'It does genuinely scare me. Why say it?'

Grazja looked thoughtful. 'Like a confessional,' she said. 'In church.'

'Are you a Catholic?' Stella asked.

'Lapsed,' Grazja said. 'Very, very lapsed.'

'Is Frank?'

'How should I know?'

Stella grinned. 'Because you seem to talk to him a lot. In Polish.'

178

Grazja snorted. 'He say something to me in Polish. Not a conversation. I do not 'talk to him a lot'.'

'Touchy,' said Stella. 'You must like him.'

Grazja rolled her eyes. 'I like him. He seem nice but it not romantic, Stella. I not interested in romance. Anyway, you think him creepy, why you want me to 'date' him?'

'He's not creepy as Frank,' Stella said. 'Only as the monk, and let's face it, he is running a ghost train. 'Creepy' is part of the job.'

'True,' agreed Grazja, 'but your painting make me curious. Maybe you have third eye.'

'What?'

'Sixth sense.'

'Shut up,' Stella said. 'It's just a painting.'

'Maybe you witch,' Grazja grinned.

'Oh God,' Stella said. 'Don't say it in public. The way Mapton's going I'll be burned at the stake.'

Nominations

From: jtaynor.mapton@btconnect.com
To: piratetom22@gmail.com

Acting Mayor Turner

So far we have received three nominations to run for councillor. I have summarised these below:

Candidate 1

Ms Gina Deidre Pontin

Independent candidate

Proposer: George Wentworth

Seconder: David Suggs

Candidate 2

Mr Anthony John Forbes

Conservative

Proposer: Dorothy Stogg

Seconder: Edward Turner

Candidate 3

Mr Andrew Wayne Timmis

Independent candidate

Proposer: Darren Bilson

Seconder: Carole Greenwood

Interesting!

Julie Taynor,
Town Clerk

'Sweet Jesus,' Tom blasphemed as he read the email. Gina Pontin! He didn't know whether to laugh or cry.

Laugh, he decided. Gina had about as much chance of being elected as a pig in a dress. She might have found a soapbox to climb on with the Mapton Knights but she was still a joke to most people he knew.

She'd put her foot in her mouth as sure as the sun would rise, and was bound to raise the hackles of half of Mapton before she was done.

Andy Timmis, now he was a possible threat. He owned a business and was generally liked. He was single, though, and seen as a bit desperate when it came to the ladies. Singletons were always a hard sell with the electorate; they whiffed of undesirability.

Tony Forbes, Tom's man, was a much better prospect. A family man, active in the Rotary club, a judge in the annual hanging basket competition, and most important, loyal to Tom.

Plus Tony had Tom to guide him through the campaign; quietly of course as it wouldn't do for the Mayor to be seen to be actively endorsing one candidate over the others. Tom had years of experience to pass on, while Gina and Andy were campaign virgins, as innocent as lambs to the slaughter.

Finally, Tom smiled, rocking back in his chair, things were looking up.

Another email from Julie popped onto the screen.

From:jtaynor.mapton@btconnect.com
To:piratetom22@gmail.com

Just seen short piece in the Lawton Post. Martha Seaton interviewed on Inside Out tomorrow. Apparently to give her chance to tell her side of the story.

Can't wait!

Julie Taynor,
Town Clerk

Tom groaned.

Breaking News

Andrew Leith had thought he was on his way to the big time when the Daily Mail had run the story but despite the journalist's promise Andrew's name hadn't appeared on the by-line, only next to his quotes inside the article.

Since then he'd encountered a certain amount of hostility in Mapton and Siltby, especially at the protest site.

Even Dennis Payton had turned down an exclusive interview, saying he didn't want any publicity right now but could Andrew call him back once the licence had been approved?

'You seem very optimistic about that,' Andrew had prompted.

'I'm a glass-half full kind of guy,' Dennis had replied, refusing to be drawn any further.

This morning he himself had been interviewed by Vanessa Baro for a special edition of the BBC's regional 'issues' show Inside Out.

He wasn't too fond of Ms Baro, who clearly thought of herself as some sort of minor star and serious journalist just because she was on local television. Still, he was quite flattered that she had approached him. She was making a programme on Martha Seaton, and as the journalist that broke the story she wanted his comments. Plus his editor insisted Andrew do it. 'It's free advertising for the Post,' he said.

Andrew was surprised when Vanessa smugly informed him that she had in fact gained an exclusive interview with Martha Seaton herself, who had previously refused to talk to him, or any press.

More rankling were the questions Vanessa asked him. How does it feel to break a story that you know will ruin someone's life? How much background checking did he do before deciding to publish? How did he respond to the vandals that had defaced Mrs Seaton's house with the word 'whore' and more recently thrown a brick through her window?

Andrew had eventually ripped off his mic and stormed out. It was rich coming from Vanessa who'd done such a nice hatchet job on the Mapton Knights and Gina Pontin.

He considered it a professional discourtesy.

And he would be watching it at nine-thirty like everyone else.

#

At nine on Tuesday night Mapton was as deserted as a Western town before a gunfight. In an era of iPlayer and on-demand TV, it was rare for the majority to watch a programme at the same time, but few in Mapton and Siltby wanted to be the last to hear Martha Seaton's side of things.

Since Dennis Payton had confirmed his intentions for the Paradise life had never been so exciting. It was just one thing after another.

Sugsy had the TV on in the bar and the room was jammed with Maptonites, including most of the Marauders.

'Turn it up,' Alf yelled. 'I can't hear it.'

'It's up,' Sugsy protested. 'Any louder we'll bust our eardrums.'

'Turn your hearing aid up, Alf,' Mildred shouted in his ear. 'It's you that's turned down.'

Alf grunted, fiddling with his aid. He jolted. 'Bloody hell, Sugsy. Turn it down will yer?'

Sugsy rolled his eyes.

He served Andy, who said to Carole: 'There's nothing she can say to make it better. Should've been honest in the first place.'

'Oh Andy, let's hear her out first.'

Andy smiled. 'You're a softy Carole. It's a very feminine attribute.'

Carole blushed. 'Stop it,' she giggled.

'What's this I hear about you standing against Gina, Andy?' Sue trundled up.

'There's no law against it,' Andy said. 'I'm as free to run for council as she is.'

'You're joking, Andy,' Sugsy said. 'You haven't?'

'He has,' Sue said.

'But we agreed,' Sugsy said. 'At the meeting. Gina's standing.'

Andy bristled. 'We got double the chance of winning the seat with two of us standing. Anyway, seriously, Gina?'

Sue chortled but Sugsy glared. 'What's wrong with Gina?'

Andy opened his mouth to retort when someone hushed them. 'Shush. It's starting.'

Sugsy gave Andy another hard stare before transferring his attention to the TV.

#

This was George's first outing since his angina attack. Rick picked him and Gina up at nine to chauffeur them to the 'castle' where they'd be watching Inside Out with Stella, Rick, and Grazja.

Gina looked taken aback to see Frank sitting in the lounge.

'Hello,' she said. 'What you doing here?'

'Rick invited me,' Frank explained.

'Dint know you were such good pals as he'd have you around his house,' Gina said.

'Gina,' Stella warned.

Gina subsided but made things awkward by squeezing herself onto the sofa between Frank and Grazja, so that Frank had to shuffle over or be sat on.

'Ay up, duck,' Gina said to Grazja. 'This is a bit exciting, ain't it?'

'Very,' Grazja said. 'Mysterious.'

'I wonder what's she's got to say for 'erself?'

Rick, who'd been hanging up coats, appeared. 'Drinks anyone?'

'Glass of wine,' Stella said. 'Whatever's open.'

'Same for me,' Grazja said.

'Gina?' Rick asked.

'Got any Babycham, Ricky?' Gina asked. 'I feel like pushing the boat out.'

'You know we keep it in just for you,' Rick laughed. 'George, Frank?'

'I'd love a scotch,' George sighed, 'but best make it tea, Rick. Doctor's orders.'

'I'll have a beer, if you've got one,' Frank said.

'Wanna give me a hand, Frank?' Rick asked.

Frank nodded, rising swiftly, looking grateful.

As soon as he'd gone, Gina turned to Grazja. 'You know what he's after, don't you?'

Grazja pretended she didn't.

'Intercourse,' Gina declared.

'With you?' Grazja teased.

'No, yer donkey, with you! I saw it the minute I walked in, the way he was snuggling up to yer on the sofa.'

'He was just sitting. There was no 'snuggling'.'

Gina snorted. 'I can always tell,' she said. 'Can't I George?'

George neither confirmed nor denied it.

'There will be no 'intercourse',' Grazja said.

'That's what I said,' Gina cackled. 'And look what happened.' She winked at George, who smiled sheepishly. 'Course I was lucky. George is a good un. Probably the only good un. I wouldn't trust that Frank.'

'Why not?' Grazja asked a little sharply.

'Lives on 'is own,' Gina said.

'You live on your own; George live on own.'

'Yeah but George was a widower and it's alright for a woman to live on her own. Not natural for a man. Means something's wrong with 'em. Only thing worse is if they live with their mother.'

'Well, thank you for your advice, Gina,' Grazja said. 'I am very grateful.' She grinned at Stella who returned the grin.

'I can see you laughing at me. It won't be so funny when he's got you alone in a dark room. And for God's sake, don't let him get you on that ghost train.'

'He seems alright to me, Gina,' George chipped in. 'It would be nice for Grazja to have a gentleman friend.' He smiled fondly at Grazja.

Before either Grazja or Gina could answer, Rick and Frank returned bearing drinks, and it was almost time for the programme.

From the baby monitor on the coffee table came the sound of Gerta chattering in her sleep, followed by a squeaky sigh as she turned over, and then silence.

Everyone smiled. Rick settled next to Stella, giving her hand a squeeze.

The anchor appeared onscreen. 'Hello, welcome to this special edition of Inside Out. Tonight we meet the former mayor of Mapton-on-Sea, who recently resigned amid a blaze of scandal and hear her side of the story. Because of the shocking nature of some of the subject matter this edition is screening after the watershed. A helpline number will appear at the end of the show. Vanessa Baro investigates.'

'That cow!' Gina shouted.

'Shhhh,' came the collective hiss.

'Well, I'm just saying,' Gina grumbled. 'She won't get a fair hearing from her.'

'We won't know if we can't hear it,' Stella snapped.

Gina flattened her lips into a thin line, crossed her arms, but kept quiet.

Martha Seaton came on screen in a long shot, sitting in a café with Vanessa, nursing a cup of coffee. Vanessa's voice-over filled the viewers in on the situation. Then the view changed to a close-up of Martha. She looked thinner but as immaculate as ever. Yet, even make-up couldn't disguise the dark circles under her eyes, or the haunted look in them.

Vanessa, opposite her, said: 'Thank you for speaking to Inside Out, Martha. I know this is very difficult for you, but I think a lot of viewers will be very surprised by the experiences you're going to share.

'First of all how did it feel when the Lawton Post broke the story?'

'Terrible,' Martha said. 'I'd spent a lot of years working to put the past behind me, and to have it dragged up so publically has been devastating. My house has been vandalised, a brick thrown through a window, and my reputation shredded. But far worse, for me, and for my family, is the knowledge that what has been reported is a very skewed picture of what I actually went through when I was younger.'

'And you want to put that picture right?' Vanessa said.

'I do. I've thought about it a great deal, and it's not easy for me; I'm naturally a private person, but it's time for people to know the truth. They can decide for themselves what they think of me afterwards. It will be a weight off my mind and I hope I'll be able to move on.'

Vanessa nodded sympathetically.

Martha began. 'I was born and raised in Mapton. My parents were Catholic, and I was a good girl, very inexperienced with boys, careful to do my homework, and, looking back, very naïve. When I was seventeen I met Michael Courier …'

Martha's Story

Michael Courier looked as though he would be as good to taste as the candyfloss Martha was selling in her dad's booth.

She was seventeen in the summer of '82, and full of romantic dreams.

Michael, with his startling blue eyes, and smooth tan, was actually buying candyfloss for another girl, the first time she saw him, but he turned and gave her a wink as he walked away that fluttered her heart.

He had definitely noticed her.

During his two weeks of holiday in Mapton he courted Martha as though he were a prince wooing a princess in a tale of old.

That's how it seemed to Martha. Although she couldn't imagine a prince being such a great kisser. His kisses made her as hot as fresh sugared donuts. They left her sticky and yearning for more.

She knew it was love. He told her it was.

On the second Wednesday of his holiday she lost her virginity. They laughed at the blood on the caravan bedsheets. Michael said he didn't care if he lost his deposit. Still, he asked her if she could try washing them out. It would be better if he didn't have to lose it.

She used hot water, so the stain set in. It was only later she learnt she should have used cold.

That was the day that she cried into his chest; she couldn't bear the thought that he would leave at the end of the week.

He couldn't bear it either, he said, but he had a new job waiting for him. A car salesman job in Southend, with commission. It was the chance he'd been waiting for.

By the time Friday came Martha was almost wild with grief at the prospect of losing Mike.

She asked if he had a girlfriend back home. He admitted he did, but he'd be breaking up with her the moment he got back.

Martha was the only one for him. If only…

'If only what?' she'd wanted to know.

If only Martha would come with him.

On the Saturday she did, running away from Mapton and her parents, her A levels and her friends.

It wasn't easy but it was easier than living without Mike. And if he went without her, what would stop him forgetting her?

She packed her case, left a note for her parents, and crept out in the early hours.

Mike was waiting in his Ford Capri.

#

Mike was ten years older than Martha. She'd known he was older - it was part of his glamour – but had assumed it was only by two or three years.

It didn't matter. Only love mattered, but there were occasions when it made a difference. Occasions, for example, when they got together with his friends.

His friends, and their girlfriends, all seemed so much older and sophisticated to Martha.

One night she and Mike went for a curry night at his friend Graham's flat. His current squeeze,

Joanna, was there, as well as another couple, Ian and Sally, who Martha had never met before. After the curry and a few beers, Graham slid a video into his new VCR.

'Movie night,' he announced.

'What are we watching?' Martha asked.

'Something educational,' Graham winked.

Martha snuggled up next to Mike on the sofa. Ian and Sally sat on the floor with their backs to the sofa, while Joanna waited for Graham to start the video before she settled on his lap in the armchair.

It was a blue movie, the likes of which Martha had never seen before.

She was mortified and rigid with embarrassment.

The others seemed to be enjoying it.

Joanna started to rock on Graham's lap.

Mike took her hand, she thought to reassure her, then placed it on his groin.

Martha didn't move a muscle. She felt sick and stupid and very young as images she hadn't even imagined flickered. She didn't look at Mike, who was tugging her hand.

It wasn't until Ian (or Sally) slid a hand up her calf that she could finally move, leaping up so quickly she stamped on a hand.

She fled to the bathroom.

Mike followed her in. He shoved her hard against the sink. 'What the fuck was that about?' He unzipped his fly.

The evening got worse from there.

And after that everything got worse.

Years later, Martha could look back and see how it all happened, how one thing had led to another and just how isolated she had been.

Only one time did she turn to another woman – one of the more sympathetic girlfriends passing through – and confide to her what had happened in that bathroom and numerous times since.

Linda laughed and said, rather bitterly. 'That's just the way it is between men and women, love. Men can't help it. They're animals. But we love them anyway.'

And Martha told herself she still did love Mike. He could be so sweet, buying her flowers, and splashing out on gifts. For their second wedding anniversary he bought her a gold bracelet inscribed 'Forever Mine.'

Yes, he had married her. What more proof could she need that he loved her?

They'd gone up as a party to Gretna Green, and afterwards the honeymoon was a shared affair, but that didn't bother Martha too much, as she did what she always did for their parties. She took Valium, prescribed by her nice doctor when she'd gone to him about her 'nerves', and then whatever else might be on offer.

She might have left Mike earlier but for two reasons.

First her father had cut her off, refusing to have anything to do with her. He took her running away as an unforgivable crime, and living unwed as the sin of all sins. Martha's mother did write occasionally but only to tell her how outraged her father still was.

Martha had no true friends, no job, and nowhere to go. Mike made good money as a car salesman – he must do with the cash he flashed around – and controlled all the finances. He bought them a house but Martha only ever had what he gave her for the weekly food shop.

He'd even taken to going clothes shopping with her. He liked to dress her.

Secondly, her brain was scrambled.

That was how she thought of it later.

It wasn't the addiction to Valium. She took that to ease the scramble. Of course it made it worse over the long term, but it wasn't the cause.

The cause was meeting Mike – a type she learnt was a classic abuser – at seventeen. Older, stronger women had fallen prey to such men. What chance had she had?

Abusers know how to brainwash their victims. It isn't learnt on their part, more of a natural ability. The key is to set the honeyed trap and overwhelm the woman with attention; to make them feel special; to charm them with the true meaning of 'charm': to enspell. And what is a 'spell' but a dirty trick and illusion?

This part has to last long enough to truly ensnare them. Months, maybe years.

Next comes the Jekyll and Hyde game. One moment nice, the next nasty. Undermining comments, exaggerated compliments. One day a caress, the next day the fist.

Confusion is crucial to break a mind.

Mike nearly broke Martha. Then a thing happened that ultimately saved her. Something that both of them had begun to assume couldn't happen.

Martha became pregnant.

Mike made sure Martha took her pill every morning with orange juice. He didn't trust her to remember, and he never forgot. He found out that taking the pill continuously without a break meant no periods.

Mike hated periods.

The pill wasn't fool proof. And Martha was often sick.

Neither of them read the fine print in the contraceptive instructions that said diarrhoea and/or sickness could prevent absorption of the pill.

Because she didn't have periods, it wasn't a missed one that alerted Martha to her situation; it was morning sickness.

Her first trimester she had it bad and finally went to the doctor. He confirmed she was pregnant.

'No more Valium,' he said.

Martha didn't argue. But she hadn't known what an addict she was until she stopped taking it. It was probably a good thing that she hadn't known or she wouldn't have gone straight home from the doctor and flushed her pills down the toilet.

Withdrawal was hell. Martha endured it because of the new life in her womb. Pregnancy changed her. For the first time in years she cared about something beyond her own survival. She had hope.

For two weeks she took to her bed and told Mike she had stomach flu. He believed her. She sweated and retched, got the shakes, and looked terrible.

Her left her alone, and during the weekly parties he put an 'out of bounds' notice on their bedroom door. He certainly didn't want anyone seeing her like that.

Finally Martha told him she was pregnant. She was just beginning to show.

Mike was furious. He didn't want kids – at least not yet. Later maybe.

'You stupid bitch,' he said. 'You've done this on purpose. You better get rid of it.'

'I asked the doctor,' she lied. 'It's too far on for an abortion.'

'Legally maybe, but there are other ways.' Suddenly he punched her in the stomach.

Martha doubled over. Her baby!

Mike had punched her in the solar plexus, missing her womb. She never knew if it was by luck or design.

The next day Mike came home from work, whistling. He brought her flowers and a bottle of champagne. 'To celebrate,' he said.

He changed his mind. He wanted a son. One day he'd hand over the business to him.

Martha, head clearer than it had been since she was seventeen, thought to herself that Mike didn't have a business to hand over. He didn't own the car dealership, even if he was the star salesman.

The dealership wasn't the business Mike meant.

As her pregnancy progressed, Martha began to see things she'd never noticed in her sedated haze.

The swinger parties still took place but Mike allowed Martha to drop out sexually. She still acted as hostess, refilling drinks and handing out canapes, but now she had time to observe the guests.

Most of the old gang had gone. Some of the usuals – the Spellmans for example – were still in circulation but the atmosphere had changed. Whereas it had previously been established couples on the scene, men arrived with girls she'd never seen before. At twenty-one Martha saw herself as old. The girls arriving were as young – if not younger – than she'd been when she met Mike.

She felt protective towards the girls, but most of them seemed to regard her as a fat old joke. A heifer bearing a calf. That's what Mike called her at the parties.

And the girls were in the honey-trap stage. The men gave them jewellery, money, attention; things they'd never had. They supplied them with drugs and plied them with alcohol.

After a few weeks familiar girls would disappear, replaced by new ones.

Strange men came in the middle of the night. Bundles of cash exchanged hands.

By seven months Martha was huge. The doctor thought it might be twins.

She didn't tell Mike. She hadn't forgotten that warning punch. She wanted out. She wanted a new life for herself and her child or children.

But she had no one to turn to. Nowhere to run. She'd given up on her parents. She had no money of her own. Mike controlled it all. She couldn't even drive.

She was trapped.

And without the Valium Martha had begun to feel like a terrible person. The things she'd done and allowed to be done to her. She'd been raised a Catholic and guilt bore down upon her. It was pulling her down as surely as concrete weights would a swimmer. She would drown.

She couldn't drown. She had life growing inside her. She wouldn't let herself drown.

In the end it was her Catholic guilt that would be her salvation.

Martha went back to church,

Her feet were swollen, her stomach huge, and she could barely go half-an-hour without a pee, but somehow she managed the walk to St Helen's.

It was the confessional box she sought.

The End of the Story

'I was so lucky,' Martha said to Vanessa, coming to the end of her story. 'It could have been any other priest who took the confession that day. Not all of them are kind or sympathetic. He listened and encouraged me. I ended up telling him far more than I meant to. To cut a long story short he called social services and they couldn't get me into a shelter soon enough - I had never even heard of such places – so he arranged for me to stay with his sister. Both of them were saints. He gave me some money – no strings attached. I walked into that church and never went back.'

'Were you scared Mike would come after you?'

'Terrified. But only two days later he was raided by the police. You know the rest. He went to prison and died in there from a brain haemorrhage a year later. I had twins – a boy and girl. It was tough but with a lot of help from wonderful people I got through. I went back to college to learn to type, got a job as secretary and then a P.A. and upwards.'

'And you met your husband, John Seaton?'

Martha smiled. 'I did,' she agreed. 'I went from marrying a terrible man to marrying the best one in the world. I count my blessings every day. Once the twins were at uni I had a yearning to come back to Mapton. My parents passed on a few years ago, but we were reconciled through the grandkids – and they loved John. I wanted to come home, so we took early retirement and moved back.'

Vanessa said: 'And have held the office of mayor for five years. It's very unusual for one councillor to be voted in so many years running.'

'It's been an honour to serve my community,' Martha said.

'Do you feel that community has betrayed you?'

Martha frowned. 'Not at all. The people of Mapton and Siltby have been going through a terrible time lately. They felt I had betrayed them. I hope by telling my story they will understand that, in my eyes at least, I didn't.'

'And finally,' Vanessa said. 'Would you ever consider running for office again – or accept reinstatement?'

Martha smiled ruefully. 'The answer to both those possibilities is no. Actually, I'd already decided this would be my last term anyway. I'm ready for a quiet life.'

Divided Opinions

Andrew Leith was as green as a Granny Smith with envy. What an interview coup. Why hadn't he thought of offering Martha Seaton a 'tell all' in the Post?

Television could do some things so much better. The way they'd used actors to recreate some of the scenes as Martha spoke was a great touch. And then that helpline and website address at the end for women in abusive relationships was a stroke of genius. Martha came out of it looking like a heroine in some soppy TV movie of the week.

Andrew was rather relieved by the fact that his interview hadn't been used at all in the final cut.

Vanessa and the producer quite rightly recognised that Martha's story was the gold. Other than a little polish it didn't need any embellishment.

And he'd have come out of it looking like a shit.

He needed a way back into this story; something that would make him shine like a dogged reporter fighting for justice, instead of a heartless hack ruining a good person's life.

\#

Tom Turner almost threw his whisky at the screen.

Martha Seaton had done it again. She was like a bloody phoenix rising from the ashes. All that crap about being in an abusive relationship. He was sick of hearing about it - not that he'd ever say it in public because he'd be lynched by the political correctness police – but he never believed a woman would stay in a situation she didn't want to be in. All the bloody resources the council put into help for women in recent years made his blood boil. A man couldn't even give a woman a friendly pat on the bottom without being accused of sexual harassment. Feminism had ruined this country.

He looked over at his wife, Phyllis. 'Utter rot,' he said.

'I was the girl he bought candy floss for,' she replied.

'What?'

'Mike Courier. I remember him now. I never knew his last name. He was on holiday with some mates. I only went on a couple of dates with him but I was spitting mad when he dropped me for the candyfloss girl. He really did have amazing eyes, and he could kiss like Casanova.'

Tom didn't appreciate her dreamy expression. 'You never told me this.'

'Oh, I hadn't thought about him in years,' Phyllis sighed. 'Mike was a gent, as I remember; he opened the door of his Capri for me, gave me his jacket when it got chilly. I don't believe a word Martha's said. I just can't see it. Not of Mike.'

Tom was torn between wanting to discredit Martha and pop his wife's nostalgic bubble.

'What about Cloris Spellman in that article. She claims he was a swinger.'

'I wouldn't trust a thing the Spellmans say either,' Phyllis huffed. 'Still,' she added primly. 'If

Mike had tried any funny stuff with me I'd have put him right straightaway.'

'Exactly!' Tom was delighted to be sharing more mutual ground. 'All this nonsense about being caught in a trap – didn't know what she was doing, etc. Any decent woman would have left.'

'Of course she would,' his wife agreed, and went back to looking dreamy.

#

'Wow,' Stella said into the silence.

'Poor Martha,' Rick said.

Frank surreptitiously wiped away a tear but Gina noticed.

'Aren't you the sensitive flower,' she said, drawing everyone's attention to him.

'It is a sad story,' Grazja interceded quickly. 'She rebuild her life and then one journalist take it away.'

'Not just *one* journalist,' Rick said.

'D'you believe her about not wanting her job back?' Gina asked.

Frank recovered. 'I'm fairly certain she doesn't.'

'Cos, people will probably want her back,' Gina pressed.

Stella smiled. 'Worried you won't get to run for councillor, Gina?'

'No,' Gina said quickly. 'I'm just thinking is all.'

'I feel very sorry for her,' George said. 'She's always been a dedicated mayor, even if I don't always agree with her politics.'

'So you'd like to see her back?' Gina demanded.

'Of course not,' George soothed. 'I want to see you elected. I'm just saying I've got sympathy for her. She's had a bad time of it. My daughter had a nasty first boyfriend. Lucky she didn't marry him. Put her off men for a while though.'

'People will feel sorry for her,' Gina said.

'Don't you?' Grazja asked.

Gina shrugged. 'I suppose, but I wouldn't get meself into a situation like that.'

'Right,' Stella said. 'Because you haven't made any mistakes or had any secrets in your past.'

Gina glared at her.

'Actually,' Frank interrupted. 'There's something I need to tell you Gina, but if you don't like Martha, I don't think you'll want to hear it.'

Every head swivelled towards him.

'Oh aye,' Gina said warily. 'What's that then?'

'I've a message to pass on from Martha. She doesn't want to be councillor again, never mind mayor, but she is willing to help you run for election.'

'Me?" Gina looked as stunned as the others. 'She wants to help me?'

'Why?' Stella asked.

'I don't know,' Frank said. 'She just asked me to pass the message on. If you're interested I'll put you in touch.'

'She knows a lot about campaigning,' George said. 'Much more than any of us. She knows how to handle the press.' He looked excited. 'Remember when we said needed someone who knows what they're doing?'

'But that was for the Knights,' Gina said.

'It doesn't matter,' George said. 'She might help with that too. After all standing against the sex camp is the main part of your political campaign.'

Gina sunk back onto the sofa. 'Bloody hell,' she said. 'Imagine me with a 'political campaign.''

She looked at Frank. 'Alright. Tell her we can meet to discuss it.'

When Gina Met Martha

Martha and John returned home the weekend after the interview aired.

Frank and Rick had given the whitewashed bricks a fresh coat to obliterate the graffiti and John had arranged for a glazier to fit new glass in the window.

The response to the interview had generally been a positive one. Martha was surprised by the number of well-wishers who had pushed cards through the letterbox, although there was the odd hate-letter to remind her what a terrible person she was, or that she would burn in Hell.

It was much the same reaction when she bravely ventured out to the Co-op for supplies. Most people welcomed her back. One woman called her a slut, and one man gave her a crotch salute and asked her if she fancied a bit of dogging. Someone Martha had previously considered a friend ducked into the toilets to avoid talking to her – whether from hostility or embarrassment Martha couldn't guess.

Big Pam Stimson swallowed her in a hug and began to sob.

It was an ordeal, although not half as bad as she'd expected, and being seen out and about would go a long way to reclaiming her life.

But Martha hadn't simply come home to reclaim her life; she had come home for vengeance.

Subtle revenge. Not the sort that anyone, other than the victim, Tom Turner, would recognise.

She intended to get Gina Pontin on the council because if anything would make life hard for Tom Turner it would be that.

Gina would be on him like a terrier on a rat. She'd challenge every little thing he did, steal his precious limelight, trample over carefully negotiated deals, and be tactless in delicate situations.

Tom had waited a long time to lead the town council. Martha had absolutely no doubt he was behind her downfall; she just couldn't prove it.

He was a man who liked to be in control.

Gina Pontin was an uncontrollable force.

It was Frank who'd told her Gina was planning to run for election. He'd thought it might make her laugh. It had, but inside the laughter had taken on a villainous cackle.

What she told Vanessa Baro was true; she didn't want to run for office or be reinstated. She was tired of petty grievances, bureaucratic hurdles, and windbags in meetings. She'd achieved some good things as town councillor. Being mayor was an honour but it was only really a ceremonial position, good for photo opportunities and public relations. Yet it had prestige, and it was this which Tom coveted.

Martha was ready for a change. A new hobby, perhaps, or a return to education. It was never too late to expand horizons.

She and John had talked long and hard about doing the interview. In the end they decided they had nothing left to lose. If it backfired, they would sell up and move nearer to the kids. John, particularly wanted Martha to tell her side of the story.

'There are women everywhere in bad relationships,' he said. 'If your story helps just one of them escape, that will be worth it.'

Frank had been more reticent, but he said if she felt it was the right thing to do, she must do it.

Martha felt a little guilty about Frank. He was such a good person. He'd been surprised by her suggestion that she help Gina Pontin to run her campaign, and then pleased when she'd explained her reasons. Those reasons hadn't included revenge on Tom Turner. Frank wouldn't approve, so she let him believe her motivation was altruistic.

Needs must.

On Sunday evening Martha rang Gina's doorbell.

#

Gina was unusually nervous. Much as she hated to admit it, she found Martha Seaton intimidating. The former mayor had a composure and poise that Gina couldn't even dream of possessing. She was always perfectly turned out, self-assured and quietly assertive.

'I'm all piss 'n' vinegar,' Gina said to George. 'She's like a lavender disinfectant. What's she want with me?'

By the time the doorbell chimed out 'God Save the Queen' on Sunday evening, Gina's lounge was immaculate. No slob in the cleaning department normally, Gina had hoovered and polished as though she was hosting a state visit.

She'd bought a selection pack of biscuits – some of them foil wrapped – and arranged them on her best china. The sugar was in a bowl matched to the milk jug and teapot. Teaspoons gleamed.

Ginger Rogers, unable to resist the biscuits on the coffee table, had been banned to the kitchen.

George had been telling Gina to sit down and relax for the past half hour.

She was so keyed up she almost screamed when the doorbell went.

Ushering Martha into the lounge, Gina offered her a cup of tea, almost sending the tray flying in her eagerness to be busy.

George took over smoothly, taking her coat to hang in the hall. Returning, he grasped Martha's hand warmly. 'So good to see you again, Mayor Seaton.'

'Not mayor anymore,' Martha reminded him. 'Please, call me Martha. May I call you George?'

George laughed. 'Wouldn't have it any other way,' he said. His eyes turned serious. 'We were very touched by your interview, Martha. You need to know we don't blame you a bit.'

The smile Martha gave him was brittle.

'That's right,' Gina said, handing her a cup. 'That Mike sounded like a right nasty bogger. There were a bloke once at The Palais asked me to go outside for intercourse. Course I said no. Wouldn't catch me behaving like that.'

'Of course,' Martha murmured.

Gina saw George turn red and re-ran what she'd just said through her head.

She slapped her forehead. 'There I go again with me big mouth. Don't know why you want to help me, Martha. I ain't got a chance in hell of winning.'

This time Martha's smile was genuine. 'Actually, I think we can make your 'big mouth' your winning ticket.'

Gina blinked. It was one thing for her to call herself a 'big mouth' but another for this well-dressed woman.

Then it tickled her. She guffawed. 'You hear that, George? Me big mouth is going to be my asset. Not heard that before 'ave we?'

George gave them a relieved grin.

'Martha, let me take that cup while you sit down.'

With Martha settled, cup of tea to hand, nibbling a biscuit (Gina insisting she take a foil-wrapped one) they began to talk seriously.

'I hear you've already filed your nomination form,' Martha said.

'George nominated me, and Sue Mulligan seconded.'

'And you're standing as an independent candidate?'

'I voted Labour all me life,' Gina said. 'Look at George's face; he's a bloomin' Tory. But I've had it with all them parties. They're all the same. I'm standing for Mapton.'

'Are the Mapton Knights behind you?'

'O' course they are!'

'Only I wondered as Andy Timmis is also standing. He's the Knight's treasurer isn't he?'

Both Gina and George looked blank.

'What yer on about?' Gina said. 'Don't be ridiculous. Who told you that?'

Martha nodded, as though confirming some unspoken thought. 'Julie, the town clerk. I spoke to her this morning. It's official. He hand-delivered the form to Lawton. Andy is nominated to stand.'

Gina and George stared at her. Gina leapt to her feet. 'That little sod,' she roared. 'What's he playing at? He didn't say nothing about it at the last meeting. I wonder if Sue knows?'

She reached for her phone and punched the speed dial for Sue.

'Sue, tell me you didn't bleedin' know about Andy … What? No, he's only gone and nominated himself to stand against me for councillor … yeah! Yeah! I know! …Tomorrow evening ain't it? … Let people know; we'll nobble him at the meeting. Right. Right. What? I'll tell yer tomorrow…Okay. Thanks Sue. I got a visitor so I gotta go. Bye.'

Gina sat down with a huff. 'Didn't know a thing about it, she says. Ooh, he's a sneaky bogger. Made trouble for Rick last week.' She looked at Martha. 'And he's no fan of yours.'

'Well then,' Martha said, unruffled. 'Let's make sure we beat him.'

She set her cup and plate aside, reached into her bag for a reporter's notebook and pen, and leaned forward.

'Tell me what policies you're planning to run on.'

'Eh?' Gina looked bemused.

'Which issues are you going to campaign for?'

'Well, stopping the swingers' camp, o' course.'

Martha nodded. 'The priority, but you need others as well. For all you know the district council will turn that licence down before the election and you'll be left without a platform. You need other issues to promote.'

George nodded approvingly. 'This is why we need your expertise.'

Gina thought for a moment. 'Cats,' she declared. 'I hate the boggers. And men in the summer going round with their man boobies out.'

Martha's pen paused over her pad. 'Right,' she said. 'I think we're going to have to work on this.'

Knights V Crusaders

The meeting of the Mapton Knights was explosive.

I got as much right as anyone to stand for councillor,' Andy flung at Gina. 'More than you, in fact. I'm Mapton born and bred. You've only been living here a few years. What gives you the right to represent us?'

'But Andy,' Sue protested. 'We all agreed that Gina would stand. You did too.'

'Yeah, well. I had time to think about it, and I don't think Gina's best for the job.'

'And why the hell not?' Gina demanded.

'Like I said, you're not one of us,' Andy said. 'And you're a troublemaker.'

'I am not!'

'Oh, come off it, Gina. You've rubbed up more people than Dennis Payton.'

'That's a lie,' Gina huffed. 'Mebbe at first but I get on wi' everyone now. Even me 'n' Pam Stimson say hello.'

'And Martha Seaton's helping Gina campaign,' Sue said. 'She's a local hero.'

Andy pulled a face. 'Half this town might have fallen for her sob story but I'm not. It's a load of cock and bull. I'm sick of women moaning about how badly they're treated by men. Bloody women's lib gone too far.'

'Here, here,' said Alf. Mildred elbowed him in the ribs.

'I ain't got nothin' against women in general,' Andy said. 'But I'm sick of this town being run by 'em. Martha Seaton was mayor for years. Sue leads the Marauders. The Knights were fine with George at the helm but since he's off sick, it's all started falling apart.'

'I beg your pardon,' said Sue. 'It has not. The protest is running fine.'

'But it's not, Sue,' Andy said. 'It's a shambles. People turning up when they like, misspelled signs, no proper rota. It needs organising properly. A strong hand on the rudder.'

'Yours, I suppose,' Gina sneered.

'As it happens I've been asked to take charge by a number of people,' Andy drew himself up. 'Sue rocks up on her Rascal when she feels like it. I'm there most of the time. There's a core group of us taking it seriously. Others just see it as a bit o' fun. Once the weather turns they'll be out of there.'

'I've seen your core group,' Sue said. 'You and Darren Bilson, your cousins, Ian and Stuart, the Eardley brothers, and a few more. You whipped them up good the other week about Rick's place. If it hadn't been Ange there you'd have started a fight.'

'Rick was well out of line,' Andy answered. 'There's a good example of Mapton going downhill. Too many outsiders thinking they can tell us what to do. And a man who leaves a woman to stick up for him is not a man in my book.'

'That's my son-in-law you're having a go at,' Gina said. She curled her fists. 'You better shut up.'

'See,' Andy said, looking round the anxious faces at the meeting. 'Outsiders sticking together, telling us what to do. Thinking you're better than us. You and your hoighty toighty granddaughter married to Yankee Rick, and their foreign housekeeper. Who has a housekeeper in Mapton? And them all living together in one house. No wonder Rick won't sign the petition. He's already got himself a harem.'

'How dare you!' Gina blazed. She looked like she was about to lunge when Sugsy stepped in.

'I think you better leave, Andy,' he said. 'I'm surprised at you mate. I thought we were all in this together.'

'I only came tonight to tell you I'm resigning from the Knights,' Andy said. 'I'm starting my own group, Mapton Crusaders. You ever grow a pair, Sugsy, you come over and join us.'

As he reached the door, Sue yelled. 'And you're banned from the Marauders too.'

Andy flipped a gesture that almost made Mildred faint.

'Good riddance to bad boggers,' Gina declared.

'Now I know why Carole didn't come,' Sue sighed. 'She's a stupid cow if she thinks Andy's her prince.'

'She's lonely,' Mildred said, recovering. 'And there's not much worse than that in this life.'

#

For a week there was a relative lull in Mapton's affairs. Martha had been accepted back into the community but hadn't been seen much.

215

The locals had got as much mileage out of discussing her as they could.

'I never thought bad of her. I knew there had to be another side to the story.'

'She shoulda cried in the interview. I know I would 'ave. Made her come across as cold, like.'

'John's a lucky dog. Bet she knows some moves in the bedroom.'

There had been comments on social media, and letters to the Lawton Post editor, even calls to reinstate Martha as mayor but then the weather turned bad, early snow blowing in from Siberia, and Mapton and the weather became the main topic of conversation.

Andy Timmis had been right in his prediction that come the winter weather, many of the sex camp protesters would abandon post.

Some of the Marauders dropped out, not because they weren't loyal to the cause but because as pensioners the ice and snow was a threat to hips and health. Mobility scooters provided little protection from the elements, and even those with canopies were no good in driving snow and sleet.

The seafront in winter was no place for the frail.

Sue did her best to rally the troops, venturing to the Paradise every day, although the cold played buggery with her arthritis. It irked her to see the Knights' numbers dropping while Andy Timmis, with his army of blokey Crusaders waved their banners, sang songs and stamped their feet. They'd taken to wearing England flag tabards over their layers.

Ange was still loyal, and many of Mapton's mums came out while their kids were in school. In the summer almost everyone would be working but this was the off-season.

Two groups began to form. Male and female. Sue noticed that the men left in the Knights' camp had begun to shuffle gradually towards the Crusaders.

Banter ran back and forth good-naturedly between the genders. After all they were on the same side.

Sue and Andy studiously ignored each other. There was bad blood between them.

Bad blood had a habit of spilling and spreading.

Gina stayed away from the protest on the advice of George and Martha. She wouldn't be able to ignore Andy. Martha needed to train Gina how to handle the opposition. Apparently lobbing insults, and possibly missiles, wasn't 'proper'.

Gina was so busy going round to Martha's house to plan the campaign that she didn't mind. A new world was opening up to her.

George, on the other hand, was fed up. Not because of Gina's absence, although he did miss her, but because he was bitterly disappointed over the split in the Knights.

Since his angina attack George had been advised by his doctor to take it easy and avoid stress. The attack had gravely frightened him. He took the doctor's advice, letting Sue run the Knights. Perhaps if he had been chairing he could have talked Andy round rationally.

Women could react so emotionally.

He didn't mind that. For most of his life he'd been glad to have dominant women tell him what to do, but many men – Andy obviously – felt threatened by women. He would have responded to George. A quiet man-to-man word in his ear might have done the trick.

He'd tried to persuade Gina not to go to the meeting but she'd ignored him. Thank God she agreed to stay away from the protest.

Martha was clearly already having a strong influence on her.

George felt like a wimp. Blow the angina; he should have gone to that meeting.

He was bored too. The weather had him trapped at home; he was sick of doing crosswords; he'd stopped having the Daily Mail on principle after their disparaging article. He found the Express a bit downmarket.

Ginger Rogers often kept him company but she wasn't much of a talker.

He was glad on Wednesday when Sue rang his doorbell. For once he didn't mind her yattering his ear off, although listening to her talk about the Crusaders got his blood pressure up.

On Thursday he called Stella to see if Grazja would bring little Gerta around. She did, and they had a great time playing peek-a-boo, but gosh, he was exhausted after an hour and needed his nap. It made him feel like a right old geezer.

Sue came around again on Friday, bringing a very bundled up Scampi.

'Could you look after her for the day?' she asked George. 'I'm so busy I worry she's getting lonely.'

She's not the only one thought, George, as he lifted Scampi gently onto the sofa.

Swingers Strike Back

The Lawton Post

Letter to the editor.

Sir,

As chairman of the UK Swingers' Association I feel it is time to address the bad press swingers have recently been getting due to plans in Mapton-on-Sea to introduce a caravan and camping park dedicated to swingers. This, along with the very misleading BBC programme, Inside Out, has perpetuated the damaging myth that swingers are degenerate and perverted.

Nothing could be further from the truth. Swingers are merely ordinary people who have unshackled themselves from the prudery of societal norms. Whereas many of those who condemn swingers are guilty of illicit affairs, adultery, and deceit, swingers usually have strong, loving, open partnerships, free from hypocrisy.

The swinging community is made up of a higher proportion of successful professionals than other sections of society, including doctors, vets, dentists, nurses, teachers and lecturers, army officers and police officers. All the people who work so hard to keep our country running in fact. It may well be that a strong sex drive is perhaps linked to intelligence, ability, and motivation to succeed.

While I have every sympathy with the plight of Mapton's former mayor, Martha Seaton, the Inside Out programme gave the impression that swinging is linked to abusive relationships. Nothing could be further from the truth. Neither Mrs Seaton nor her first husband, were swingers in the true sense. Mrs Seaton was forced into a compromising lifestyle by an abusive, manipulative man. He was clearly using sex as a weapon. This is fundamentally in opposition to the swingers' code of ethics. Sexual partnering is always a free decision between all parties. Coercion is not tolerated.

Drugs are most definitely not part of the swingers' scene. Neither drugs nor alcohol are encouraged as they affect sexual performance. Many swingers' clubs do not sell alcohol at all.

Neither is prostitution part of swinging. Where is the need when sex is given freely and joyfully? Martha Seaton's husband was not a swinger; he was a criminal.

It is time swinging lost its social stigma. Why is it wrong for law-abiding, respectable adults to responsibly enjoy consensual sex with multiple partners?

Yours, sincerely,

A Stephens
UK Swingers' Association

Damned by Association

Andrew Leith was on it quicker than a pet-jumping flea.

His article appeared the next day.

SWINGERS QUESTION MAPTON'S IMAGE
By Andrew Leith

Residents of Mapton and Siltby fighting an application for an entertainments licence that will allow the Paradise Holiday Park to transform into a club for swingers will be surprised to know that many swingers would turn their nose up at Mapton.

Following a letter published in the Lawton Post, claiming that swingers are misrepresented, reporter Andrew Leith, contacted the UK Swingers Association for further comment.

Andrew Stephens, who wrote the letter, is joint chair of the association, along with his wife Joyce. They describe themselves as fit, healthy, late-fifty somethings, with children who have flown the nest, and a zest for life. Both are retired professionals.

Mr Stephens was only too happy to talk to the Post.

'We've been following the Mapton situation carefully. As is too often the case, the prospect of a swingers' facility has been whipped up by the media and a bunch of Little Englanders into a frenzy of faux moral hysteria.'

According to Mr Stephens the majority of swingers tend to be mature couples of professional standing who want nice surroundings and a harmonious environment in which to meet like-minded people.

Mr Stephens explained: 'When we heard about the plans in Mapton my wife and I decided to visit for the day. The Paradise Holiday Park will need a lot of work to get it up to the standard our members would expect. It leaves a lot to be desired.'

The couple went into Mapton central, took a stroll along the beach, and visited a local café.

'The beach is lovely,' Mr Stephens said. 'But to be honest Mapton isn't the prettiest seaside resort. There's a lot of tat for sale, and it seems a bit downmarket for our members. There are other resorts with far better facilities.'

Mr Stephens added: 'It's ironic that the Mapton protesters argue that a swingers' club would send the town downhill. If anything it's the other way round. They need to improve Mapton to attract us.'

However the Stephens' impression of Mapton wasn't all bad.

'We overheard an argument in an American-style diner,' Mr Stephens said. 'The owner, Rick, was standing up to one of the protesters, so not everyone in Mapton is small-minded. Also the food was delicious. If everything in Mapton was as good as The Last Resort Diner, our members would love the place. As it stands, Mapton needs to take a hard look at itself before casting aspersions on others.'

#

'Great,' Rick groaned, as his friend Jill laughingly showed him the article on her iPad. 'I don't believe my luck. How was I to know they were swingers? They just seemed like a nice, middle-aged couple on a day out.'

'Not just swingers,' Jill sniggered, 'But the chair of the UK Swingers' Association. The swingers all other swingers look up to.'

'Yeah, laugh it up,' Rick said. 'You don't how hard this is going to make my life.'

Rick was in Lawton, prepping in Jill's kitchen for their pop-up restaurant at Jill's deli, Delicious.

'You should move to Lawton,' Jill said. 'We're much more cosmopolitan.'

'So you keep saying.'

'There's a gay scene.'

'Really useful if I was gay,' Rick acknowledged drily. 'And speaking of that, have you started seeing someone?'

Jill dropped her eyes coyly. 'What makes you think that?'

'Oh, I don't know. A certain spring to your step. A newfound cheeriness. A little glow.'

Jill blushed. 'Well, there might be someone.'

Rick swatted at her with a tea towel. 'I knew it. C'mon, details. Spit it out.''

'Her name's Suzanne,' Jill said. 'But I don't want to talk about it yet. I'm afraid I'll jinx it.'

'I getcha,' Rick said.

His phone buzzed. He looked at the screen. 'Gina,' he said. 'Bet she's seen that article.' He rejected the call.

Ten minutes later the phone buzzed again. This time he answered it.

'Hey Stell … Yeah, I seen it …Yeah, well tell her it's none of her business.' He pressed a hand to his forehead. 'They didn't have stickers saying Swingers United on their foreheads, how was I to know?' He listened. Nodded. 'Yep, good times ahead. How's the painting today? … Great. You're enjoying this aren't you? All grist to the mill.' Rick laughed. 'You little sicko… Okay, see you tonight. Bye.'

He grinned at Jill. 'Poor Stella's just had an earful off Gina. Thank God I'm in Lawton today. Yet again there is outrage in Mapton.'

His phone buzzed again. He rolled his eyes. 'Ange. No way,' he said, pressing reject. 'I'm gonna text Stella,' he said. 'Tell her to ring you if she needs to get hold of me.' He texted then switched his phone off.

'You might have a point about moving to Lawton,' he said.

A moment later Jill got a text. She laughed. 'Stella says to tell you you're a chicken.'

'That's me,' Rick said cheerfully. 'And I'm gonna clucking stay that way.'

#

'Stella thinks it's funny,' Gina said, slamming her phone down on the table. 'Stupid girl.'

'Perhaps it's better to see the funny side,' George said wearily, not looking like he saw anything humorous at all.

'Funny side? It's bloody disgustin' is what it is. How dare they have a go at Mapton? All that la-de-da language don't hide the fact they're knicker-swapping perverts. You should ha' heard everyone in the Co-op. Whole of Mapton's up in

225

arms. And Rick! What was he thinking? He'll ruin my chances if he don't stop arsin' around. He's a bleedin' embarrassment.'

'He wasn't to know,' George said.

'I woulda known,' Gina said. 'If I'da been there I would have known straight away. I got a nose for perverts. I'da told 'em where to get off, believe you me.'

George did believe her.

'Maybe I'll write a letter to the Lawton Post,' he suggested.

Gina nodded. 'That's a good idea,' she said. 'But don't bother yerself, George. It should come from me cos I'm running for councillor. I'll get Martha to help me write it.'

'Oh,' George said. 'Well, if you think that's best.'

'Yes,' Gina said, jumping up. 'I've got a meeting with her now. I'll ask her what she thinks. Don't worry about walking Ginger. I already took her out.'

After Gina had left George looked at Ginger. 'Looks like neither one of you needs me today,' he said.

Ginger responded by hopping onto the sofa and curling up against him.

First Strike

As it happened, Martha advised Gina not to write a response to the Lawton Post (and risk getting into a slanging match) but to concentrate on getting their campaign leaflet organised.

However, it was actually Andy who got his leaflet out first.

He beamed out from a photograph.

ANDY TIMMIS
Independent Candidate
Leading the Fight to Keep Mapton Decent

I have lived all my life in Mapton-On-Sea and never wanted to live anywhere else although I have been given many opportunities to leave. As a local business owner of Andy's Fancy's I know what it is like to struggle to keep a business afloat in a seaside town, very difficult. I love it though and won't quit, I am not a quitter. I am active in the community as president of TOM Townsmen of Mapton, you probably know us from when we hand out presents to the local kiddies at the Christmas parade. Now I have started a new action group The Mapton Crusaders to fight the arrival of sleeze and corruption in Mapton. You might think we are the same as The Mapton Knights, we are not. The Knights have lost the leadership of George Wentworth and now have Gina Pontin running as a candidate. Gina Pontin has never contributed to the community in the less than ten years she has lived here. Furthermore her campaign manager is non other than Martha Seaton our recently disgraced mayor with a swinging past, on top of that it came out yesterday that Gina's American son in law Rick Blake welcomed swingers in his diner The Last Resort.

If you vote for me I promise to:

- STOP DEAD the plans for a sex camp at The Paradise Holiday Park.
- NOT allow swingers into Mapton at all.
- Make sure that <u>people from Mapton</u> get first choice to run our businesses, not outsiders and foreigners.
- Restore BRITISH HERITAGE by bringing Punch and Judy back to our beaches.
- ALWAYS put Mapton peoples needs first.
- NOT associate with dodgy people.

VOTE FOR ANDY, YOU KNOW IT MAKES COMMON SENSE.

#

Martha's reaction to Andy's leaflet floored Gina, who was livid.

'Brilliant!' Martha declared. 'Exactly what we wanted.'

'It's bloody insulting,' Gina said. 'I'm gonna kill him.'

'You're going to beat him,' Martha chuckled. 'This is terrible.'

'I know,' boiled Gina. 'He's made a laughing stock out of me.'

Martha stopped reading and looked at Gina surprised. 'No, I mean his leaflet is terrible as in it's really bad. Laughably bad. Look at these errors.' She grabbed a pen and started ringing punctuation and spelling mistakes.

'Ooh, I was so mad, I didn't notice,' Gina said, perking up. 'But we can't let him get away with what he says about me and Rick. And you.'

'We can,' Martha said. 'It's negative campaigning. People don't like it. Oh, you'll get some who'll repeat this nonsense. Andy will have his supporters and they'll be loud and given more attention because of it, but privately most people won't buy it. You've heard of the 'silent majority'?'

'I've heard o' it but I don't know what it means,' Gina admitted.

'It means that a lot of people don't like to voice their opinions. They don't say which way they'll vote, especially if their choice would make them unpopular with their friends and neighbours, but when the time comes they'll vote the way they really feel.'

'Like all them people who voted Tory at the last election after the polls said they wouldn't?'

'Exactly,' said Martha. 'Or in the Scottish referendum.'

'How does that help us?' Gina said.

'It might not help us at all,' Martha said. 'But I want you to remember that when Andy is making

229

a lot of noise and getting some Maptonites stirred up, the majority will be looking at those daft points and stupid mistakes and making their own minds up. Our job is to run a calm, clean campaign.'

Gina flopped into a chair. 'I'm not known for being calm,' she said.

'True,' Martha agreed. 'But we're going to concentrate on your other well-known quality – telling it like it is – while showing Mapton that you can control your temper. Andy is going to be the perfect way to show that.'

'So we're going to let Andy insult us to help us win,' Gina said. She thought about it. 'That's bleedin' genius,' she said, cheering up.

'Our main rival is really Tony Forbes,' Martha said. 'He's Tom Turner's man. He's solid as far as I know, and Tom will be guiding him. He's a bit dull, but a known quantity so people will trust him. He's a family man too, and established.'

'Sounds like you think he'll win,' Gina said.

'Not necessarily,' Martha replied. 'But you've got to know your enemy to beat them, strengths and weaknesses.'

'What's his weakness?'

'Like I said, Tony is a little dull. He doesn't have charisma or personality.' She looked at Gina. 'Personality is something you have in spades.'

#

Tom Turner was also tickled by Andy's leaflet. He showed it to Tony. 'If Gina's campaign is as bad as this you'll be sailing onto the town council, matey.'

230

Bun Fight

Rick was decidedly not pleased.

A few of Andy's Crusaders had decamped from protesting at The Paradise to hanging around outside The Last Resort. They'd brought a couple of 'Keep Mapton Decent' banners with them, and were handing out Andy's campaign leaflets to passers-by.

The cold snap had broken, bringing a few days of early December sunshine, so townsfolk and a few day-trippers walked the promenade, making the most of the lull in the weather.

'C'mon guys,' Rick said, stepping out of the diner. 'You're intimidating the customers. There's no need for this.'

'We're just giving them the truth,' Darren Bilson said. 'You should be serving the people of Mapton, Rick, not perverts. Anyway, it's still a free country. We're just practising that right.'

Rick held his hand out for a leaflet. 'Let's see what Andy's saying.'

Darren begrudgingly let him have one. As Rick scanned it he began to chuckle.

'What's so funny?' Darren demanded.

Rick snorted.

'Give that back,' Darren snatched for the leaflet and tore it out of Rick's hand.

'Aw, c'mon man, it was just getting good,' Rick said.

Darren bristled. A younger man, he was well muscled. He drew up to Rick.

'You wanna watch what you say, Rick. One of them bricks sent through Martha Seaton's could come your way.'

Rick stopped smirking. 'Was that a threat, Darren? The police want to know what coward lobbed that brick. Are you saying it was you?'

It was Darren's turn to smirk. 'I don't know nothing about that. I just know it would be a shame to see it happen to you.'

Rick looked beyond Darren to the men behind him. He singled out Stuart Timmis, Andy's youngest cousin.

'Nice company you're keeping, Stuart. Sorry you can't come in and have a cinnamon bun – the ones you love. I just got a fresh batch outta the oven.'

Stuart looked at his feet, and his brother Ian looked away.

Rick gave them all a disgusted look before turning to go inside.

'If you're thinking of ringing the police, we ain't done nothing illegal,' Darren said. 'We're not stopping no one coming in.'

Rick didn't bother to reply.

Frank, who was sitting tensely at the counter, said: 'You need some back-up?'

'No,' Rick said shortly. 'But ring Grazja and tell her to keep Gerta away from the diner today.'

'I don't like it,' Maria said. It was her shift. 'I'm scared.'

'I'll deal with it,' Rick said. He disappeared into the kitchen. Ten minutes later he reappeared with a plate of cinnamon buns and coffees.

'Get the door for me, will you?'

Frank hurried to let him through.

'Right,' Rick said, laying the tray on one of the outside tables. 'Darren, I don't know you, and I don't much like what I've seen, but you two have been my customers for years. I've never had a problem with you or you with me. So, I'll lay it out for you. I didn't know that couple were swingers but they coulda been bloody Martians for all I care. I don't question my customers about their habits, because if I did I'd probably learn a few things about my neighbours I don't want to know. I'm learning things I don't like today. Secondly, I didn't sign that damn petition because I hate feeling bullied into doing things and because I never believed and still don't believe a swingers' camp is ever gonna happen at the Paradise.

'One thing I do agree with you on, however, is liberty and freedom of speech. Call me a crazy, old-fashioned American. So, although I don't agree with your methods, as a gesture of goodwill I am leaving you these coffees and fresh baked buns. It's up to you whether or not to accept them. I just ask you to think about what you're doing to a Mapton business while you decide.'

#

Stuart was the first to break. He grabbed a cinnamon bun. 'Fuck it,' he said. 'Rick's right. I don't like doing this. We been coming here for years.'

Darren snarled. 'Put it back. He's buying you off.'

'Nah,' Ian piped up. 'I'm with Stu. I feel bad. Me 'n' Leanne had our first date at Rick's – the old

233

diner what blew up. I say we go back to the Paradise.' He too took a bun, and reached for a coffee.

'I don't believe it,' Darren barked. 'You frigging wusses.'

'Watch it,' Ian said. 'And what was all that about chucking a brick? I don't hold wi' that.'

He stood up and his brother stood with him. They were wiry but tough-looking lads.

Darren eyed them. 'I was just saying it,' he said. 'Didn't mean nothing by it. Heat of the moment.'

The fourth man, Jim, who had been silent all through the whole exchange, took a bun and said. 'I'm bored outta my mind. Let's get back to the Paradise where all the birds are. I fancy me chances with that really big-knockered one.'

'What, the one from the church-group? Pious Pauline?' Ian asked.

Jim nodded. 'Church girls are good goers. Not much in the looks department but plenty of frustrated energy.'

They all snickered. Darren gave in. 'Alright,' he said. 'We'll forget the diner. But don't tell Andy.'

They all agreed, and started to move off.

'Oh, fuck it,' Darren said, hurrying back. He grabbed a bun and a coffee to take with him.

#

Twenty minutes after the Crusaders left, Sue rode up with the Marauders fanned out behind her.

She tooted her horn.

Rick came out to them.

'Ricky,' Sue cried. 'We came to help you. We heard you got trouble.' She looked bewildered by the scene of tranquillity that met her eyes. A few hardy people were dotted around the outside tables enjoying the rare sunshine.

Peter Moss raised his mug to her.

'Oh thanks, Sue,' Rick said. 'You missed it. Four 'Crusaders' protesting outside the diner.'

'Mildred rode past this morning,' Sue said. 'She called me, said they looked nasty, but it took me a while to get the Marauders together.'

'We were so worried, Rick,' Mildred called. 'But we couldn't find Alf's back brace.'

'Where was it?' Rick asked.

'Down back of the settee,' Alf said, rolling his eyes.

'What happened?' Sue puffed. 'Was it a standoff?'

'Actually,' Rick said. 'It was more of a bake-off.'

'Tell us then!'

The Marauders loved 'bake-off'. Alf kept repeating it to anyone who'd listen.

'Seriously, though,' Rick said more quietly to Sue. 'I don't like that Darren character. He threatened to lob a brick through my window. Mentioned Martha Seaton's house.'

'You think it was him that did it to Martha?'

'Yeah. I do.'

'You should tell the police,' Sue said.

'I probably will,' Rick said. 'But isn't Sergeant Johnson one of Andy's buddies in TOM?'

'Yeah, but's he's alright. Turns a blind eye to rumble nights.'

'When Andy was in The Marauders,' Rick pointed out. 'Didn't you chuck him out?'

Sue looked alarmed. 'That's a point. Hope we don't get no police harassment now.'

'Do you know Darren?' Rick asked.

'Not well,' Sue said. 'Used to be a bouncer for the Shalimar disco before it shut down. Went off to Skeg for a bit and moved back here recently. Seems to have been a bit of an influence on Andy lately. He never used to be such a twot, did Andy.'

A Night to Remember

Stella stepped back from the canvas. She'd been painting all day and needed to get ready to go out. They were having a rare night out, a meal with Grazja and Frank. Gina was babysitting Gerta – another rarity; since she'd been preparing to stand for council Stella had hardly seen her. Tomorrow she would launch her campaign.

Stella hadn't let herself dwell too much on what that might entail. Whatever it might be, the next few weeks would be interesting to say the least. Life around Gina was never dull.

Nor was life in Mapton at the moment, especially for her husband.

Stella was already itching to paint the 'bake off,' but she still had a few finishing touches to add to the Paradise canvas.

As she cleaned up, Rick knocked on her studio door and entered.

'Hey,' he said, giving her a kiss. 'Nearly time to go. Gina's already here.'

'I heard her,' Stella said. 'I'm just cleaning up. Have I got time for a quick shower?'

'Sure,' Rick said, moving to look at the painting.

'Wow,' he said after a moment. 'That's incredible, hon.'

Stella joined him, gazing at her work critically.

Beneath the billboard of the frolicking carefree couple protesters thronged before the shabby Paradise. In the foreground Sue, proud on her

Rascal Vision, stared out of the painting, grasping a flag emblazoned with St George on his steed.

Flanked around and behind her were groups of people; some held banners, mouths wide to chant and shout. Others laughed with each other, chatted, or ate sandwiches, enjoying a day out. A tight knot of men stood to the left, glowering. Menace emanated out of them; a threat of violence about to erupt.

Other than Sue none of the faces were instantly recognisable as Maptonites, but if you knew what to look for the tell-tale signs were there. A glimpse of orange hair and a leg exiting the picture signalled Gina's departure. A man politely tipping a smart cap to a woman was George.

'Darren Bilson,' Rick said pointing to the lead man in the threatening group. 'It's not his face exactly but you capture his aggression.'

'I've never actually seen him,' Stella said. 'I've just let myself paint what came up.'

Rick peered more closely. In the background a barely visible hooded figure stood with his head bowed.

'Frank?' Rick turned to Stella. 'As far as I know he's not been down to the site.'

'It's not him exactly,' Stella said. 'It's just a watcher on the side-lines.'

Rick looked again. 'He looks sad,' he said. 'And ghost-like.'

'Come on,' Stella said suddenly brisk. 'I'd better get ready or we'll be late.'

#

They went for pizza at Giovanni's Pizza Steakhouse. Joe, who owned the restaurant, was Mapton born and bred but his father, the eponymous Giovanni, came over from Naples in the 1950s. Joe always claimed his father had been escaping from the Mafia but no one ever believed him, despite the fact that in a Golden Coast Radio poll, sixty percent of callers believed in UFOs.

Joe was a fan of Rick's pop-up in Lawton while Rick was a fan of Joe's secret pizza-sauce recipe.

Tonight Joe ushered them in and served them himself.

'That stupid Andy Timmis,' Joe said. 'What's he put you in his leaflet for? Stirring up trouble. My papa was a foreigner and we're the longest running business in Mapton.'

'Ah, forget about it,' Rick shrugged. 'It'll all blow over. Tonight I don't want to think about it.'

'I hear you, Rick,' Joe nodded. 'You had trouble at the diner?'

'Nothing serious,' Rick said. 'I handled it.'

'I heard you threw cream buns at them,' Joe laughed. 'Scared them off.'

'I didn't throw anything at anyone,' Rick said.

'No? That's what they're saying. You bombarded the bad guys with cream buns, quick as a machine gun.' He mimed the action, making machine gun noises.

Rick laughed. 'God, now I wish I had.'

Joe said. 'If Andy Timmis, Darren Bilson or their buddies come in here I'm gonna throw pizzas at them, like this...' He made a noise like a ninja hurling Frisbees.

Stella choked out: 'I hope they do. I really want to see that Joe.'

Joe grinned and took their order.

'I not come here before,' Grazja said, eyeing the décor – a mixture of Italian cliché meets Mapton Artex.

'It's Mapton's best surprise,' Rick said. 'Great pizza. It's his sauce.'

'I like the dough,' Frank said. 'You can taste the olive oil, and it's not too dense and bready.'

'Do the Polish eat pizza?' Rick asked Grazja.

'Yes,' she said. 'But we like ketchup on it.'

'Ketchup?' Stella smiled.

'Yes, ketchup. Why so strange?'

'It just seems weird,' Stella said. 'It already comes with a tomato sauce.'

'Not so weird as vinegar on chips,' Grazja said. 'Salt and ketchup, yes. Mayonnaise okay. Vinegar no.' She wrinkled her nose, shuddering.

'I try to keep my mind open when it comes to food,' Rick said.

'Well, you were top French chef,' Grazja said. 'You eat snails and frogs legs. Etcetera.'

There was a small pause.

'I didn't know you were a chef, Rick,' Frank said. 'Obviously you run a great diner...' He trailed off, noting Stella's wary expression and Grazja's sudden blush.

'A long time ago,' Rick said casually. 'I don't really talk about it. Bit too hectic a lifestyle for me.'

Frank smiled. He picked up his glass for a toast and the others followed suit.

'To positive changes and easier lives,' Frank toasted.

'I can drink to that,' Rick said. They toasted and moved on to other things.

After a leisurely meal and a few too many glasses of vino, they decided to go for a nightcap at The Diving Helmet.

The pub was busy.

'I forgot it was Karaoke night,' Stella said. 'It's so long since I've been out.'

They found a recently deserted table. If anyone gave them odd looks or presented a frosty shoulder they were too merry to notice.

Sugsy was working the bar with his wife, Tina.

'Good to see you. Not seen you both in the Helmet for an age.'

'Not since I had Gerta,' Stella replied.

As Sugsy sorted her order, he said. 'Get Rick to sing. Used to be a real crowd pleaser when he did a turn. Great voice.' He winked at her. 'Popular with the ladies.'

Stella laughed. 'I remember. I'll ask him. I notice you didn't ask me to sing.'

Sugsy pulled a face. 'I love looking at you sweetheart, but it breaks my heart when you sing. And my ears.'

'Cheeky bogger,' Stella said in Gina's voice, making him grin.

Returning to the table with a tin tray of drinks, Stella told Rick. 'Sugsy wants you to sing.'

'Nah,' Rick shook his head tipsily. 'Been too long.'

'Oh go on,' Grazja said. 'I remember when you sang 'Gentle on my Mind.' You brought house down.'

'That was the night you and Gina sang Summer Nights,' Stella chuckled.

'I remember that too,' Frank surprised them.

'I didn't know you were there,' Rick said.

'I came in for a pint and to watch the karaoke. Makes me laugh. Freda Lightfoot is the best. She wears a monkey backpack and during the instrumental bits she turns around and makes it dance.'

'I can't believe you remember me. Was years ago.' Grazja said.

'It was the first time I noticed you,' Frank said, smiling at her.

Grazja went all shy, like Gerta when she met a stranger.

'Hey,' Rick said. 'You do the karaoke with me, Frank. We can do a song together.'

Frank protested until he saw Grazja smiling at him, pink-cheeked and girlishly coy under the influence of wine.

'You take the lead,' he said to Rick. 'I'll do back up.'

They all got up, none of them too steady, to make their way to the back room.

Stella gave Sugsy a thumbs up as she passed.

Ange's ex-husband, Des, was DJing the karaoke. Rick and Frank spoke to him as Pam Stimson, dressed in a Britney Spears schoolgirl outfit, wailed out 'Baby One More Time.'

'Good job Gina's not here,' Stella said to Grazja. 'This could set off their war again.'

After Pam tottered off stage to a round of applause, Des stepped up to the mike. 'Yes, yes, yes. That was our own Pam S shaking some Britney booty. And now for something completely different on 90s night. A welcome return to the stage for Mapton's only American, Rick Blake, and a first time round of applause for Brother Frank of ghost train fame. They'll be channelling a bit of Pulp tonight, folks, wiiiiiiiiiiith … 'Common People'.

There was a smattering of applause.

The opening bars chimed in, then Rick began to sing 'She came from Greece/She had a thirst for knowledge …' Frank hung back, swaying along. Rick motioned for him to come forward but he shook his head until the chorus when he burst in with: 'I want to live like common people/I want to do whatever common people do …'

Stella whooped. 'Go Frank.'

Halfway through the song she noticed a man moving around some of the tables, bending to whisper in ears, pointing towards the stage, but it meant nothing to her. She didn't know him and she thought he was probably trying to persuade some of his mates to get up next.

Frank and Rick really went for the key change crescendo at the end, belting it out together.

They ended in a triumphant, boozed-up glow of joy.

Stella and Grazja clapped enthusiastically, and a few others less so. Then a slow clap started and began to build as people joined in.

Rick and Frank looked confused.

The man Stella noticed moving around the tables stood up and shouted: 'Bit of a piss-take ain't it Rick, you singing about the common people?'

'It's just a song, Darren,' Rick said into the mike.

'Yeah,' Darren said, turning to look at the other customers. 'Just a song. Take a look, Rick. We *are* the common people, and proud of it. We don't need you condescending to us, with your snobby wife and yer housekeeper living in that pretend castle without a worry in the world.'

There were a few grumbles of assent.

'You're talking bollocks,' Rick said, making his way unsteadily off the stage.

'Don't sound like bollocks to me,' Darren's friend, Jim called. 'You won't stand up for Mapton when it needs you. Serving swingers in your café. Got a posh restaurant in Lawton. You're not common people.'

Stella gripped Grazja's hand. The atmosphere had turned tense.

Rick scowled as he moved towards Darren, Frank shadowing him closely.

'Listen, dude, you can have a pop at me, but don't mention my wife.'

'Or what?' Darren sneered, squaring up.

Pious Pauline, who'd been knocking back cider in the erroneous belief (fuelled by Jim) it was non-alcoholic, gave an excited squeal.

Stella stood up. 'Don't Rick. Let's go. He's just trying to start a fight.'

Grazja echoed her. 'Yes, let's go. We no need this.'

Her Polish accent sounded more pronounced in this company.

Darren shot her a smirking look. 'If you really care about Mapton,' he proclaimed, 'you would've hired a local to keep your house, not brought in a cheap Polack to steal our jobs. You're probably banging her too.'

Frank was in front of Rick in a second. He sprang into a boxing pose, fists cocked. Suddenly his Irish accent sounded much broader. 'I've reached maximum umbrage, young man. You don't insult the lady.' With that he popped Darren a punch to the jaw that knocked him down.

'Sinner,' Pious Pauline screamed.

'You don't know the meaning of the word,' Frank snapped back.

Suddenly he started to shake. Rick looked bewildered.

Sugsy ran into the room. 'Break it up,' he said. 'I've called the police.'

Out of the Blocks

The next campaign to hit Mapton doormats was Gina's. Her letter dropped through letterboxes the morning after the fight.

Under a headshot of Gina smiling (Martha had taken her to a professional photographer in Lawton) it read:

Dear Maptonites,

My name is Gina Pontin and I am running as independent candidate for town councillor. I grew up below the poverty line with an alcoholic father. As a single mother in the fifties and sixties, I knew about discrimination and how tough raising a child on your own can be.

I worked full-time all my life, raising first my daughter, then after her tragic death, my granddaughter. It was tough, but I am a tough woman, and I had a dream to keep me going: to retire one day to Mapton-on-Sea.

My family couldn't afford a week away each year but we always did a daytrip to Mapton. As a child I thought it was paved with gold.

Living here for almost ten years I can honestly say there isn't another place on this earth that I'd rather be. But now I know it isn't paved with gold and has its problems and I want to do my bit to solve some of those problems.

As a mother and grandmother I know how important it is to keep Mapton as a safe, family-friendly resort. That's why I co-formed the

Mapton Knights Action Committee to stand against proposals to introduce a sex camp to Mapton. I will fight to my last breath to stop that happening.

As a pensioner I understand the needs of an ageing population in Mapton and will campaign to lower kerbs in the town for easier mobility scooter access.

I don't take no for an answer. You'll remember that for years the council did nothing with the dilapidated huts on the west promenade. The beach was neglected, and businesses shut down. Now it is thriving and tourists love it. Why? Because me and my granddaughter, Stella, painted our beach hut, and helped others to do the same. My son-in-law opened his new café there, taking a big business risk. As a family we believe in Mapton.

That's the can-do spirit I'll represent you with. I will always fight for what is best for Mapton. The district council give the majority of the money to the farmers, neglecting Mapton and Siltby. I won't stand for that.

I won't stand for a sex camp. I won't stand for injustice.

I stand for Mapton.

I hope you'll stand with me.

Yours, sincerely,

G Pontin

Gina Pontin

#

Stella stumbled to open the door, nursing a hangover.

Gina pushed her way past her. 'I've just bloody heard,' she said. 'I start my canvassing and I have to be told by Mavis bleedin' Gratton while I'm standing on her doorstep, that my closest family got in a drunken bust-up last night. Well thank you so bloody much.'

Stella limply trailed after her in to the kitchen, where Rick slumped dispiritedly over a mug of coffee.

The blare of cartoons came from the garden room where Gerta was watching TV. Not even a visit from Grandma Gina would break her away from that enchantment.

Thank God, thought Stella. Whilst the shrill sounds pierced her hungover brain, this morning they were better than trying to keep Gerta entertained. What had parents done before the hypnotic draw of television on kids?

'Keep it down, Gina,' Rick said. 'My head's thumping.'

'Serves you right,' Gina snapped. 'You've done nothing but embarrass me since this whole sex camp thing started. Why aren't you at work, anyway?'

Rick gave her a murderous look, gathered the shreds of his dignity, and stalked out of the kitchen.

'Gina!' Stella said. 'That's not fair.'

'He's been against us since day one,' Gina huffed.

'He hasn't been against anyone,' Stella sighed. 'Anyway he didn't throw the punch last night; it was Frank.'

'Frank! He wouldn't say boo to a goose.'

'Last night he knocked out the goose,' Stella said. 'Defending Grazja's honour. Sort of.'

Gina transformed from being angry to avidly interested.

'Grazja?'

'Darren Bilson called her a Polack.'

'That's racialist!' Gina said, ignoring the fact that in her first meeting with Grazja she'd called her a 'dirty Polack'.

Stella nodded. 'And he said Rick was 'banging her'.'

Gina gasped. 'That dirty bogger. Why didn't Rick hit him?'

'I thought he was going to,' Stella said. 'It all happened so fast. Suddenly Frank leapt in and floored Darren. And then Sugsy ran in saying he'd called the police. It took hours to sort it out. We all got taken to the station. Darren wanted to charge Frank with assault, but he dropped the charges when Grazja threatened she'd press charges against him on the grounds of inciting racial hatred. A couple of people had filmed it on their phones too, so she could back that up.

'In the end Frank got let off with a warning. It was a horrible night.'

'Frank Manning,' Gina said, amazed. 'Didn't think he had it in him.'

'Apparently he used to box,' Stella said. 'Darren Bilson's not a lightweight, but he took him out with one punch.'

Gina's eyes gleamed. 'He's a dark horse, that one. Where's Grazja?'

'Dunno,' Stella said. 'She came back with us last night but I haven't seen her this morning. Probably in bed with a hangover like we should be.'

'I'll catch up with her later,' Gina said. 'Here, have a look at me campaign leaflet.'

Frank's Confession

Grazja wasn't in bed. She'd hardly slept all night. She rose early and walked down to the seafront to let the cold sea wind sweep out her head.

After some time she turned towards town.

Frank lived in small flat above Kleen and Gone, the launderette.

Grazja had never been there before; she wasn't sure she should be here now, but after a moment's hesitation she rang the doorbell.

Footsteps clomped down the stairs. Frank opened the door, peering out warily. His smile when he saw Grazja was relieved.

'I thought you were the police calling to say Darren had changed his mind and decided to press charges.'

'No,' Grazja said. 'I sorry, it's early but I wanted to see you.'

'It's fine,' Frank said. 'Please, come up.'

Grazja followed him up the narrow stairs to his flat.

She looked around with interest. His lounge was tidy, but lined with bookshelves. A small table with two chairs filled the window nook; a wooden slatted blind, partially open let in the weak winter morning sun. A laptop sat on the table, next to a fruit bowl and a vase of chrysanthemums

A battered sofa stood against one wall, opposite the fireplace with its log-look electric fire. The TV was modestly tucked away in a corner.

Photos of the sea and paintings jostled for position with the books on the shelves.

'So many books,' Grazja said.

'I do a lot of reading. Would you like a cup of tea, or coffee?'

'Have you got milk?' Grazja asked.

'Yes.'

'Then I have tea, please. But strong. Not like your weak tea.'

'My fly's piss?' Frank grinned.

He disappeared into a galley kitchen, leaving Grazja to peruse the books.

There were classics, modern thrillers, books on art and photography. Poetry, Shakespeare. An entire two shelves of Terry Pratchett. Books on flora and fauna, sea-life, geography. A mini library on various religions and theology, as well as a range of other subjects.

Grazja was fascinated. She jumped when Frank spoke; she hadn't heard him return. He held two mugs.

'Sit on the sofa or at the table?'

'Table,' she chose.

As he was setting down the mugs she noticed his bruised, swollen fist.

'Ouch, that looks painful,' she said.

He looked ruefully at his hand. 'I feel pretty stupid,' he said. 'I don't condone violence.'

'Me neither,' Grazja agreed. 'I don't know whether I grateful or angry at you.'

Frank simply nodded.

'You put ice on that?' Grazja asked.

'Last night, when I finally got home.'

They sat in silence for a moment.

'I wanted to see you are okay,' Grazja finally said.

Frank's smile was quick. 'Thank you. I am. Are you? Rick and Stella?'

'I fine, except for hangover. Not know about Rick and Stella. Curtains still closed when I went out.'

'Rick's not at the diner today, at least. He's over at Lawton later.'

'Good thing. Everyone want to talk to you and him, I think. Me and Stella too.'

'I'm going to keep a low profile today,' Frank said. 'Let the gossip blow over.'

Grazja hesitated, cradling her tea. 'Frank,' she said. 'I need talk to you. I not want romance.' She looked at him compassionately. 'I not want to lead you on.'

Frank didn't wince. 'Grazja,' he said softly. 'I'm not about to push you into anything you don't want. I am very attracted to you, I won't lie. I've not got much experience at these things but I think you like me too – romantically, I mean. But it's not the most important thing to me. Your friendship means as much.'

Grazja smiled wryly. 'Men say things like that, but not my experience. Really, they want to sleep with you.'

Frank reddened. 'That's probably true. But relationships are complex, and sex is an element of them, not everything. In fact I'm glad you came over, Grazja. I've been thinking all night, and I've made up my mind. I want to tell you who I really am.'

Grazja looked alarmed. 'No,' she said. 'No need, Frank. Everyone got secrets they don't want to share.'

Frank smiled. 'I know about secrets better than you can imagine. Most people do want to share them; they're just too afraid to.'

Grazja looked uncomfortable. 'Please, not tell me …'

Frank put his hand over hers. 'I want to, 'he said. 'You're the first person I wanted to talk to about it. Don't worry. I am not a terrible man, just a weak one.'

Grazja looked dubious. 'Alright,' she sighed, extracting her hand. 'I listen.'

'I'm assuming, being Polish, you were probably raised Catholic?'

Grazja raised a quizzical eyebrow. 'Yes. But I lapsed a long time ago.'

'I was a priest.'

Grazja closed her eyes. 'You not a paedophile?' she said quietly.

'No! I am not,' Frank said. 'Despite what the news might suggest. Most priests aren't. Not the majority I hope, although recent revelations make me despair that I might be wrong. And...' He stopped. 'I'll come to that,' he said. 'I'll start with Martha Seaton.'

'Mayor Seaton!'

'Yes. Remember the priest she went to for confession?'

'That was you?' Grazja looked at him wide-eyed.

'That was me,' Frank said. 'I was a young priest, not long out of seminary. I believed in God,

254

in the church, and I thought I could make a difference in the world. Southend was my first parish.

'When I heard Martha's confession I knew I had to help her. The seal of confession is sacred so I asked if she would be willing to meet me face to face and seek help for her. The confessor has to give permission, as you probably know.'

Grazja nodded. Her mother had been very keen on confession.

'Even though I hadn't technically broken the sacred seal, my superiors disapproved. By approaching social services, and then arranging for Martha to stay with my sister, they felt I'd involved the church in something unsavoury. Martha was a married woman. No matter how terrible her husband, her duty as a wife was to endure her situation. And the Couriers had a reputation in town. In the church's eyes Martha was less a Mary Magdalene than the Whore of Babylon.

'I found their attitudes callous and unchristian. It didn't make me very popular in the diocese hierarchy. The bishop decided it would be best to post me elsewhere.'

'Warsaw?' Grazja asked.

'Close,' Frank smiled. 'Birmingham. I liked it. It was a more progressive parish. I loved the people. As a boy from just outside Dublin I hadn't much experience of living in a multicultural society so Brum was a shock. For a few years I thrived, managing to stifle my doubts about the church, about religion.'

'You had doubts as a priest about God?' Grazja sounded shocked.

'Less rare than you might think,' Frank said. 'But at the time it was less about God, and more about some of the teachings of Catholicism. In all honesty, I'd started to question it in seminary school. I couldn't admit that at the time. My mother is a fervent Catholic. I have two sisters and three brothers, and it was always expected I'd go into the priesthood. It's what I thought I wanted. I loved the ritual, the sense of community, the 'high theatre' of mass, and the release of confession. In fact, I still do. But other aspects began to bother me and I kept pushing them down. The thought of dropping out and crushing my family's expectations just wasn't a consideration.

'Anyway, my Birmingham years were happy ones for the most part until something completely unexpected happened. I fell in love with a woman in my congregation.'

'Ah!' said Grazja.

'Celibacy is never easy. In my teens I pretty much thought about sex every two seconds and wondered how I'd ever survive the priesthood, but as an adult it wasn't so bad. Difficult, but suppressible with a very busy schedule.

'Until she came. Rachel. Then, as the cliché goes, all the love songs suddenly made sense. I fought it, and fought it, and fought it but I burned with love and with lust. Popping the wafer into her mouth at communion became an act so erotically charged I felt everyone in the church would feel it. It shook me to my very core. We would sneak moments together, arrange illicit meetings, and talk about me leaving the priesthood so we could marry.

'After a year I couldn't bear it any longer. I had to be with her; I had to leave the priesthood. It would break my mother's heart but what could I do? Rachel was everything.

'I talked to my superior. He was sympathetic but dismissive. He told me to wait, not do anything hasty. All priests were tested at some point. I must pray for strength.

'I was adamant. I wrote to the bishop explaining my situation, begging for dispensation.

'Then something happened. Something I'd never imagined could happen.'

'What?' Grazja asked.

'Rachel fell in love with another man.' Frank said. 'Seemingly overnight.'

'No!'

Frank nodded ruefully. 'With hindsight I think it was the excitement of an illicit affair with a priest that drove her relationship with me. Once the reality of me leaving the priesthood to marry her started to look real she lost interest, or got scared. One or the other. Six months later she was married to someone else.'

'And you?' Grazja probed.

'I was in Warsaw,' Frank said. 'Rachel left me heartbroken and humiliated. I'd never felt pain like it. My senior priest said it was God's will. He wanted me for the priesthood, and in time I would thank Him.

'I withdrew my request for dispensation but requested I be posted elsewhere with a new role. I felt too bitter and shattered to be a comfort to my parishioners, and I had betrayed them with my affair. Not that they knew. I least I hope they didn't. We were very careful.'

'Somebody always knows,' Grazja said. 'So they sent you to Poland.'

'Exactly,' Frank said. 'I think they saw it as a punishment, but for me it was exciting. Warsaw, even a few years after the collapse of the USSR, was chaotic. A city in transition, new possibilities opening up, new buildings, a buzz in the air.

'They sent me to a school to teach English. I didn't speak a word of Polish and my pupils very little English, so at first it was a struggle. But Fr Tomasz, who ran the school, did speak English. He taught me Polish. He was a fantastic teacher. A wonderful man, and very popular. He'd been a vocal supporter for Solidarity in the eighties – a brave thing to be after the Communists murdered Jerzy Popieluszco.'

Grazja nodded.

'Fr Tomasz was a hero to me. He restored my faith – temporarily at least. I discovered I loved teaching. As well as English, I taught the boys to box. I'd learnt it as boy and teenager - was pretty good at it...'

'Now I understand your knockout punch,' Grazja interrupted.

Frank looked sheepish. 'Yes. Some things you don't forget how to do.

'Boxing is good for adolescent boys. Everything is so confusing at that age. You have too much energy, too much aggression; your sex hormones are going mad but if you're Catholic you have all the guilt to contend with too. Boxing is a safe outlet for the aggression, the frustration. It provides discipline. Not for all boys of course, but for a lot of them. Our boys came from tough backgrounds. It gave them somewhere to go.

'I ran the local club. Even boys who didn't attend our school came along. And I didn't run it alone. Other priests coached too. Fr Tomasz had been a prizefighter in his youth.

'One boy, Jarek, stood out with talent. He had speed, grace, strength, and incredible coordination.

'He was only eleven when he joined; by thirteen he'd started to shoot up, put on muscle and was taking on boys much older than himself.

'Saturday matches drew crowds – parents and priests – as our boys competed against other clubs. Jarek was the star attraction. Out of the ring he was an amiable lad, but as he got older he became increasingly moody, and in the ring he began to behave as though he was trying to kill his opponent, not just beat him. I tried to talk to him about it a number of times but he was sullen and tight-lipped. Being stupid and naïve I put it down to adolescent moodiness.'

'It wasn't?' Grazja asked.

Frank sighed. 'It seems obvious now, in light of all the terrible revelations about paedophile priests in the news, but until only a few years ago it was never talked about. Oh, you heard whispers, rumours – especially in the seminary – but it was taboo. I suppose those in the know shared it with each other, but not one priest ever mentioned it to me. Certainly the victims didn't talk about it. Every Catholic child sees priests as almost godlike. A mini god, not to be questioned.

And shame is the most powerful silencer in the world. It's an overpowering system – corrupt – and until recently entirely without answer to any other authority than itself. A self-protecting insulated monster.'

Frank sounded bitter.

Grazja touched his sleeve lightly. 'Go on,' she said.

'I discovered it by accident,' Frank said heavily. 'I left my wallet back at the boxing club one night. I thought everyone had left; it was dark. I switched on the light and saw Jarek being … well, I won't go into details. He was being abused by one of my junior coaches, Fr. Borys, a priest I worked with, laughed with, ate my lunch with. Not a good friend but a colleague.

'We were all frozen to the spot. Then my colleague sprang back, yanked up his trousers and rushed from the gym, leaving me with Jarek. The poor boy was beyond humiliated. I turned my back to give him time to get sorted and then we talked.

'You can imagine how hard that was for the boy. It was as though he was spitting up hard knots of wire wool. His emotions were everywhere. Tears, fury, shame, terror, guilt – he ran the gamut.

'It had been going on for over a year. Fr. Borys had fed him all the usual lies, messed around with his mind the way abusers always do. I'd heard it before in confession – the confused way the victim always blames themselves - I heard it when

Martha came to me. But I'd never heard it from a child. Perhaps I'd been lucky. How many priests do hear it in confessional but bound by the seal never act? How many children have 'confessed' and never received the help they needed?'

'What did you do?' Grazja asked.

Frank looked at her. 'Jarek begged me not to tell anyone. He was so ashamed. He couldn't face his parents knowing. Couldn't face anyone else knowing. And besides, he said, they wouldn't believe him. Not about a priest. If I could just stop Fr. Borys that would be enough.

'I didn't think that was enough, but for the moment I reassured him I'd find a way to figure it out. I would see it didn't continue, that was for sure.

'I walked Jarek home and went back to my rooms at the school. Borys was waiting for me. He had the guilty look of a puppy who's peed on the carpet and expects to be mildly punished – *wants* to be punished – and then forgiven. I wanted to kill him.

'He wheedled and pleaded. 'It was a moment of weakness.' 'Jarek kept coming to me, tempting me.' All the crap. All the usual, stupid crap. 'He would never do it again. Surely, I understood about the temptations of the flesh. Rumour had it that I had broken my vows with a parishioner back in England.

'I grabbed him, crashed him against the wall. 'With an adult, Borys. A woman. Never with a child.'

261

'Jarek's no child,' he said. 'You can see that, surely. It's been him who's been chasing me. I'm not a homosexual. He's perverted me.'

'I thought about strangling him. 'You're *not* a homosexual, you're a paedophile.'

'He started to choke and I realized I was strangling him. I let go and stepped back.

'He rubbed his throat. 'What are you going to do?'

'I'm not going to let you get away with it. I'm taking it higher.'

'He bent over as though he was going to be sick, and said: 'You won't get anywhere. I'm not the only one.'

'His words froze my blood. 'What do you mean?'

He began to stagger away. 'Nothing. You won't get anywhere. You'll see.'

Frank was trembling.

'I get you glass of water,' Grazja said. 'Your tea is cold now.'

She disappeared into the kitchen while Frank regained his equilibrium.

When she was seated again, he said. 'I've only ever told one other person all of this. Are you sure you want to hear the rest?'

'I have to,' Grazja said. 'There is no going back.'

Frank nodded.

'I went to Fr. Tomasz. He was the head of the school, had years of experience and there was no one I respected more. He listened gravely and carefully, heard me out. At the end he put his hand on my shoulder and said. 'It is good you came to me. I'll deal with Fr. Borys.'

'My relief was huge. Fr. Tomasz believed me and was willing to do something.

'The next day Borys had gone. I assumed he'd been suspended while the case was being reviewed, and that it would be taken up with the police. Jarek didn't come into school but I thought he'd need some time off.

'I broached the subject very carefully in my English class, telling the boys that if in any circumstances they felt an adult – a priest – touched them in a way they felt uncomfortable with, they could tell me. It was awkward. Some of the boys made a joke of it. Others looked like I was insane, while others looked at me as though they saw a potential molester.

'The next evening a boy slid a note under my door. He assumed it was anonymous as he hadn't signed it but I taught him and recognised his handwriting. He didn't name the priests but he indicated there was more than one paedophile in the school. When I tried to talk to him he clammed up and denied ever writing the note.

'Another boy did come to see me. He was fourteen and another victim of Borys.

'I went back to Fr. Tomasz, showed him the letter, and said another boy had come forward. I confided I was worried it hadn't just been Borys.

'This time Fr. Tomasz wasn't so sympathetic. 'It's all round the school that you are stirring up trouble,' he told me. 'You plant a seed like this in a young boy's head it will grow like a weed in his imagination. I'm surprised you've not had fifty notes. Boys make things up. And as for this other boy, well, even if what he claims about Borys is true it is not our problem anymore. Borys has been relocated, and I doubt we'll see him again.'

'Relocated? Not to another school, surely? He should have been reported to the police.'

'Fr. Tomasz waved me away. 'The police! This is a church matter. We deal with our own. There is no need to wash our dirty linen in public. The Pope, and above all God, is who we answer to.'

'But Borys committed a crime, not just a small sin he can say a few Hail Marys for. A hideous crime against children.'

'They are not children,' Fr. Tomasz dismissed me. 'They are adolescents. Their minds are already filled with licentious thoughts.'

'He softened. 'Frank, you and I are good friends. Let's not fall out over this. When you've lived to my age you've seen the weakness of the human flesh time and again. We all know of priests – good men – who love youth too much. You yourself sinned with a woman. We are frail beings who try our best, but sometimes we fall. It is between us and God whether we truly repent and enter Heaven or suffer the flames of damnation. Only God can judge and know our hearts.

'When I see evil in my school I try to root it out, as I did as soon as you told me about Borys. I have done this a number of times over the years, Frank, and I can honestly say, as long as these boys repent of their part in the sin, they grow up and move on into manhood with no lasting damage.'

'His expression was kindly. He actually thought he was comforting me.

'I stumbled out of his room completely bewildered, sick to my stomach. I didn't sleep all night. The following morning I'd made up my mind to go to the police, but first I wanted to talk to Jarek. He still hadn't been back to school or the boxing club. His mother answered the door and seemed pathetically grateful to see me.

'Oh, Fr. Frank, how good of you to come. Perhaps Jarek will do penitence for you.'

'Penitence. What for?'

'She gave me an odd look. 'For being a bully, of course. That's why he's on suspension. He's been hitting the other boys so hard lately. I don't know what's wrong with him. He used to be such a good boy.'

'Jarek had been suspended to keep him out of the way. My heart sank. He would think I was responsible.

'He did. I found him in the yard, a bundle of barely reigned in fury.

'You said you wouldn't tell,' he hissed.

'I said I would figure out how to deal with it. Fr. Borys is gone, Jarek.'

'And I am being punished. They know. They all know.' His tears were hot with fear and humiliation. 'They don't say it but that is why I am suspended.'

'Only Fr. Tomasz knows,' I said. 'No one else.'

'They all know,' he repeated. 'And Fr. Borys hasn't gone far. My cousin told me yesterday that he has a new PE teacher at his school, and asked me if I knew him.'

265

'I stared at him, horrified. It made me more determined to go to the police.

'Jarek,' I said. 'I want to tell the police about Fr. Borys. What he's doing is a crime. He needs to be stopped.'

'No!' Jarek looked terrified. 'No one else can know. Not my parents. They will hate me. They will call me a pervert and unclean. Please don't, Fr. Frank.'

'But what about your cousin, Jarek? Do you want the same thing to happen to him?'

'Jarek shook his head. 'I told him there were rumours about Fr. Borys, and he must never be alone with him. Besides, Aleksy is ugly; Fr Borys will not notice him.'

'It was desperate reasoning but I didn't want to push him further. Jarek was close to breaking.

'Alright,' I said. 'I'll tell the police what has happened but I won't tell them your name. I am a priest too; they will trust my word.'

'Jarek wasn't happy but I felt I must do something. Fr Borys couldn't be let loose in another school.

'So I went to the policja. As a priest I was treated deferentially and dealt with straightaway by the junior commissioner of the station. He listened politely and took notes. I was surprised he didn't press me for the name of the boy involved but relieved too. At the end he thanked me, shook my hand, and said it was a very serious issue and they would look into it.

'When would I hear back, I wanted to know. Soon, he reassured me and ushered me out.

'It was an oddly deflating experience. I returned to my room at school, excusing myself from taking my class with a migraine. I needed time to think. Old doubts were resurfacing, along with more worrying new ones.'

'You were thinking about leaving?' Grazja asked.

'I was certainly having a crisis of the soul,' Frank admitted. 'But I wasn't thinking of leaving the church – not yet. Where would I go? With Rachel I had someone to go to; I was overtaken by the euphoria of love. I was building romantic castles in the sky. This was a very different crisis. In fact, if Rachel had taught me anything it was that the church was my family, my community; It was the thing that I clung to after she broke my heart. Fr. Tomasz particularly had provided deep friendship.

'So, I wasn't on the verge of leaving at that moment.'

'But you did eventually,' Grazja said.

'Oh, much sooner than 'eventually',' Frank said with a wry smile. 'The next day I was summoned to Fr Tomasz's office. To my surprise the bishop was there.

'Fr Tomasz took my hand and held it for a moment. His smile was sad. My first thought was that my mother or a member of my family had died. But why involve the bishop?

'Fr. Manning,' the bishop said. 'The police commissioner kindly contacted me yesterday. He voiced concerns about your mental well-being, saying you had concocted a dangerously wild story about a fellow priest. Fortunately we have a close relationship with our esteemed policja, and he had the good sense to contact me.'

'I told him the truth,' I said.

'The bishop stopped me with a gesture. 'I'm sure you think you did,' he said. 'Fr. Tomasz has explained that recent events have overly disturbed you. They have been dealt with yet you cannot let them go.

'This seems to be a pattern. First your inappropriate behaviour with the woman in Southend …'

'Inappropriate! I helped her as a priest should do.'

'Rubbish,' the bishop snapped. 'You helped her leave her marriage – a sacred covenant in God's eyes – and came close to breaking the seal of confession but for a technicality. Your English bishops are softer, I think. I would have been rid of you. And how did you thank your church? You entered into an affair with a member of your congregation! You broke your vows of celibacy!'

'He tapped a fax on the desk. 'I have the evidence here: your letter begging for dispensation, as well as a written statement from your senior priest in Birmingham confirming you admitted to fornicating with this woman.'

'That was a private conversation,' I said.

'He snorted. 'It did not take place under the seal of confession. According to his report you were not repentant. You wished to abandon your mother church for this woman, and when she rejected you, you clung instead to our skirts. Sent here by your soft bishop, given into the compassionate care of Fr. Tomasz, you sucked the milk of our kindness, only to now spit it back in our faces.'

'I felt too weary to protest.

'We, the church, have fed you, clothed you, housed you, loved you,' he went on. 'We have forgiven you when you trespassed against us. And now, you who have sinned so often, dare to judge us on one priest who has fallen to temptation once, repented and been forgiven as we have forgiven you who has not repented. You try to tear down our house with your visit to the policja. It is too much.

'I am stripping you of the priesthood. You are not worthy. You are to be laicized.'

Fr Tomasz put his head in his hands and wept.

'I stood in total shock.

'Laicized. Stripped, effectively of the priesthood, forbidden to perform the duties of the priest, no longer 'Father Frank' but a layman with no place in the church, nowhere to live, no income.

'No identity.

'I opened my mouth to argue but nothing came out.

'You have a week,' the bishop said. 'To make your arrangements. Then you must be gone.'

Grazja reached out her hand for his. 'Oh, Frank. I am so sorry.'

Frank blinked. He enfolded her hand into his and gave a weak smile.

'I was in a daze,' he continued. 'It was as though I had a communicable disease, the way people avoided me. The other priests and staff. I wasn't allowed to say goodbye to my students. My daze gave way to anger. I had nothing else to lose, so I organised a meeting with a journalist from the Warsaw Voice. I wanted some sort of justice for Jarek and the other boys who'd been – probably were being – abused.

'Again, the journalist listened, sympathised, but said: 'There is not a newspaper who will print this, or a TV programme that will run it. The Catholic Church is simply too strong in Poland. One day, perhaps. But we are a Roman Catholic nation. We all know of bad priests, but we do not want to believe they exist in our neighbourhoods.

'Maybe in future years it will change. But for now, no; no editor would touch it. And not from you, I'm afraid – a laicized foreign priest. It would be you under scrutiny. You would be ripped to shreds. You have made sure the boy is safe. Leave it alone and go make a new life.'

'I took her advice, I'm ashamed to say. I gave up and came home to stay with my sister, the one who helped Martha. I went into a state of deep depression and shock. It took me months to tell my mother I'd been laicized; she still doesn't talk to me.

'I don't know how my sister coped with me. She's a wonderful person. Eventually she got me a job at her local B&Q. I didn't want to be round people anymore but it was the best thing for me. It gave me a routine and a regular income. People came to me for help with easily answerable questions. Where could they find a wrench? What was the correct fitting for this kind of tap? I had always been pretty handy at DIY; even in the priesthood I'd been the go-to-guy to put up a shelf, or fix a leak. My dad had worked as a handyman, so I'd picked it up.

'It felt good to have the simple answers to simple problems. No soul-searching, no confessions, no moral conundrums; just good practical advice.

'Gradually I picked up the pieces of my life.'

Frank looked at Grazja. 'Like I said, you're only the second person I've told *all* of this to. Do you know who the first was?'

'Your sister?' Grazja said.

'No. Some obviously, but not all. It was Martha, I told.'

'Martha!' Grazja looked surprised.

He nodded. 'We stayed in touch during all those years. I don't even know why. She wrote to say thanks for my help and I wrote back. And we continued writing throughout the years, then emailing, occasionally meeting up. We became friends. I liked John and her children. Apart from my sister, I felt that they were more my family than my parents and siblings were.

'A couple of years after my disgraced return to England, I got a letter from Fr. Tomasz. I don't know how he traced me but he did. He was writing to tell me some sad news. Jarek had killed a boy in the boxing ring. He had punched him so hard in the head the other boy had suffered an epidural haemorrhage.

'The news devastated me. I felt I had abandoned Jarek to his pain and rage as much as the church had. As much as Fr. Tomasz. Now Jarek would have to live with this burden too.'

271

'You did what you could,' Grazja said. 'More than anyone else.'

Frank shook his head. 'I could have tried harder. Fought on until someone listened. Or sent my address to Jarek so he could at least write to me when he needed a person to talk to.

'I was the lucky one with someone to confide in. I visited Martha in Mapton and told her the entire sordid story.

'She thought I needed a change of perspective and a new start. She told me that the Formans had an ad in the trade paper for someone to take over the lease of the ghost train. It would be perfect for me. It would be fun; I'd see people but not have to interact too much. I'd be near to her and John. More importantly nobody would know who I was; know I'd been a priest. People knew in Southend where I lived with my sister. Of course they did; it was where I'd started off. I was the subject of gossip and speculation when I returned broken and 'defrocked'.

'A fresh beginning appealed to me. Working in a fun fair would be novel. So I applied and the rest, as they say, is history.'

'But you didn't leave past behind, did you?' Grazja said.

He cocked his head. 'Why do you say that?'

'You dress as a monk – close to a priest, yes? – you say: 'Dare you face your sins in the dark?'

Frank's smile was sad. 'Ah, you've got me there. It was something Fr. Tomasz wrote in his letter. He said: 'I thought about you a lot after you'd gone. I came to see you as brave. I told myself I had acted only to protect my beloved church and truly believed that any transgressions my boys occasionally endured were but fleeting moments to be forgotten. When I encountered an errant priest I admonished him, or sent him to another post with promises to start afresh and a soul washed clean by repentance. I told myself it was enough.

'In the daytime I believe it. But during the night, when I can't sleep, such as now, I see Jarek's face, and that of the boy he killed, and I wonder if you were right. I ask myself: do I dare face my sins in the dark? Can I be a brave man like you?'

'It is such a *serious* question to ask happy holidaymakers,' Grazja said.

'It is,' Frank agreed. 'But I run a ghost train, and what are ghosts if not the remnants of past sins that appear in the dark?'

Grazja shuddered.

Frank smiled again, but this time his smile was like opening the door to spring after a cold, hard winter.

Grazja couldn't help smiling back.

'There is a happy ending of sorts,' Frank said.

'There is?'

'I did get back in touch with Jarek. At first I thought my letters weren't reaching him. But then, after some months of writing every week, I received a short reply. He'd got into more trouble – stealing – and was in a juvenile detention centre. He was only writing back to let me know how much he hated me. So he said, but I sensed differently, so I continued to write to him.

'Letter writing is becoming a lost art; emails are much more convenient but don't have the depth. Jarek didn't have access to a computer so letters were the best way to communicate. And they give you time to think, what to say, how to respond. Over time, Jarek opened up. His guilt about taking a boy's life was immense. It threatened to drown him. He'd never imagined it could really happen; the boxing ring had seemed the only safe place to let out his rage; his pain. After I'd left, a new coach took over the club and he'd encouraged Jarek's aggression in the ring.

'Jarek saw the boy's face in his dreams. The boy had been the only child born to a middle-aged couple, a gift that had come late to them.

'Jarek was doubly haunted, by the memory of his abuse, and by the boy he had killed.'

'Poor boy,' Grazja said. 'I thought this story had a happy ending.'

'It does,' Frank replied. 'Jarek survived. He turned his life around. He is a builder in England. He makes better money here, and what he makes he sends home, not to his mother and father, but to the mother of the boy he killed. She is a widow; a woman of enormous compassion. Jarek wrote to her too, while in detention, not to beg forgiveness – he thought that too much to ask – but to express his enormous regret for what he had done.

'She came to see him; forgave him. If I still believed in miracles I would think that one. Today he is more a son to her than to his own parents.

'And, as if that weren't enough, last year Jarek and I travelled back to Warsaw together. The policja had opened an investigation in historic abuse cases by Catholic priests. Fr. Borys was on the list. We both testified. Borys is behind bars. Jarek wasn't his only victim, or his last.

'That is the sin I face in the dark; that I left Poland knowing Borys was still working with children.'

'You went to the police and the media,' Grazja said. 'What else could you do?'

Frank shrugged. 'That's the question I ask again and again. I still don't know the answer.'

Twits and Pieces

The video of Frank punching Darren went viral in Mapton, Siltby and surrounding areas. Tweets flitted back and forth in the twittosphere:

@Suemarauder: Gentelman Dfends honor of lady. Tru Knight.

@seasaltlicks: OMG! Just peed pants. Sooooo funny. Mapton rocks.

@Lawtonmummy: Once again Mapton people act like animals. Drop into sea Mapton. Good riddance to rubbish.

@Suemarauder: @Lawtonmummy u shutup. This man fights for his lady. No one would fight 4 u!!!

@deckchairdude: @Lawtonmummy keep stuck up nose out of our business bitch or I'll come sort you out good.

@Lawtonmummy: thanks for proving my point@deckchairdude. Crawl back into the primordial slime.

@cobstopdan: Was there. Rick Blake totally took piss singing Cmon People. No respect. Deserved a twatting. Buoycot his diner!

@MrBig: Frank Manning is my hero! What a right hook. Bilson deserved it. Cock.

@barflyD: stop slagging off the competition@cobstopdan. So obvious. No, u wasnt there.

@Pamdoll: I was there. Darren Bilson stirring up trouble. Been doing it all over town. Deserved wot he got. End of.

@Suemarauder: @Pamdoll well sed Darren made trouble at diner too. Needs taking down.

@seasaltlick: Ha ha ha! Watch this CHEESE:www.youtube.com/watch?v=KswPEy9hG2

Seasaltlick had set the video of the fight to Peter Cetera's The Glory of Love. The lyrics blared out over the image:

Off social media the fight was as much the subject of gossip in Mapton. Far more people claimed to have been in the Helmet than could have possibly have fitted in the entire pub, never mind the function room. In an autumn that had seen one sensational topic after another hit the town, Maptonites hadn't lost their appetite for scandal or tongue wagging.

Opinion was, as usual, divided, but people seemed to be swaying towards Frank's side, especially women, who, never having given him more than a glance before, suddenly saw him in a whole new light. Rick too; although he hadn't swung the punch, he had squared up to Darren and defended Stella. But Rick had often caught the eye of more than one Mapton woman; with his sexy accent and crinkly blue eyes he'd always been a draw until he married that artist from London. Frank, on the other hand, was a revelation. Soon, his relationship with Grazja was the subject of much speculation – a larger than life romance bloomed in the minds of Mapton dreamers. Who knew that such passion existed beneath his mild exterior?

'Blimey,' Gina remarked to George. 'I'd never have seen Frank as a gusset-quiverer.'

Gina's leaflet in the form of a letter was causing quite a stir too.

The personal touch pleased many and irked others.

'I'd forgotten how rundown them beach huts used to be,' Paul Ferguson said to his friend Bob.

'Aye, council didn't even send tractor down that way to clean the sand,' Bob said. 'Not till Gina and Stella started doing up them beach huts. Then Gina were after them every day to do that part of the beach. She don't give up, I'll say that for her.'

'Well, I won't be voting for that woman,' Marjorie Suspring announced, as she served Paul Ferguson on the Co-op checkout. 'She accused me of overcharging her once. Made a right scene, and in the end it was her fault. She didn't read the price of a packet of Persil – wanted the 1kg for the price of a 500g pack. Screamed blue murder, she did, and never apologised after the manager came and showed her she was wrong. I nearly died of embarrassment. Everyone was watching.'

Somehow the news of the fight became inextricably linked in Maptonites' minds with Gina's campaign. They appeared in the local collective consciousness at the same time, and the fight involved Gina's family and friends.

But it also had something to do with the growing feeling of dislike towards Darren Bilson.

Older folk remembered that Darren had been a brawler in his teens. He'd appeared to have matured upon his return to Siltby but recently he'd been strutting around like a pumped-up cockerel, shaking his tail feathers and crowing in people's faces. His new commitment to a moral cause like the sex camp protest caused a few raised eyebrows but he seemed to be serious. Indeed, he'd gathered a little following of men impressed with his bluster, Andy Timmis one of them.

But Darren had made mistakes lately. Rick may have been a silly bugger in his refusal to sign the petition, but he was well liked throughout town. Plus, his business partner was Ange. She was a Mapton girl through and through. Rick had given her the chance to half own the diner – allowed her to buy in for less than what it was worth if rumour was true – and Ange was able to leave her ne'r-do-well husband Des and make a good life in her home town. So, Darren's first mistake had been his attempt to boycott the diner. In doing so he also alienated the younger Timmis boys, popular lads in the town, who'd begun to make it clear they were no longer on his team.

The fight in The Diving Helmet showed Darren up as a bully. Either he'd forgotten about phone cameras or he simply hadn't understood how he'd come across, but it didn't work to his advantage. Yes, he had his supporters, but overall the damage was done.

Andy Timmis had hitched his horse to the wrong wagon. Everyone knew he'd been hanging out with Darren.

Yet, that wasn't Andy's only trouble. Carole had finished with him.

So it was that Rick, taking a walk on the mostly deserted beach the Sunday morning after the fight, spotted Andy sitting miserably on the prom steps in the rain, staring out to sea.

At first Rick was going to avoid him, but something about Andy's disconsolate posture made him reconsider.

'Hey Andy,' he said, approaching. 'You okay, man? This ain't the weather to be sitting out in.'

'You're out in it,' Andy said.

'Yeah, but I'm bundled up and on my way home. What about you?'

Andy squinted up at Rick, as though only just recognising him. Various emotions scudded across his face before settling on abject misery.

'I been an idiot, Rick,' he said. 'A total twat.'

'Yeah?' Rick said. 'Can't say I've noticed.'

Andy, digesting this, gave a weak smile. 'She broke up with me.' He looked as though he was about to cry.

Rick tentatively sat down next to him on the cold concrete. 'Who? Carole?'

'Carole,' Andy sighed her name like a prayer. 'Last night. Said she liked me – had liked me for longer than I knew – but she didn't like what I was becoming. It was your fight with Darren that did it.'

'Hey,' Rick held up his hands. 'I didn't start that.'

'You didn't end it either,' Andy said. 'Frank did that. I watched it on YouTube. Darren came across like a right prick.'

'They say the camera never lies,' Rick said. 'But I don't see what it had to do with Carole. You weren't involved.'

'Yeah, but since I've started to pal on with Darren, she said he's been a bad influence.'

'Is she right?'

'Mebbe. I suppose so. Darren got banned from the sand racing last winter for being too aggressive. Should've let that tell me somethin'. I been thinking about it all night.'

'About Darren?'

'No! About Carole. Never used to take much notice of her in The Marauders. I go for good-looking birds usually. Not had much luck with 'em.'

'Carole's nice-looking,' Rick said.

'Yes! Yeah, she is,' Andy said enthusiastically. 'Funny I didn't notice before. Cos she let her hair go grey and don't wear much make-up. But when you look at her – really look at her - you see she's pretty. And nice too. Kind. Considerate.'

'That's Carole,' Rick agreed. 'Sounds like you really like her.'

'I do,' Andy said glumly. 'I didn't realise it till she broke up wi' me. Didn't even realise we were together actually, not like a proper couple. I think... I think I were using her a bit.'

'Then good for Carole,' Rick said. 'She deserves better.'

'She does,' Andy hung his head. 'She said she'd made up her mind; she'd rather be alone than with someone she can't respect. Said she'd been going along with me because she liked me and didn't want to lose me but she didn't want to do that anymore.'

'I like her more and more,' Rick said.

'Me too!' It was almost a sob. 'I think I love her. I effing love her, and I've been so stupid I couldn't even see it.'

'Wow,' Rick whistled. 'That's big. So what you gonna do about it?'

Andy stood up. 'I'm going to start by apologising to you, Rick.' He stuck out his hand. 'I should never have said the things I did. I been listening to the wrong people and letting my head get turned. I'm sorry I been such a prat.'

Rick rose to accept his handshake.

'Apology accepted. Now what do you say I open up the diner just for you. I'll whip up something that'll give you the energy to go get your woman back.'

Paradise Lost

Since the first week of the protest Dennis Payton had mostly kept his head down, only being seen as he drove in and out of the site. Work went on renovating The Paradise despite the protesters. One person had been zealous enough to lie down across the entranceway, and his mother had given him such a clip round the ear for the mud on his anorak that even he only did it once. No one else seemed to much fancy it.

The Paradise hadn't been so lovingly looked after since its early days, long before Dennis had taken over. The protesters watched as skips filled up with old fittings, scarred tables, wobbly chairs, and manky carpet tiles, and new ones arrived. A timber-framed sauna and jacuzzi extension was half built already.

If it wasn't for the intended purpose of a swingers' club, Mapton would have welcomed the changes.

In fact, although it remained a 'hot topic' general interest in the coming and goings at The Paradise were on the wane. Christmas was looming, the days were short and the nights long. Only the dedicated core of protesters held the line, Knights and Crusaders pitted as much against each other as against Dennis.

Andy had re-joined the Knights after withdrawing his name from the electoral race, leaving Gina in direct contention with Tony Forbes. He had won Carole back by metaphorically prostrating himself before the

Knights and thus, The Marauders, and begging forgiveness. This was magnanimously given.

Sue, with open arms: 'Oh, come here yer great lunk.'

George: 'We all make mistakes but it takes a big man to admit it.'

And Gina: 'You stupid bogger. Don't bleedin' do it again.'

The Crusaders shrunk in numbers. Some slunk away, others shuffled over the invisible line that separated them from the Knights, and rejoined the women.

The core group that remained took on an almost rabid demeanour. Darren, humiliated by Frank, had something to prove, and channelled his aggression into the protest. He lobbed eggs at Dennis's car, and once he jumped on the bonnet, pounding on the windscreen before his friends dragged him off.

Jim stuck with him, as did Pious Pauline, who, seeming to think she was Joan of Arc, had begun to turn up in chainmail and a helmet, a metal cross the size of Coke can clanking across her considerable chest.

The district council refused to speed up a decision on Dennis's application or be pressured into turning it down.

Then, after weeks of staying low, Dennis made another bid for most hated man in Mapton.

On the night of the big Christmas switch on, when Maptonites gathered to see Acting Mayor Tom Turner, and local celebrity crooner, Dusty Velvet, hit the switch to the high street festive lights, Dennis Payton switched on his own.

It was a Christmas cracker alright.

Dennis had parked a delivery lorry in front of The Paradise entrance during the day, and brought in a couple of his old buddies from his biker days to stop any nosy protesters from sneaking a look round the sides. One of them Sam 'Wolf' Hodson, brought his Husky, Killer, with him. Everyone knew Killer was as soft as a cuddly toy, but Wolf wasn't. Even Darren Bilson gave him room, although he did a lot of 'barking' from a distance.

The amount of banging, sawing, and drilling that came from behind the lorry piqued the curiosity of the onlookers, but by the time the Christmas light switch was thrown in Mapton centre, only Pious Pauline and Jim were left on site, playing serious tonsil hockey in the back seat of Jim's car as he fought to break into her chainmail.

'It's wrong, it's wrong,' shrieked Pauline as she grabbed Jim's buttocks and pulled him against her vast bosom. 'Lord forgive me!'

She screamed as the car was suddenly flooded with light, dazzling her. 'I am blinded! I repent. I repent, Lord. I am coming.' She scrambled out from beneath Jim and tumbled out of the car, stumbling toward the light.

The next thing Jim heard was Pauline's squeal of rage. 'Sinner. Blasphemer! You will burn, burn…'

Jim clambered out of the car. He saw Pauline, silhouetted before an enormous flashing sign.

WELCOME TO PARADISE
PLEASURE CAMP FOR ADULTS

OPENING SOON

Flanking the sign were two couples etched out in bulbs. The bulbs flashed sequentially. One moment the couples were clothed, the next the women were bare breasted with the men cupping their breasts and winking.

Next to them two Christmas trees twinkled merrily. Strangely this last touch seemed like a two finger salute in the context of their surroundings.

Jim grinned. He flicked open his phone. 'You're not going to believe what that bastard Payton's done now. You better get yerself down here.'

Word spread fast. Maptonites, enjoying the Christmas buzz with their kids, family, and friends started to hear about the display up at The Paradise.

Tom Turner heard about it. 'Bloody idiot,' he murmured to his wife.

Gina, out and about with Gerta, Stella and Rick, was glad-handing like a pro-politician when she heard about it.

'The dirty bogger,' she exploded. 'I'll put a stop to that.'

Stella looked at Rick.

'No way,' he said. 'I've seen enough trouble. You go if you want to; I'll stay here with Gerta and have us some fun.'

'I have to see this,' Stella said, eyes guilty. 'And someone needs to control Gina.'

'Like you can do that,' Rick snorted. 'Go on. Just be careful. If it looks like it's going to get nasty, leave. Immediately.'

Sue heard; the Marauders set off along the prom in battalion formation.

Frank, enjoying a mulled wine with Grazja at one of the stalls, noticed the growing number of groups heading out of town towards the seafront.

Sugsy called to him as he went past. 'C'mon Frank, we're going to need your right hook.'

Frank looked at Grazja, who shrugged.

'Something's going on,' he said.

'Yeah,' Rick said, appearing beside them with Gerta. 'Trouble, that's what.' He told them about Dennis.

'We stay here,' Grazja said resolutely, taking Frank's arm.

'Definitely,' Frank agreed.

Andrew Leith, feeling despondent at being back on the reporting-beat of small-town events, caught the scent of a story, and took off at a sprint towards the Paradise.

As the groups joined together on their march to the Paradise, no one brandished burning torches but quite a few glow sticks purchased at the Christmas market waved around in the crowd.

The mood was swiftly turning mobbish as the Paradise's illuminations came into view.

Dennis was waiting for them, standing on the wooden block steps normally used to reach the stage in the clubhouse. He was flanked by Wolf and three of his tattooed biker buddies. One, Paul 'Harley' Davies, was as large as a grizzly. Like Killer, his looks belied a soft nature, but his sheer size was enough to intimidate. They stood with their arms crossed, enjoying the chance to look mean.

Darren Bilson, who'd been drinking in The Swan when he got the call from Jim, pushed his way to the front where Pious Pauline was already ranting at Dennis about fornication and the hell fires waiting for him.

'You pushed this too far now, Dennis,' he shouted. 'You're taking the piss.'

'Language Darren,' Dennis said into a loudspeaker. 'I notice some kiddies here.'

He was right. In their eagerness to see what was going on, some parents had come with their kids.

'You shouldn't be talking about kids,' someone shouted. 'Not with what you're doing.'

'Can't you read the sign?' Dennis replied. 'It says 'for adults'. Shame on you for bringing your kiddies.'

'Shame on us?' Gina shouted, jostling to the front. 'Shame on you, yer dirty bogger. What sort of sign is that? Disgustin'. You did this on purpose, Dennis Payton, stealing the thunder from the Christmas lights.' The crowd growled in agreement.

Dennis smiled lizard-like. 'I'm just being civic, would-be-councillor Pontin. Putting my lights up like everyone else.'

'Civic my arse,' Gina said. 'You wanted us all here, din't yer? Why?'

'You're not as stupid as you look,' he said. 'As a matter of fact I've got an announcement to make.' He paused dramatically. Everyone leaned in.

'Go on,' someone cried. 'Tell us yer bastard.'

'It's not official yet,' Dennis projected his voice. 'But I have it on good authority that my licence application has been approved.' He waved to his flashing sign. 'So as you see, Paradise Pleasure Camp will be opening soon.'

The bulb girls cheekily flashed their breasts.

'Tear down the sign,' a man yelled.

Darren suddenly charged, leaping up the steps before Wolf's men could stop him, knocking Dennis off his podium. Behind him the mob surged forward towards the illuminated scaffolding, roaring. Kids dragged along with parents started to bawl. Some people scrambled to get out of the crowd.

Sirens wailed and blue lights whirled, as two police vans screeched to a stop and officers piled out.

It was all over quite quickly.

Gina was knocked over in the surge, and was lucky no one actually trampled her. Stella, who, sensing trouble had moved to the edge of the crowd, saw her go down and fought her way to her.

Gina, despite a shallow gash to her forehead, was conscious. Stella pulled her to her feet and tried to hustle her out of harm's way but Gina yanked herself free and climbed the podium, grabbing the discarded megaphone on the way.

'Oy,' she roared into the megaphone, causing it to squeal feedback.

The frenzied mob seemed to freeze in to a tableau at the sound of her voice. Alf, who'd just knocked down a Christmas tree with his scooter, braked guiltily. Even Pauline, wrestling with Harley, turned to look.

Gina, illuminated by various blinking lights, blood trickling down her face, threw out her arms imploringly. She didn't need the megaphone.

'Look what you're doing,' she bellowed. 'This ain't no way to go on. You got children here. Can't you hear them crying? I'm a pensioner and I've already been knocked down. You should be ashamed of yerselves.'

Dazed, people blinked at her, looked around at each other and at the smashed bits of glass and wood on the ground. They seized their kids and hugged them.

'It were Dennis's fault,' a woman called weakly.

'And Darren Bilson's,' someone else added. 'He made the first move.'

'You were none of you far behind,' Gina said. She looked at one of the police officers, recognising him as Sergeant Johnson. She'd had dealings with him before when as a PC he'd been investigating Gina's dog, Bing Crosby, for criminal activities. 'You got here quick,' she said grudgingly.

'We had a tip-off,' he said approaching the podium. He climbed up beside her. 'Might have known you'd be involved,' he said quietly, then, as grudgingly as she had, he added. 'Well done for calming things down. Quick thinking. You need to get your head looked at; you're bleeding.' He turned. 'Officer Warren, escort Ms Pontin to the first aid kit.'

Gina reached up to touch her gash, saw her fingers covered in blood and squealed. She fainted at the sight.

Sergeant Johnson gallantly caught her. 'Get an ambulance out here too.'

#

Dennis had been bruised but was basically unhurt by Darren's attack. Luckily for him, Wolf had done his job, grabbing Darren and throwing him to the ground. When the police vans squealed onto the scene, Wolf paused before he put the boot in. Darren scrambled up, fleeing into the night, chased by Killer, who was more excited than vicious, and thought it all a great game.

The police put out an order to pick up Darren for questioning but he didn't go home or reappear anywhere public that night.

The entire incident was a difficult one for the police. A number of people had done criminal damage to Dennis Payton's property but establishing who did what was near impossible. The Paradise's sign, lights, and Christmas trees were beyond repair.

Pauline wanted to charge Harley with assault, yet Harley seemed the worst off, with a huge welt in the shape of a cross imprinted across his cheek.

The paramedics when they arrived were kept busy, not only with Gina's gash – less serious than all the blood had implied – but also with numerous cuts, bruises, and splinters, mainly to hands. One man had broken his toe trying to kick down the sign scaffold.

It was, as Sergeant Johnson said quietly to his officers, 'a clusterfuck'. The only thing that most people agreed on was that Darren Bilson had attacked Dennis. Most were also convinced that just before leaping on the podium, Darren had yelled 'Tear down the sign.' A couple of others disagreed, saying that it came from someone else, but they couldn't say who had yelled it.

In the end Maptonites were allowed to slope off to their homes, by foot or by scooter. Many hung their heads.

Andrew Leith wasn't one of them. He left head held high. As far as he was concerned it had been a fantastic evening.

But it wasn't over. In fact the unfortunate event was only a prelude.

In the middle of the night the Paradise clubhouse burnt down.

Ashes to Ashes

Rick woke to the sound of sirens. Climbing quietly out of bed he crossed to the window. Opening the curtains a crack he saw the unmistakeable flicker of orange in the night sky that signalled a fire. A large one – most likely a building – over by the seafront.

His first thought was for the diner.

'Stella,' he said, gently shaking his wife. 'Wake up! There's a fire.'

'What!' Stella sat bolt upright. 'Gerta!'

'No, no. Sorry. Not in the house. Somewhere by the seafront. I'm going to check it's not the diner.'

'I'll come,' Stella said, kicking her legs out of the covers. 'Oh, no, I can't leave Gerta.'

'You stay here,' Rick said. 'You've had enough excitement for one night.' He was pulling on his jeans and a sweater as he spoke.

Stella crossed to the window. More sirens split the night. 'Oh God,' she said. 'But I don't think it's the diner. It's too big.'

They looked at each other. 'The Paradise,' they said together.

For the second time in one evening Rick found himself observing groups of Maptonites flowing towards the Paradise. This time he followed them. He heard his name being called and looked back to see Frank hurrying to catch up to him.

'It never rains but it pours,' Rick said.

Frank nodded grimly.

As they reached the promenade they could see flames roaring up into the sky. Black smoke billowed. Even before they reached the site they could feel the heat. The air was acrid; ash floated.

Police and the fire service had set up a boundary to keep people well back from harm's way and let the fire crew work unimpeded.

'I hope no one was in there,' Frank said.

'Those bloody lights he put up probably set it off,' Dave Suggs said, joining them. 'Electrical fault.'

'I heard they were destroyed in the riot earlier on.'

'Wasn't quite a riot,' Sugsy said. 'Gina stopped it. Hero, she was.'

'They're not going to save that,' Frank said, gazing at the fire.

'Nah,' Rick said. 'It's gonna burn to the ground. After all that work too.'

'Good riddance,' Sugsy said. 'Not the way I wanted it to end but it's going to be hard to rebuild from scratch. Maybe Dennis will reconsider.'

'Hope he's got insurance,' Frank said.

'He will have,' Sugsy said. 'Can't run a place like that without it.'

Sue trundled up on her scooter. 'Never a dull moment lately,' she said.

'That's an understatement,' Rick replied.

'Well, he's gone too far this time,' she said.

'Who?'

'Darren Bilson of course. He'll be the one who started it. Bet you my scooter. You'll see. I pick up police radio – like to listen when I can't sleep. They're on the look-out for him.'

'You never fail to amaze me, Sue,' Rick said.

Sue nodded. 'I got a lot of hobbies, Rick. Like to keep me mind sharp.'

#

If the Paradise had previously been considered an eyesore between Mapton and Siltby, now it looked a hundred times worse. By morning the clubhouse was little more than a charred shell, and three of the old wooden chalets, a hangover from the seventies, had gone up too. Firefighters were still damping down the smouldering remains in the morning to minimize the risk of any more of the chalets or caravans catching fire. The sea breeze whipped black ash into the air. Dennis, talking to the police and fire service looked pale and dazed.

He wasn't the only one.

All of Mapton was in shock.

Tom's Torment

Once again Tom Turner stared down at another newspaper headline, this time in the Lawton Post.

GREAT GRANDMOTHER RISKS LIFE TO STOP RIOT

By Andrew Leith

Brave pensioner and great grandmother, Gina Pontin, risked her life yesterday evening to stop an angry mob turning into a riot at the Paradise Holiday Park.

Gina, who is currently running as a candidate for town councillor in the Mapton by-election, was pushed to the ground when out-of-control townspeople, angered by plans to turn The Paradise into a sex-club, surged forward to destroy a newly erected sign.

Suffering a nasty gash to her forehead, Gina still had the courage to climb up on the platform where Dennis Payton had been announcing his plans, and command the mob to stop.

One person, wishing to remain anonymous, said afterwards: 'Gina reminded us to be human. She pointed out there were children present and it was no way to behave. What's more, everyone knows Gina is dead set against the sex camp but she still stopped us destroying it. She made us do the right thing.'

Dennis Payton who owns The Paradise, and who was assaulted by an angry protester, also paid tribute to Ms Pontin's courage. 'There's no love lost between us, but if Gina hadn't stopped folk, I shudder to think what could have happened.'

Mr Payton spoke to The Post while he was being checked by paramedics just after the incident that saw both him and Ms Pontin injured.

The crowd became angry when Mr Payton chose the same night as the annual Christmas lights switch-on to put on his own X-rated lights display, as well as to announce that the district council had approved his adult entertainment licence.

Police arrived very quickly on the site, but it was the great-grandmother who saved the situation from becoming even nastier, as Sergeant Johnson acknowledges. 'It was very quick thinking on her part to grab the megaphone. Gina holds a special place in the hearts of this community, so they listened to her. She is known to be quite vocal.'

However, despite Ms Pontin's courageous act, Mr Payton wasn't so lucky later on during the night when The Paradise went up in flames (see front page).

So far the district council has provided no comment on Mr Payton's claim that they have granted his licence to operate as a sex-club.

Tom ground his teeth. He'd already read the front page.

He'd seen the fire even from Siltby and had run down to the scene on his Drive Royale.

He truly couldn't decide whether it was a disaster or a blessing that the clubhouse had burnt down. At least it had happened out of season.

297

Of more concern to him at the moment was the positive coverage Gina Pontin was gaining. It was campaign gold. Boring Tony Forbes didn't stand a chance against headlines like that.

Martha Seaton must be gloating. He'd landed her in the shite and she'd come up smelling of bloody roses.

When he'd heard she was helping Gina run for councillor he'd laughed aloud. Even Martha couldn't make a silk purse out of a sow's ear. Then he'd read the campaign 'letter'. It was just the sort of crap people fell for – personal, 'straight-talking' – pushing all the right emotional buttons. In contrast he and Tony had put together a perfectly professional, conventional leaflet. Perfect for Siltby, he realised in retrospect – he himself represented Siltby on the town council – but not for Mapton West, which was the seat Martha had held.

Tom picked up the paper again and almost growled. It was the photograph that really stuck in his craw. Gina Pontin captured in a saintly pose, hands outstretched pleadingly, blood trickling down her face. Somehow, by a trick of the light, she appeared to be framed by a halo.

Tom ground his teeth together so hard he felt the expensive crown on his back molar crack. It made a nasty crunching sound as it broke away.

He was having a very bad day.

The Usual Suspect

There was little doubt in the minds of the police and the fire service that the fire had been arson. It was the most obvious case they'd ever seen. The thick, black smoke during the fire suggested an accelerant, such as petrol, immediately. Investigations, once the site had been declared safe, revealed three petrol cans in different locations and traces throughout. Windows had been opened to let in more oxygen, suggesting the arsonist knew what they were doing.

Usually suspicion would fall on the property owner, for insurance fraud, or on local teenagers. This time the police already had one clear suspect in mind.

Darren Bilson hadn't been seen for a few days. The police wanted to question him about his attack on Dennis Payton. Now the matter was entirely more serious.

Sergeant Johnson paid a visit to his old sarge, Derek Tomlinson, who'd walked the local beat for years before he retired. There wasn't much Derek didn't know about the citizens of Mapton and Siltby.

'What d'you know about Darren Bilson, Sarge?' Johnson asked.

'What don't I know?' Sarge said. 'Cheeky little blighter when he was a kid. Dad moved away. Lived with his mum, Delia. Always in some trouble or other. You fancy him for this fire?'

Johnson shrugged. 'It was arson. Bilson's been agitating outside the Paradise for weeks. His aggression towards Dennis Payton escalated from insults to egg throwing, and to jumping on his car. Then the 'riot'. He assaulted Payton and fled before we caught him. Same night place goes up in flames.'

Sarge inhaled on a vape. 'Never thought I could give up smoking till I met one of these,' he said. He chewed the tip like it was a pipe, thinking.

Johnson waited. He knew Sarge was searching his long memory.

Sarge sat forward. 'Bilson does have a history of fire-starting,' he said slowly. 'He had a phase of it, briefly, when he was about ten.' He ruminated some more. His face shone suddenly as though receiving a revelation. 'Funnily enough that was around the same time Delia started seeing Dennis Payton.'

'So he has a history with Payton,' Johnson said eagerly.

'Aye,' Sarge said. 'Delia was a fine-looking woman – still is, just got a bit rougher round the edges like the best of us. Didn't think Dennis Payton could care for anyone but I think he was genuinely sweet on her. Went out for over a year. There was talk of them getting married. Then Delia broke it off. Apparently Darren didn't take to Dennis, or the other way round.'

'It was probably mutual dislike,' Johnson said.' Can't say I like either of them. Tell me about the fires.'

'He only did it about four times. At least one of them was about Dennis. He'd stayed over the night at Delia's and young Darren took it on himself to sneak into their bedroom in the early morning and swipe Dennis's clothes. He was caught burning them on that piece of scrubland over the dyke. Milkman saw the fire and called 999. Got a bit of a laugh at the station, the thought of Dennis having nowt but Delia's dressing gown to get home in. Darren got a bit of a taste for setting small fires. He did it three more times – not with Dennis's clothes – but soon as Delia gave Dennis the boot he stopped, so I reckon he was doing it to get his mum's attention.'

'So he's got a grudge against Dennis. Makes sense now, him joining the protest against the Paradise. He just saw the opportunity to make trouble for Dennis. It never quite fit – Darren taking the moral high ground.'

'He looks likely,' Sarge agreed, as Johnson rose to go. 'But think about it the other way round too. Payton's got a grudge against him.'

'For what?'

'Ruining his relationship with Delia,' Sarge said.

Johnson thought about it. 'Can't see Dennis Payton being broken-hearted,' he said, already dismissing the idea.

He never gave it another thought once his colleagues, paying another visit to Delia Bilson, who swore Darren wasn't there, discovered petrol tanks in her shed that matched the type left at the scene of the fire.

'It's for Darren's motorbike,' Delia had explained. 'Him, and his mate, Jim, are doing one up. It's a nice hobby for him. He loves the sand racing. Got to have petrol for that hasn't he?'

George in the Doldrums

George was struggling with three things. First was an overwhelming feeling of doom caused by the spiralling catastrophe of the past couple of months that had culminated in the near riot and the fire at The Paradise; to George it felt as though anarchy was running amok in Mapton.

Secondly, he felt resentful.

Third, he felt guilty about feeling that way.

His resentment was towards Gina. It hurt him; he'd thought he was a much bigger man than that, but the truth was as Gina's star was rising he felt his own sun to be setting.

The night in the hospital had scared him badly. It was strange that he had survived his wife's death some years ago without any real thought to his own mortality. But recently when he woke in the middle of the night he could almost see the spectre of Death leaning over him.

He didn't talk to Gina about it. He came from a generation where men didn't verbalise their fears. And Gina was never much help when it came to emotions. Even if she had been she was never around anymore. If she wasn't discussing 'strategy' with Martha, she was knocking on doors canvassing, or meeting with the Knights, or saving the day during a riot.

He knew he wasn't being fair. After all, it was he who had encouraged Gina to run for councillor. He'd always believed she was destined for more.

But George had imagined he'd be her rock; the one behind her campaign, still chairing the Knights, still keeping up with her bombastic energy.

Now Martha ran Gina's campaign far better than he ever could. The Knights continued without him. And Gina seemed to have moved beyond him.

George was mostly left alone with his fear. The doctor advised he start some gentle exercise, yet George felt the threat of chest pain, or thought he did, whenever he did too much.

Most of the time he stayed at home with Ginger Rogers, who practically lived with him since Gina was so busy. He and Ginger were settling into a routine of sloth that delighted Ginger, but was sucking George down into a bog of lethargy and depression.

The only person who seemed not to have forgotten him was Sue, who still popped in most days.

George had actually begun to see her as a bright spark in his day.

The Fugitive

Frank approached the ghost train with other thoughts on his mind.

Mainly he thought about Grazja. He thought about her a lot. They'd spent more time together since he'd told her his life-story, just hanging out together being friends.

That their feelings extended – mutually he was sure – beyond friendship was palpable between them, but Frank wasn't going to push it. He was content, for now, to have Grazja's friendship. It had been a long time since he'd shared even that much intimacy with another human being.

They had gone to the cinema together – Mapton's tiny picture house with its old-fashioned loveseats along the back row which Grazja had determinedly rejected – to watch a dreadful movie. Then they'd stayed up half the night talking about how great films used to be.

They'd walked along the beach wrapped against the biting winter wind, Frank fighting the impulse to take her hand.

They'd even been to Rick's pop-up restaurant in Lawton for an astoundingly great meal.

And most days they saw each other when Grazja brought Gerta into the diner.

Whenever she walked into a room Frank felt his face split into a big, stupid smile.

Wrapped up in his thoughts, it took Frank a few moments to realise that the padlock he'd fitted the key into wasn't actually attached to two ends of the chain. Or rather it was, but one chain had been cut through, leaving the padlock redundant and the door to the ghost train – boarded up for the winter – unlocked.

Frank felt a spasm of anger that kids might have broken in to vandalise his beloved ride. Without thinking about any danger to himself he stepped inside and turned on the light.

A man cried out.

Darren Bilson, scrambling to get out of his sleeping bag, tripped and banged his head against one of the train's cars.

'Darren,' Frank exclaimed. 'My God, this is where you've been hiding out?' He could virtually see the cartoon birds whistling around Darren's head, and went to help him up, guiding him to sit on one of the car benches.

Darren, dazed, and still a little blinded by the bare bulb after sleeping in total darkness, blinked up at him.

'Don't turn me in,' he begged. 'I didn't set that fire.'

'Why are you on the run then?' Frank asked. 'If you didn't do it?'

'Cos they think I did,' Darren said miserably. 'Seems like the sort of thing I'd do.'

Frank agreed with him silently. He studied Darren under the harsh bulb and saw a boy – not a very nice boy, but a boy all the same – instead of the bullying man Darren presented to the world. He hadn't realised how young Darren actually was – somewhere in his twenties –under the menacing shaved head and ugly swagger.

Unexpectedly he felt pity for him. 'How long have you been in here?'

'Couple of days,' Darren said. 'Sneaked out at night. Slept during the day.' He looked embarrassed. 'Sorry, I had to piss in the corner.'

Frank could smell it. 'And the other?'

'Eh?'

'Where did you defecate?'

'Oh,' Darren said. 'I shat in some bushes. Didn't want to sleep near it.'

'Thank God for small blessings,' Frank said. 'Have you eaten?'

'Me mum dropped me a bag of sandwiches 'n' stuff into the bin at the entrance. Texted me to say they were there. Didn't want to come in. Says the coppers are watching her. That were day before last. I'm hungry again now.'

Frank handed him the paper bag he was carrying with a muffin from Rick's. He'd intended it to be his snack later.

Darren swooped on it. 'Aw, good on yer.' After stuffing half in his mouth, he looked up. 'Are you going to turn me in?'

'You should turn yourself in,' Frank said. 'It'd be for the best. If you're innocent you've got nothing to worry about.' It seemed like a good thing to say even though he didn't believe in either Darren's innocence or that justice worked for the righteous.

'I'm not going down for life for something I didn't do,' Darren said.

Frank smiled. 'I think arson's about three years, more or less. Less, probably, if no one was hurt.'

Darren looked surprised. 'Oh,' he said. 'But I still didn't do it. I been stitched up. Mum said the coppers found my tank of petrol in the shed and it was the same kind used in the fire.'

'Well, why d'you have petrol at home?' Frank said.

'We was fixing up Jim's bike,' Darren said. 'Needed the petrol to run it, didn't we?'

'You need to tell the police that,' Frank said. 'Your friend Jim will back you up.'

'He's not answering my calls,' Darren said. 'There's that saying: when the going gets rough your friends piss off.'

'I'll talk to him for you,' Frank said. 'Where's he live?'

'Dunno,' Darren shrugged. 'Bugsby I think. Or another village. Only known him a few weeks. Showed up at the protest.'

'Do you know his last name?'

Darren pulled his face. 'Nah,' he said. 'Funny ain't it?'

'Funny,' Frank agreed.

Darren finished the muffin, slid out of the car and stood before Frank. There was an awkward silence.

'What now?' asked Darren.

'You should leave,' Frank said.' I won't harbour a fugitive, and I can hardly force you to stay while I call the police. I don't want another fight.'

'It was hardly a fight,' Darren admitted. 'I went down like a puff.' He looked chagrined.

'Well,' Frank said kindly. 'I had the element of surprise.'

Darren nodded. He perked up. 'Yeah, you did.' He made to move, stuck out his hand, and said: 'Er, thanks for the muffin, and yer know, sorry about the piss.'

Frank shook it and let Darren slip out of the door. He gave him a couple of minutes before ringing the police.

Still, he wasn't unsympathetic to Darren's predicament. It might be worth checking out this Jim fellow. And if the police weren't interested he thought he knew who might be.

Scampi's Goodbye

'Gerald told me emphatically that no one had approved the application for The Paradise,' Martha told Gina. 'That was just Dennis stirring the pot, and look where that got him. Still, if he hadn't, you wouldn't be so far ahead in the race.'

Gina had heard this before but never grew tired of it. She hadn't stopped to think what she was doing the night of the near-riot; she had simply reacted, and by some strange magic, acted in the best interests of the town.

Her actions, amplified by the media coverage and the extraordinary photo of her haloed plea shot her popularity up like a Roman rocket. Because it happened the same night, the fire became tangled up in people's minds with Gina's heroism, so that many pictured her braving flames, as well as a raging mob, to single-handedly prevent a riot.

'With The Paradise burnt down we would have lost the immediate threat of the swingers' camp, and a main campaign issue,' Martha continued. 'Now you are a shoe-in to win next week.'

Gina glowed.

'Unless you do something really stupid, or Tony Forbes does something amazing,' Martha said, catching her eye.

The two women laughed.

'I can't believe it,' Gina said. 'Me! A councillor. I'da never have thought it.'

'Tom will be so mad,' Martha said happily.

Gina looked at her. 'Is that why you helped me, to annoy Tom Turner?'

Martha smiled. 'It was one of the reasons – well a main one; he's such a smug bastard – but the more I've seen how you've got organised and campaigned the more I've come to realise you're just what the council needs. You'll shake them up a bit, I think. And you won't let county and district push you around.'

'No one pushes around Gina Pontin,' said Gina.

'Exactly,' Martha said, and they clunked their tea mugs together in a toast.

#

George was doing some light hoovering in the bedroom when he heard the pounding on his door.

'No need for that,' he muttered as he went to answer it. 'I'm not deaf.'

He opened the door to find Sue in a state of distress. Mascara streaked her cheeks and she was trembling. Her Rascal Vision was abandoned by the kerb. She clutched a box to her chest.

'Sue!' George took her elbow. 'Whatever's wrong?'

'I been knocking for ages,' Sue gasped. 'I knew you were in; I heard your hoover but you didn't hear me.'

She began to cry. George ushered her into the lounge.

'Sit down,' he said gently, guiding her to the sofa. 'Let me take that for you.' He reached for the box but Sue clutched it tighter.

'It's Scampi,' she wailed.

311

'Scampi?' George asked. 'Is she ill?'

'Noooo,' Sue sobbed. 'In the box. Scampi – she's dead.'

'Dead! Oh, Sue,' George sat down next to her. 'I'm so sorry. Poor little Scampi.'

'I… I came home from me morning run out to the diner and found her. I thought she were asleep – she sleeps so much – but then I saw she wasn't breathing.' She began to shake. 'Oh, George, Scampi died alone. I shoulda been there for her. I been out so much lately. I let her down. I let me own little baby down.'

She broke down completely.

Gently, George took the box away from her and placed it very carefully on the coffee table. He opened it gingerly, just to check it wasn't some awful mistake and Scampi really was asleep.

Scampi was curled up in the box, looking peaceful. She wasn't breathing. Tentatively George touched her. Rigor Mortis was just beginning to set in.

'Good Scampi,' George whispered. 'Rest in peace.'

Respectfully, he closed the box, then put his arm around Sue and held her while she cried.

Eventually, as her sobs died into sniffles, he said: 'What do you want to do with her?'

'Bury her in my garden,' Sue said. 'I'll build her a little shrine.'

'I'll help you,' George said. 'We'll hold a ceremony. Invite the Marauders.'

'Scampi would like that,' Sue sniffled. 'She were such a sociable dog. Everybody loved her.' She snuggled into George. 'I remember when she were just a puppy. She were the cutest thing I ever saw. She never nipped or bit, even before she lost her teeth. She were friendly to everyone.' She began to cry again. 'What am I going to do without her? I got no one else. She were the only one to love me.'

George squeezed her. 'Now c'mon, that's not true. You've got lots of friends. The Marauders, the Knights... me.'

Sue turned her tearstained face up to his. 'You were the first person I thought to come to,' she said. 'You're such a good man, George.'

Their faces were inches apart. Sue, face washed clean by tears, trembled in his arms. George felt needed; masculine. Their eyes met. Sue stretched up to kiss him and George met her lips with his.

A moment later he sprang back, suddenly realising what they'd done.

'Sue,' he said. 'We can't. I'm Gina's.'

Then the lounge window shattered and Sue screamed as glass flew in.

Something Stupid

Gina bought another pasty to take home for George. He'd been trying to follow his rabbit food diet since the angina attack. A pasty would be a tasty treat for him.

She also bought it to salve her intermittent conscience. She'd hardly paid much attention to him lately, being so wrapped up in her campaign and local celebrity. It would be nice to sit down and have a bit of lunch together like they always used to do.

She was feeling happy as she walked up their cul-de-sac. With only a few days to go to the election, Gina was confident she would win; Martha certainly thought so.

She paused at the sight of Sue's scooter, frowning. How often did Sue drop in on George? He mentioned it sometimes, but Gina hadn't taken it in.

It always rankled with Gina to see the Rascal Vision, as though Sue had managed to trick her out of it rather than the reasonable price Sue had actually paid her.

She sniffed at the ludicrous soft toys and various ribbons Sue had chosen to decorate the scooter with. Ridiculous.

She wasn't going to invite Sue to stay for lunch. These pasties were meant for her and George. Sue could bog off.

Thinking this, Gina continued up the path towards the front door. She glanced through the lounge window expecting to see Sue nattering at

George but what she saw instead was them in a clinch on the sofa, Sue gazing up into George's face. The next moment they kissed.

Gina saw red.

She didn't stop to consider; she grabbed the first thing to hand – a stone gnome – and hurled it at the window.

Running round to the side of the house, she seized a plant-pot and smashed it through the tiny window of the downstairs loo, and on she went, finding objects and lobbing them through glass until all George's windows were smashed and all the neighbours were out on the street trying to figure out what was going on.

George ran out of the bungalow in his slippers.

'Gina, 'he yelled. 'Gina! Stop! This is madness.'

'Don't you talk to me,' Gina raged. 'Don't you come near me you bastard. I saw you in there. I saw you with that bitch. I shoulda known never to trust a man. Intercourse; intercourse is all you all want. Don't matter who with.' Her voice rose to a shriek.

'Gina, no. No. It's a mistake,' George pleaded. 'Scampi died. I was just comforting Sue.'

'With your lips,' Gina screamed. 'It looked like you were trying to mount her. Bog off, George. I never want to talk to you again.'

She pushed past him. 'What you all looking at?' she yelled at the neighbours, and continued to her own bungalow. Once she managed to get her key in the lock she disappeared inside and slammed the door.

Stella sat with Gina, holding her hand. She had picked her up and brought her home to their house.

George had called her, shaken and almost unintelligible, saying Gina needed Stella and she must come immediately. She couldn't understand what he was trying to tell her – something about he'd made a terrible mistake – glass everywhere... Gina locked in the house.

Grazja kept Gerta entertained while Stella jumped in her car and drove over to Gina's, heart pounding.

George had been waiting for her on the kerb. His bungalow looked like the scene of a shootout. Stella's mouth went dry at the sight of it.

Was Gina hurt?

Neighbours milled around on the cul-de-sac but there was no sign of the police or an ambulance.

'What happened?' Stella leapt out of the car.

'Gina broke all of my windows,' George said.

'What! Why?'

George led her away from the onlookers. 'Er, Gina saw me and Sue kissing.' He hung his head.

'What! George! How could you?'

George's head dipped lower. 'It was a mistake,' he said. 'Scampi died today. Sue was upset and needed comfort. We got confused. It just happened for a second. I stopped it, but it was too late – Gina saw us through the window.'

'And broke every window you've got,' Stella said, gazing around at the destruction. 'A moderate Gina reaction.' She shook her head in disgust. 'Stupid George. Very stupid. Where is she?'

'Locked in her house,' George said, shame-faced. 'She's double-locked the front door.'

Stella had a spare set of keys to the front and back whilst George only had one to the front. Gina had left her key inside the lock so the front door couldn't be opened by him.

Stella went round the back and let herself in. 'Gina,' she called. 'It's me, Stell.'

All the rage had drained out of Gina. Stella found her lying on her bed, pale and exhausted. Even her hair looked faded. Ginger Rogers was lying with her muzzle on Gina's stomach, making little whining sounds.

'He cheated on me,' Gina said quietly. 'George cheated on me.'

'I know,' said Stella. 'I'm gonna pack a few things and take you and Ginger over to mine. I don't want you staying here on your own.'

For once Gina didn't put up a fight.

At Stella's, Gina had her cry. 'I swore I'd never trust a man after Carl,' Gina lamented. 'I really thought George were different, but they're all the same. Think with their todgers. But with Sue?' She made a sound of disgust. 'And she pretended to be my friend. I wonder how long it's been going on?'

'I don't think it has,' Stella said. 'Scampi died today. Sue was upset. It got out of hand that's all. George is sorrier than you can imagine.'

'Sorry he got caught,' Gina retorted. 'I don't believe a word of it.'

Stella looked at Grazja for help. She had put Gerta down for her nap and joined them.

'George love you,' Grazja said. 'I not defend what he do, but he is human.'

'He's a man!' Gina spat.

'I think they human too,' Grazja said.

But Gina was having none of it.

'I don't need George Wentworth,' she said, sitting up. 'Soon I'm going to be Councillor Pontin. I'll be too busy to care.'

'You have to win first,' Stella said.

Gina puffed out. 'Martha reckons it's in the bag. She said I'll only lose if I do something really stupid before the election.'

Stella and Grazja looked at her in disbelief.

'What?' Gina protested. Her face changed. 'Oh flippin' 'eck,' she said, crestfallen. 'I done something really stupid, ain't I?'

Playing Detectives

'I'll be glad to see the back of this year,' Peter Moss said as Rick handed him his change. 'It's been one daft thing after another. I moved to Mapton for a quiet life.'

'I hear you,' Rick replied.

''ow do you put up with that Gina?' Peter asked, shaking his head.

'She's not so bad,' Rick said. 'Most of the time she's fine.'

'Can't believe she smashed all those windows. Mind you, I wouldn't have believed George and Sue Mulligan going at it like rabbits.'

'There's nothing to believe there,' Rick said quickly. 'All a misunderstanding. Nothing going on. No rabbits.'

'Bit of an extreme way to react to nothing then,' Peter smirked. 'In fact, bit of an extreme way to react to *something* going on. I was actually thinking of voting for Gina but she's lost my vote.'

'She hasn't lost mine,' Ange said. She was standing precariously on a diner chair, hanging Christmas decorations. 'Can't abide a cheating man. Deserved what he got. There'll be a lot of women feel the same way.'

Rick and Peter raised their eyebrows at each other but said nothing.

'I'd best brave it,' Peter said. 'That wind out there'll cut you in half.' He pulled his cap down and his scarf up as he headed for the door.

'See you, Pete,' Rick called.

'Looks great Ange,' he said.

Ange climbed down to admire her work. Satisfied, she started to clear away the loose ends, scissors, and tape.

Outside the December afternoon was losing what little light there was. Sleet was beginning to fall, slanting sideways in the wind.

'We might as well shut up early,' Ange said. 'No one else will come today in this.'

'I'll hang on another hour, but you should get going.'

'Think I will,' Ange said. 'I enjoyed being in with you today though. We don't do the same shift often anymore.'

'Me too,' Rick said. 'Like old times.'

Rick sat down with a coffee and a sigh after Ange had gone. Calm now, the diner had actually been buzzing for the past couple of weeks. First everyone wanted to ask him about the fight in the Helmet; then it was to talk about Gina and the riot and the fire. Sightseers, coming to look at the burnt carcass of the clubhouse, walked along to the diner, the first café en route into town.

Good for business, bad for his stress-levels, Rick thought. Winter was usually a good downtime. He kept the diner open and it ticked along, but he enjoyed the breathing space after the holiday season was over – not that Mapton ever got really crowded; that's why he liked it.

This autumn and winter had been like wading through a minefield of gossip-bombs perpetually being tripped.

He breathed in the quiet. The diner, warm and bright, sealed against the freezing sleet, aromatic with coffee beans, held him in a temporary cocoon.

It didn't last. The door opened, letting in an icy blast, and Frank came in.

'Ah, it's lovely and warm in here,' he sighed, shaking off his coat and removing woollies.

'Afternoon,' Rick said. 'Not like you to come so late in the day.'

'I've been busy,' Frank said, settling himself at the counter. 'Tea, please, Rick. Any cinnamon buns left?' He looked around. 'Where is everybody?'

'Gone home,' Rick said. 'They're battening down the hatches.' He made Frank's tea and plated a bun. 'So,' he said, sliding them across the counter. 'You and Grazja seem to be getting pretty close. Anything I should know?'

Frank smiled. 'We're friends,' he said. 'Maybe it will develop, maybe it won't. I won't push. I don't think Grazja's got over the death of her husband.'

'That must have been a few years ago,' Rick said. 'I know she's a widow but she never talks about it, not even to Stella or Gina.'

'Everyone has things they keep close to their heart,' Frank said.

'True,' Rick agreed. 'So what's kept you busy all day?'

'I'm playing P.I.,' Frank said, cupping his tea. 'Did I tell you I discovered Darren Bilson hiding out in the ghost train?'

'No!' Rick leaned on the counter. 'I heard he'd been finally picked up and charged with arson. When did you find him?'

'That day,' Frank said. 'I called the police, but I'm not sure he set the fire.'

'C'mon,' Rick protested. 'The man's a complete psycho. It's right up his street.'

'I thought so too,' Frank said,' but now I'm not sure.' He described his encounter with Darren. 'It was what he said about his friend, Jim. Can you remember seeing him around before all The Paradise stuff started?'

Rick thought about it. 'Never,' he concluded. 'I've hardly noticed him. I mean, he was with Darren and the Timmis boys that day they tried to boycott the diner, but he didn't say anything. Darren was the ringleader. Then he wound things up a bit at the karaoke but again it was mostly Darren I took notice of. And Pious Pauline.'

'I've been to see her,' Frank said.

'Pious Pauline?'

Frank nodded. 'I don't think we should call her that,' he said. 'I think she has mental health problems. Perhaps a borderline personality disorder.'

'Something weird's going on in her head, that's for sure. Why did you go to see her?' Rick asked.

'She's been seeing Jim,' Frank said. 'I wanted to find out more about him. Turns out since the night of the fire she hasn't seen him. She was beside herself, saying he was Satan come to tempt her and she had succumbed. Like Darren, she didn't know his last name, or where he lived. She met him on the protest line.'

'Mysterious,' Rick said. 'What else have you discovered, Manning, P.I.?'

'Same thing with the Timmis boys. Thought Jim was from one of the local villages but not which one. Didn't have much to do with him. Said he was tight with Darren. Assumed Darren had known him for years. Haven't seen hide nor hair of him since the fire.'

'So what are you planning to do with this information?'

Frank twisted his mouth. 'I asked Andrew Leigh to help me investigate.'

'That creep,' Rick exclaimed. 'Why not the police?'

'He's not a creep,' Frank said. 'Just ambitious.'

'That's not what you said last time,' Rick reminded him. Andrew had pestered both of them for interviews after the karaoke-night fight, and before that Rick had told him to clear off when he asked for a statement on Rick welcoming the chair of the UK Swingers' Association into his establishment.

'I thought I needed some evidence before I went to the police and told them I thought they'd got the wrong man. Andrew might not be my cup of tea but he knows how to ask questions and get information.'

'When are you meeting him?' Rick asked, just as the door to the diner opened and Andrew Leith was flung in with a flurry of sleet.

Rick gave Frank a sardonic look. 'Question answered.'

Andrew took off his hat, and approached the counter warily. 'Are you going to tell me to 'clear off' again?' He asked Rick.

'Depends on what you ask me?' Rick said.

Andrew picked up a menu. 'How about I ask you for a burger and fries?'

'No can do,' Rick said. 'It's too late in the day to fire up my fryer and grill, and I'm not going in the back to leave you two to talk. Frank's been filling me in, so I want to hear what you've found out.'

Andrew sighed. 'Can I at least have a coffee and one of those?' he said, pointing to Frank's cinnamon bun.'

'That I can do,' Rick said, reaching for a mug.

'You were right to be suspicious about Darren's friend, Jim,' Andrew said, turning to Frank. His eyes gleamed. 'So, I went to see Darren's mum, Delia. Told her I thought Darren might be innocent and she was only too happy to talk. She didn't know much about Jim – had just met him a couple of times. The first time Jim came round to the house with a beaten up old sand-racing bike. He'd heard Darren was good at rebuilding them. Darren said he'd do it up for a price and then they became mates.

'She didn't know Jim's second name or where he lived. What surprises me is around here people know everyone else, unless they're tourists, and Jim didn't give that impression. Delia assumed he was from somewhere local because he was protesting at The Paradise with the other locals. That's what everyone has assumed.'

'That's what I found too,' Frank said. 'It's weird.'

'Not weird,' Andrew said. 'Planned. I know who Jim is and it's going to surprise you.'

'Well, c'mon on then, tell us,' Rick demanded.

But Andrew knew how to tell a story. He wasn't giving them everything at once.

'I had one lead,' he said. 'The motorbike. I thought it was possible that Jim had bought it around here, so I contacted the sand-racing club. They run a page online where enthusiasts buy and sell.

I was lucky. They'd run an ad about six weeks ago selling a knackered bike cheap in need of a lot of work. They still had the seller's details.'

'See,' Frank said to Rick. 'I would never have thought of that.'

'Because you don't make a living poking your nose into other people's business,' Rick said sourly.

Andrew rolled his eyes. 'A free press is the foundation of democracy,' he said.

Rick opened his mouth to retort when Frank interrupted.

'So,'he said. 'Stop keeping us in suspense. Get to the punchline.'

Andrew dropped his eyes from Rick to regather his thoughts. 'The seller had the email Jim sent him. It contained his surname – Sutcliffe. I tried it in Facebook under Jim Sutcliffe first – plenty of them but not him – so I tried James Sutcliffe and bingo, up he came, photo and all.'

'I'm not on Facebook,' Frank said.

'Me neither, 'Rick said. 'Whole thing makes me shudder. Giving away your whole life, shouting 'Look at me'!'

Andrew gave him the look – the one young people give older people; a mixture of disgust and pity at their 'stick in the mud' ways.

'Lucky for us Jim doesn't feel the same way,' he said. 'And lucky he doesn't bother with the privacy settings. He lives in Derby, so not a local at all. I was able to trawl through his friends. His mum's on there – Sheila Sutcliffe – and I went through her friends list too, and that's when I found an interesting name. Ray Payton.'

Rick exchanged a look with Frank. 'Payton? As in Dennis? Could be a coincidence. There must be loads of Paytons.'

'It's not,' Andrew smiled smugly. 'I checked the birth certificate records. Dennis, Ray, and Sheila are siblings, mother Moira, father William.'

'Which means,' Frank said, thinking it through, 'that Jim is Dennis's nephew.'

Rick whistled. 'Now that's definitely not a coincidence.'

Achy Breaky Hearts

George was heartbroken. Gina refused to speak to him. She had practically moved in with Stella in a bid to avoid him.

One stupid, weak moment between two lonely, vulnerable people had ruined four years of happiness.

He hadn't heard a peep out of Sue since the incident either. According to Andy, who'd been surprisingly sympathetic to George's plight, Sue had buried Scampi in her garden but had hardly been seen since. Mildred said Sue was scared of being branded a scarlet woman and a homewrecker.

'What you need to win Gina back is a grand gesture,' Andy advised. 'Gina's not the sort of woman to respond to subtlety.'

If George had been in a better state of mind he might have questioned taking advice from Andy Timmis; Andy was with Carole now, but his long-term record with romance was abysmal.

However, George was desperate so Andy's words resonated. A grand gesture?

George thought about it for hours. It would have to be grand indeed to make Gina forgive him.

Finally, he clicked his fingers. By God, he had it. It would be risky but what had he to lose? His reputation and his happiness were already in shreds.

#

Sue was in an equal state of abject misery. The house felt so empty without Scampi; her basket in the kitchen seemed to stare at her balefully, yet Sue couldn't bring herself to get rid of it.

She was mortified about the incident with George and Gina. Somehow she felt she had defiled the memory of Scampi – not just the memory of her but her very death. There, with the body of her little dog still cooling, she had tried it on with George, knowing full well he was someone else's man.

The actual moment of the kiss had been spontaneous, born out of grief, need, and intimacy, yet Sue knew, forced herself to admit, that she had been dreaming of such a moment for months. George was much older than she but he was such a nice man – a gentleman in the true sense of the word – and she'd felt he was wasted on Gina who wouldn't know the difference between a diamond and a rhinestone.

Sue had never been sure whether Gina was her friend or enemy. Now she was convinced Gina had been her friend; a difficult, prickly, rivalrous friend to be sure, but still one. And she, Sue, had broken the cardinal rule of friendship. Thou shalt not make a move on your friend's man.

Of course Gina had reacted with Gina-like extremism. Being inside the bungalow with missiles shattering the windows had been terrifying. It also meant that everyone knew what had happened. Gina didn't keep her pain to herself. Mapton thought that Sue Mulligan was a slutty homewrecker who'd used the death of her dog to wriggle into George Wentworth's pants.

She hadn't wriggled into his pants, hadn't even French-kissed him, as they used to giggle at school, but people would believe the worst. She would in their situation. There was nothing she liked more than a bit of naughty gossip.

'Oh Scampi,' she wept. 'If only you knew what a mess yer mummy's made of everything.'

#

Gina was up in Stella's studio staring gloomily at the finished canvases stacking up.

'You've been busy,' she said.

'I've been inspired lately,' Stella said, washing out her brushes.

'You're making Mapton look like a freak show,' Gina grumbled.

'A circus,' Stella said. 'A circus of madness.'

'Same difference,' Gina said. '

Stella changed the subject. 'Are you ready for your interview on Monday?'

'Nearly,' Gina said. 'Martha's helping me prepare.'

'She's forgiven you then?'

Martha had not been impressed with Gina's antics.

'She says all we can do now is damage limitation. Anyway, I don't care about anything anymore.'

'You do,' Stella said. 'Talk to George instead of moping about.'

'Not this again,' Gina flared. 'You shouldn't be taking his side, you should be on mine.'

'I am on your side,' Stella said, settling next to Gina on the sofa. 'I just think he made a stupid mistake. You're happier with George. He's so sorry and so miserable.'

'What if it had been Rick? What about when you went flouncing back to London when you thought he'd done the dirty with Ange. You didn't even see him. I saw them, Stella, locked together like two limpets. They're lucky all I broke is the windows. Should have been their heads. And that Sue – haven't heard a peep outta her. No apology, nor nothin''

'Would you accept it?' Stella asked.

'No, I bleedin' wouldn't,' Gina said. 'But that ain't the point.'

'Let's just get the election out of the way,' Stella sighed. 'Hopefully things will calm down. Maybe you and George will sort things out before Christmas.'

'Don't hold yer breath,' Gina said. 'I hate him.'

Big News

Frank was tinkering in the ghost train shed when a shadow appeared at the door.

The shadow morphed into Darren Bilson as he stepped inside.

Frank stood up, not sure what to expect. He had been the one to call the police, so Darren might be seeking revenge.

Darren looked equally unsure of his reception.

'I assume the police let you go,' Frank said. 'You haven't escaped again?'

'Nah,' Darren said. 'They've dropped the charges on the arson. Gave me a final warning on public disturbances and assault. Said even the sniff of it and I'd be doing time.'

'That's good,' Frank said. He hesitated. 'Listen, it was me let the police know you'd just left here. I looked into what you told me though – about your friend, Jim.'

'I know,' Darren said. 'They told me you and that reporter got them to change their minds. Don't know how you did it.'

'Do *you* know that Jim is Dennis Payton's nephew?' Frank asked.

Darren's eyes bulged. 'You're joking? That bastard! They were just bringing Dennis in to the station when I was leaving. He *did* try to stitch me up. I'm gonna…'

'No,' Frank said firmly. 'Whatever you think you're going to do to him, you're not. Remember you're on final warning. Let the police handle Dennis.'

Darren visibly took a deep breath. 'You're right,' he said exhaling. 'That's what I came to tell you. When I heard what you done for me, I decided to turn over a new leaf. Start afresh. No more Mr Nasty. I'm gonna start a business doing up bikes. Make me mum proud of me.'

He looked emotional.

Frank felt a little emotional too.

'That's great, Darren,' he said. 'Just you remember that when you're about to lose it. The only person you've got to prove anything to is yourself.'

'Yeah!' Darren said. There was an awkward silence.

'So,' Frank said.

'So, yeah, I just wanted to say thanks,' Darren said. He said it as though he'd tasted a new flavour and wasn't yet convinced he liked it. 'Thanks.'

'No problem,' Frank replied. 'Glad I could help.' He watched as Darren turned to go.

Suddenly, Darren turned and within a stride was in Frank's face.

Frank startled back, thinking Darren was about to hit him, but instead Darren pulled him into a clumsy hug.

Then, wordlessly, he left.

Later, Frank sat in Grazja's tiny little kitchenette as she cooked them a meal, and told her about it.

'You think someone can change just like that?' Grazja asked.

'Probably not,' Frank said. 'But I think he genuinely wants to.'

The day before the election the big news broke. It ran as the lead story in The Lawton Post.

Exclusive!

POST EXPOSES INSURANCE SCAM IN SHOCKING MAPTON SEX-CLUB TWIST

By Andrew Leith

Following an investigation by the Lawton Post, Dennis Payton, 55, owner of the Paradise Holiday Park in Mapton, has been charged with arson and insurance fraud after trying to frame an innocent man for the crime. His accomplice, James Sutcliffe has been charged with accessory to the crimes.

After a series of scandals, protests, and bitter divisions, Mapton is once again at the centre of a storm. We can reveal that Dennis Payton, of 69 Dunes Way, a controversial figure in Mapton since announcing plans to turn the Paradise Holiday Park into a sex camp for swingers, never intended to open a sex camp. Instead he hatched a diabolical scheme to fool local people into thinking he was serious, when all along he planned an insurance scam. By deliberately planting an 'agent provocateur' among the protesters, Payton framed Darren Bilson for arson. After the Paradise clubhouse burnt down, police arrested Siltby man, Bilson, for the crime.

'We matched petrol containers in Darren Bilson's workshop to those found on the site of the arson,' said Sergeant Adrian Johnson.

Bilson was an obvious suspect; a well-known local troublemaker, he had been an aggressive member of vigilante group the Mapton Knights, who'd organised the anti-sex camp protests. He also had a history of fire-starting as a boy, which Payton knew about from a previous relationship with Bilson's mother.

However, the Lawton Post wasn't convinced of Bilson's guilt. Following a tip-off our reporter investigated the sudden disappearance of Darren's friend, Jim, following the fire. Mysteriously, no one, including Darren, knew Jim's last name. Nearly everyone our reporter spoke to assumed Jim lived in a nearby village but didn't know which one. Even more suspiciously, Jim had only recently appeared in Darren's life, bringing him a motorbike to fix up. Darren's mother said: 'He seemed like a nice lad. He and Darren spent loads of time together. It was him that got Darren interested in the protest. I thought it was good he'd encouraged Darren to get involved in the community.'

The Post can exclusively reveal that Jim is actually James Sutcliffe, 23, of Derby, unemployed, and the nephew of Dennis Payton. In fact, James had been secretly staying at Dennis's house the entire time. James befriended Darren in order to stir up his volatile nature and re-ignite the animosity Darren had felt towards Payton as a boy. Then he ensured that the type of petrol containers Darren used for his motorbikes matched those used in the arson attack.

In the weeks leading up to the fire, Payton had made considerable improvements to The Paradise Clubhouse, and upgraded his insurance to match. On the night of the fire he staged an event he knew would incite the townspeople, particularly Darren Bilson, to violent protest, making the subsequent fire appear an act of vengeance.

If not for the Lawton Post's investigation, Payton would have got away with his evil scam. Once we had presented the new facts to the police, charges against Darren Bilson were dropped.

#

Rick rolled his eyes, passing the paper over the counter to Frank.

'No mention of you,' he said. 'The Post, i.e. Andrew Leith, takes all the credit.'

Frank smiled. 'It doesn't matter. The truth's come out, that's what counts.'

Rick snorted. 'You're a bigger man than me, Frank. I'll be telling anyone who comes in it was you helped Darren.'

'Darren's already started telling people,' Andy Timmis said from the booth he was sharing with Carole. They had the Post spread out on the table between them. 'I don't like how Leith's called the Knights a 'vigilante group'. Darren never joined us; he were in the Crusaders.' Andy said this perfectly straight-faced as though it wasn't himself who had actually formed the Crusaders in the first place.

335

Rick sent Frank the barest of raised eyebrows before disappearing into the kitchen.

His muffled laughter rang back to them.

'He's in a good mood,' Andy said. 'Summit must've tickled him back there.'

#

Tom Turner was sweating. Beads of it popped out on his forehead; his armpits turned swampy.

He swabbed his face with a large handkerchief. It wasn't hot. Tom was worried.

Dennis Payton charged with arson and insurance fraud! He had never dreamed, three months ago, when he had asked Dennis to play along with a rumour of a swingers' camp, it could come to this.

Would come to this.

Jesus!

Had Dennis played him? Had he conceived of the scheme the moment Tom had popped the idea into his head, or later?

And what had he told the police? That Tom had suggested it? That Tom had wanted to make trouble for Martha Seaton? That he never would have thought of the scam without Tom's idea?

Maybe Dennis would make a deal with the police or the lawyers – isn't that what happened on American crime shows – singing like a canary about an illegal meat trade in return for a softer sentence.

Tom's heart began to palpitate.

Calm down, he told himself. Easy now. No need to race ahead. Dennis only suspected. Tom had never admitted anything. Besides, Dennis would only further incriminate himself.

'I'm fine,' Tom whispered. 'Everything is absolutely fine.'

#

Gina's interview took place in front of the burnt out Paradise. It wasn't the original plan but the local TV news thought it would be a great idea with the arrest of Dennis Payton for fraudulent arson.

Of course that news changed the focus of the interview to Gina's advantage. Instead of grilling her on her anti-social window-smashing meltdown, they were initially more interested in discovering what she knew about Dennis.

'I always said he were a bad one,' Gina told Vanessa Baro. 'Ask anyone who knows me.'

'Is it true you were the first one to challenge him when the rumours of a swingers' camp at The Paradise arose?' Vanessa asked.

'It is true. I went to see him straight away. 'Dennis,' I said. 'You will be running a sex camp in Mapton over my dead body. Mapton's a decent place for families, not perverts. That's when I started the Mapton Knights to stop him.'

'And you didn't have any inkling it was all a scam?'

''course not,' Gina said. 'No one did.' She looked thoughtful. 'Though I should have, really. Dennis is a lazy bogger. Makes sense he'd rather burn down his place for money than go to the effort of running it properly.'

'Mapton sometimes has a reputation for a being a little downmarket,' Vanessa said. 'Do you feel recent scandals have damaged its reputation further?'

Gina stiffened. 'Mapton's not for snobbish people. If you'd rather have humus than good old British fish 'n' chips then Mapton's probably not for you…'

'Isn't humus soil?' Vanessa interrupted. 'I think you mean hummus.'

'Well if you know what I mean why are you asking?' Gina demanded. 'Humus/hummus – wouldn't surprise me if it is soil. Never eaten it, never will. Give me an English pie. That's all I'm saying. In Mapton we stand for traditional values. You say has this scandal damaged our reputation? I say no. When crunch came to shove Mapton folk stood up for what's right. We said no to the swingers, we said no to Dennis Payton, and we got off our arses and did summat about it. And that's the sort of people I want to represent.'

'You want to represent the people of Mapton,' Vanessa said. 'But do they want you? Let's talk about your behaviour. First we see you stopping a near-riot single-handedly, the next you break every window in your lover's house, which is an act of criminal damage, not to mention a dangerous one. Why would anyone vote for you?'

Gina almost curled her pink lips into a snarl before seeming to catch herself. She forced a smile. 'I'm glad you asked me that,' she said. ''It wasn't a criminal act – there were no charges brought against me, but it was a very foolish one.' If that sounded a bit rehearsed, the next words were all Gina. 'I can be a daft bogger,' she admitted. 'But I'm real. I feel things very passionately, and I'm very honest. If something's not right I won't put up wi' it. It weren't right to let good Mapton people turn into savages so I stopped it. I don't put up with liars and cheats, so I stood up to Dennis Payton. They were good things I did. Breaking all them windows was a bad thing. Stupid. But I did it for the same reason. I don't put up with lyin' and cheatin'. The people of Mapton know what they're getting with me is genuine. It's Gina Pontin, like it or hate it. And if someone, or something – like business, or government – try to cheat them I won't stand for it. I won't do it; it's not in my nature. So if they want Tony Forbes who will toe the line and play the game, they can have him. Of if they want someone with a bit of fight, they'll choose me. That's it.'

The Final Countdown

George was ready. Nervously he straightened his tie, patted the ring box in his pocket, and took a deep breath. He'd positioned himself near the front of the crowd.

Mapton's community hall was as packed as it had been the night Mayor Seaton announced Dennis Payton's application to turn The Paradise into a sex camp.

In a few minutes Gina and Tony Forbes would find out which one of them had been elected. George had placed his vote for Gina in the ballot box that morning. Julie Taynor had given him an odd, almost sympathetic look. 'Did you see Gina's interview last night?' she'd asked. George hadn't. He'd been too busy and too nervous to watch, but he could get it on demand when he was ready.

Mapton's turnout for the results was unprecedented. Interest in local and national elections could be a half-hearted affair.

But Mapton had been put through the washer on spin recently. They were dizzy from sensation, scandal, and skulduggery. They needed to come together, if only to vent their astonishment at the latest revelation; Dennis Payton's scam.

The hall rumbled with discussion of it.

George hardly noticed. He hadn't even glanced at the paper or listened to the news. His focus was entirely on one thing: his big attempt to win Gina back.

He caught Andy's eye. Andy was up on the stage, fixing the microphone in place. He saw George and gave him a grin and thumbs up. He was in on the plan and had helped George set up the hall.

A huge foil banner, saying MERRY CHRISTMAS MAPTON hung above the stage. Behind it Andy had rigged up a canvas sling full of confetti to release at the right moment.

The candidates had divided into two camps upon the stage. Gina, on the right to the audience, was flanked by Martha, Dave Suggs, and Carole. Andy joined them.

It hurt George to see them. He would be up there with Gina if he hadn't messed it all up.

To the left Tony Forbes had members of the Mapton & Siltby Conservatives keeping him company, including Tom and his wife, Phyllis.

The air buzzed with anticipation.

George felt a hand on his arm and turned to see Grazja at his elbow.

She smiled up at him. 'Good to see you here,' she said, raising her voice above the general din. 'You and Gina make up?'

'Not yet,' George said. 'I'm hoping …' he touched the box in his pocket. 'I need to make a grand gesture,' he said mysteriously.

Frank came up behind Grazja, followed by Rick and Stella.

Stella hugged George. 'I'm so glad you came,' she said.

George almost wept. He hadn't seen Stella since he called her to Gina's aid.

'I went to see Sue today,' Stella said. 'She's in a bad way. She told me what happened. She feels terrible, George.'

'It wasn't her fault,' George said. 'I should have never have let it happen.'

Stella squeezed his hand. 'Gina will come round,' she said. 'If she loses this election she's going to need you more than ever.'

'Andy suggested I make a grand gesture; you know, towards Gina.'

Stella laughed. 'She certainly likes to be made a fuss of,' she agreed.

George felt his determination solidify. He was doing the right thing. Gina would love it. If she lost she would need the boost. If she won it would be the icing on the cake.

A ripple of excitement ran through the hall as the returning officer took to the stage, results in hand.

'This is better than the X Factor,' someone called, making everyone laugh.

George gazed up at Gina. She was fidgeting with her rings, the way she did when she was nervous, and he wished he could hold her hand to reassure her. Suddenly, she saw him, eyes widening.

The returning officer began to speak and Gina jerked her attention back to the results.

'I, Edward Stanton, being the returning officer for this election, do hereby give notice that the number of votes recorded for each candidate is as follows: Forbes, Anthony John, Conservative, 822 …' A cheer went up. This was one of the highest votes a candidate had ever scored in a Mapton election.

Tom pumped Tony's hand.

Edward Stanton held up his hand for quiet. 'Pontin, Gina Deidre, Independent, 1002.'

There was a moment of pure silence, then the hall erupted with noise; clapping, stamping, cheers and whooping, along with a few boos.

Mapton had spoken. Gina had won.

George, tears running down his cheeks, applauded wildly.

'Oh my God,' gasped Stella. 'I don't believe it.'

Gina appeared not to believe it either. She stood blinking on stage, looking completely dazed.

Martha grabbed her in a hug, followed by Sugsy, Carole, and Andy. They pushed Gina towards the microphone.

Andy turned, giving George a thumbs-up, and disappeared off the side of the stage.

Gina stumbled to the microphone. She faced the audience.

'Flippin' 'eck,' she said, making them laugh. She swiped at the tears forming in her eyes, and they applauded.

'I wrote a speech,' Gina began, 'just in case. But I didn't think I'd need it; then Stella's cat was sick on it, so that were that. I took it as a sign.'

More laughter. Gina looked for Stella, found her, smiled proudly. 'That cat never liked me.'

Stella smiled back, nodding her head. Her eyes glistened too.

'Everything I said in my campaign is true,' Gina said. 'I'm going to do my very best for all of yers. Even those who didn't vote for me. I love this town. I won't put up with liars and cheats like that Dennis Payton.' Loud applause. Gina opened her mouth to continue but was drowned out as a sound system cranked up, pumping out Whitney Houston's 'I Will Always Love you.'

It took George a moment to recognise his cue.

Gina looked around bewildered. A disco ball started to spin, throwing spangled lights across the stage.

George fumbled for the ring box in his pocket as he climbed the steps to the stage. All of a sudden this didn't seem like such a good idea but it was too late for him to back out now.

Gina stared at him aghast as he approached her.

The crowd gasped, sensing something sensational.

George dropped to one knee. Abruptly the music snapped off, leaving only the disco ball spinning into tense silence.

Slowly, because getting down on one knee was tricky at his age, George lowered himself in front of Gina.

There was a collective holding of breath.

'Gina,' George said, holding out the jewel box. 'I've been a fool, but I love you more than I love my own life.'

'Speak up!' a man shouted. He was hissed at to hush.

Maptonites were transfixed.

George opened the box. People strained to get a glimpse of the ring.

'Gina Pontin,' George said. 'Will you do me the honour of being my wife?'

Gina looked flabbergasted. She started to reach out to touch the diamond – because George had made sure it was a diamond – when a woman called out: 'I voted for you because you said you won't put up with liars and cheats.'

Later on, when people discussed it, it was decided that the woman in question was Trissa Vaughn, who'd just gone through a particularly bitter divorce. She vehemently denied it.

Gina's face changed. Confusion blew away and her expression hardened.

George felt his heart sink. Gina was as stubborn as that Jack Russell she used to have, and worried at a grudge like it was a bone.

She wasn't going to forgive him.

'You're right,' Gina shouted at the crowd. 'I don't put up with liars and cheats. But George Wentworth ain't one of 'em. He's just a silly bogger who kissed an ugly bird in a moment of weakness. And I love him.'

She looked surprised. 'I love you, you silly sod!' she admitted.

George felt his heart swell.

'But are you going to marry him?' another person shouted.

Gina looked at him. George saw himself through her eyes. A silly old fool barely holding his balance on one arthritic knee, holding out a ring. He held his breath.

Gina frowned. 'You know what,' she said. 'I think I bloody am!'

345

Confetti rained down on them, as Andy released the sling.

#

Rick groaned, as all around them Maptonites applauded and whooped. 'It's getting like America,' he said. 'Whatever happened to British reserve? This is so cheesy.'

'Shut up and kiss me,' Stella laughed.

He did.

#

Although George's proposal had rather overshadowed Gina's win – something George would get an earful about once Gina realised it - Martha Seaton was ecstatic.

She made her way over to Tom, after taking a moment to graciously commiserate with Tony. Tom saw her coming and tried to sidle away but she blocked him.

Tom went on the offensive. 'I think we both know the wrong man won,' he said. 'You've made the local council into a circus.'

'Woman,' Martha corrected him. 'I don't think so Tom. I think you'll find it very interesting working with Gina.'

'She won't survive,' Tom said. 'She'll either get kicked out for ballsing up, or drop out.'

'Perhaps,' Martha said. 'But you shouldn't underestimate her. Working with her has made me realise that. She'll get things done.'

Tom snorted. 'This has been a lovely little chat, Martha, but I must be going.' He began to move away but Martha caught him lightly by the elbow.

'She promised she wouldn't put up with liars and cheats, Tom. You'd best watch out.'

'What does that mean?' Tom snarled.

Martha leaned in. 'You don't have to worry about me, Tom. I have no evidence it was you who leaked my background to the paper, nor do I have evidence that it was you that started the rumour about the sex camp. You and Dennis Payton together. But I have my suspicions. If I was you, Tom, I'd be wondering what Dennis has told the police.'

'You're talking bollocks, woman,' Tom blustered.

'Am I?' Martha said lightly. 'Haven't you noticed how Sergeant Johnson keeps looking at you?'

Tom swallowed and automatically sought out the off-duty policeman.

He gulped. Sergeant Johnson *was* looking at him.

Martha smiled sharkishly. 'Everyone has secrets Tom. Mine are all finally out in the open. Are yours?'

With that she walked away.

Spring Blooms

Stella's exhibition in London was a triumph, critically and financially.

It had opened late January, the paint of the last canvas barely dry when it went up on the gallery wall.

Stella, Rick, Gina, and George had gone to the private view at Proclivity, while Grazja had stayed home with Gerta. They were joined by Stella's best friend, Lysie and her husband, Del, who lived in Camden.

'Not very private, is it?' Gina said, gazing around at all the London arty types, sipping wine and chattering. 'Look at that bloke,' she pointed to a man with high-rise hair and an elaborately coiffed beard.

Stella shushed her. 'He's a hipster,' she said in a low voice.

'A hippie?' Gina shouted. 'I thought they had long hair.'

'A hipster,' Lysie repeated. 'Men who have no identity of their own so adopt one that's trending, no matter how ridiculous.'

'He looks like a twot,' Gina declared. 'And there's another over there. And why have so many people got them black-rimmed glasses on? Ain't no one heard of contact lenses in London?'

'It all looks very nice, Stella,' George said tactfully. 'Your pictures show up very well on these walls.'

'Thanks,' Stella said.

Gina guffawed, digging George affectionately in the ribs. 'You'd make a great critic, George,' she teased. 'That were very deep.'

George smiled at her indulgently.

'Talking of critics,' Rick said to Stella. 'Isn't that Martin Salvino over there with Susan?'

Stella followed the direction of his gaze. It was Salvino, the art critic who'd written the first rave review of her 'new style'.

Susan, her agent, waved to her and started to lead Salvino towards them.

Rick said quickly. 'Gina, shall we go get a drink?'

'No point, Ricky,' Gina said. 'They ain't got no Babycham. George already asked. Besides, I want to hear what this critic-man thinks of Stella's work.'

Rick gave Stella a 'sorry, I tried' shrug. Susan reached them with Salvino in tow.

'Stella, I want you to meet Martin Salvino,' she said.

The critic, wearing the sort of intellectual, angular glasses that Gina had commented on, raised an eyebrow as he shook Stella's hand.

'So,' he said archly. 'You've completed your metamorphosis.' He swept his hand around towards the paintings. 'Gaudy, cheap, and dripping with vehemence.'

The group tensed. George put his hand gently on Gina's arm.

'I love it!' Salvino boomed, making them jump. 'The way you capture the ugly, seedy beauty of the underclass.'

'Underclass?' Gina piped up. 'Who you calling underclass? I'm in some of them paintings, and I'm a councillor, you know.' She glared at him.

'This is my grandmother, Gina,' Stella said to the critic.

Salvino turned to Gina and studied her as though she was part of the exhibition. He swept his gaze over her, expression transforming to one of wonder. 'You are magnificent,' he said, offering her an arm. 'Would you do me the honour of talking me through the exhibition?'

Gina looked at him like he was mad. 'Are you gone out?' she said. 'Stella's the artist. She should take yer round.'

'Ah,' Salvino said. 'She is the artist, but I can see that you are her muse. It is a rare opportunity indeed to meet one of those.'

'Well,' Gina puffed out. 'I have been a big influence on Stella's art, that's true.'

She accepted the proffered arm.

'Let's start over there,' Salvino said, pointing. 'Sins in the Dark.'

'I'm not in that one,' Gina said, sounding disappointed. She perked up. 'But I know everyone who is.'

As their voices trailed away, Lysie turned to Stella. 'Are you sure that's a good idea? What if Gina offends him?'

Stella grinned. 'I don't care,' she said. 'A few months ago I didn't think I'd be ready for this at all. I'd dried up. Then Grazja came back, Mapton lost its mind, and my juices started to flow again. I'm just very glad to be here.'

She took George's hand and squeezed. 'I'm so glad we're here, all together again.'

George squeezed back.

'It's a shame Grazja and Frank wouldn't come,' Rick said.

'They'll see the exhibition,' Stella said. 'I'm determined to bring it to Mapton.'

And she did.

In April, when the daffodils were fading and the tulips taking over, the exhibition came to Mapton's community hall. Although most of the paintings had been sold Stella had stipulated that none were to be shipped to the new owners until after the April exhibition.

It only lasted one day, as the issue of security and insurance proved too difficult to leave the paintings overnight in the hall, and it wasn't advertised in advance.

Stella and her team worked all night to set the show up. Only first thing in the morning did notices go up in Mapton and Siltby to announce the exhibition, and soon the gossip-chain had spread the word.

'Why didn't you advertise it?' Sue asked Stella. 'We coulda charged?'

'I wanted it to be for Mapton and Siltby,' Stella said. 'If I'd let the world know we might get flooded with visitors.'

'Oo-er, rate yerself much?' Sue laughed.

Stella, noting how much paler and thinner Sue looked, gave her an impulsive hug. 'I'm glad you finally made it up with Gina,' she said.

'I didn't think we'd be able to,' Sue admitted. 'But it were the angel of Scampi what did it.'

Stella said nothing. She thought it was Sue's courage in finally going to Gina to apologise that did it, although in a way Scampi did play a part. They'd ended up crying together about Scampi's demise. 'Losing a dog,' Gina had begrudgingly admitted, 'can send yer a bit daft.'

They would never be best friends but at least Sue felt able to show her face in Mapton knowing Gina wasn't going to publically denounce her every time they met.

In actuality, Gina was too busy as Councillor Pontin to dwell on Sue and George's moment of madness; she and Acting Mayor Tom Turner had already started to butt heads over various issues. He was such an irritable, nervy man these days. Gina delighted in provoking him into rages.

The paintings caused quite a stir. The hall was packed all day with local folk drifting in and out. People recognised themselves in paintings they weren't actually in, and often failed to identify the ones they were in. They gawped and pointed, laughed and argued, discussed, wrangled, praised and criticised.

The canvas depicting the Paradise as a sex camp with nudes frolicking on the billboard made them laugh – as though the panic over the camp had been merely a dream – while the one showing the burnt-out shell of the Paradise made them turn silent. The picture of the ghost train had people casting worried looks at Frank, while a small canvas featuring Scampi peeking out of her basket on the Rascal Vision, made Sue cry – but in a good way, she reassured Stella.

Whether they loved the paintings or thought they were 'crap' as one fifteen year old declared, most people were proud that they centred on Mapton and been feted in London by the cream of the art world.

There was the Kleen and Gone laundrette; the giant Mr Whippy cone that graced the promenade; Pam Stimpson's baby doll pyjamas wafting on the line. Here were the protesters, Knights and Crusaders, scooters and bikers, diner and chip shops.

'Mummy paint these,' Gerta told Pam Stimson proudly. 'With her fingers.'

Here was Mapton in all its shabby glory.

Grazja tilted her head to look up at Frank, as he gazed at the painting of the ghost train.

'Do I really look that creepy?' he asked.

'When you a monk, yes.'

Frank looked sad. 'Maybe it's time I stopped wearing the hood.'

Grazja agreed. 'That will be good. Let people see your lovely face.'

Frank blushed at the compliment.

'C'mon,' Grazja said, grabbing his hand. 'Let's go get ice-cream.' She led him out towards the spring sunshine.

Rick, holding Gerta, who'd fallen asleep on his shoulder, looked at Stella.

'Did you see that?' he asked. 'Frank and Grazja, holding hands.'

Stella nodded. 'I saw it,' she said.

'It's only taken them five months. Maybe in a year, they'll kiss,' Rick said. 'In five years do the dirty, in ten really get it together?'

'Maybe,' Stella smiled, reaching over Rick's arm to tuck away a stray curl falling over Gerta's apple cheek. 'This is Mapton. Anything might happen.'

About the Author

Sam Maxfield attempted to write her first full-length novel at eleven. She grew up in Canada and England. She moved seven times before she was eight years old and spent much of that time in her own imagination spinning stories. Sam holds a BA in English and History, as well as an MA in Creative Writing. She has taught English Literature for twenty years.

More than anything Sam loves stories. She devours most genres, fiction and non-fiction.

She is best known for her humorous Mapton-on-Sea series: *The Last Resort*, *Mapton Rising*, and *Must be Mapton*.

Other novels include the magic-realism Western, *West of the Sunset*, Victorian detective story *The Army of Righteous Deliverance*, and children's novel *Maddie's Magic Christmas*.

30073629R00216

Printed in Poland
by Amazon Fulfillment
Poland Sp. z o.o., Wrocław